T0208603

PRESIDENT FROM ANOTHER PLANET

Can Barzhad Osama save the universe?

ANSLEY HAMID

iUniverse, Inc.
New York   Bloomington

PRESIDENT FROM ANOTHER PLANET
Can Barzhad Osama save the universe?

Copyright © 2009 Ansley Hamid

iUniverse books may be ordered through booksellers or by contacting:

iUniverse
1663 Liberty Drive
Bloomington, IN 47403
www.iuniverse.com
1-800-Authors (1-800-288-4677)

ISBN: 978-1-4401-2959-9 (pbk)
ISBN: 978-1-4401-2960-5 (ebk)

Printed in the United States of America

iUniverse rev. date: 3/16/2009

Author's Disclaimer

There is no wish to defame, slander or libel anyone in this work of fiction. I checked out the definition of these terms in Wikipedia before I started writing, and was guided by them. Accordingly, I am convinced that they don't apply to this work. For example, all the characters, situations and events herein are entirely fictional, the pure products of my imagination; and that will be abundantly clear to readers.

At the same time, the book is about the real circumstances of politicians, politics, and American governance at a critical juncture in our nation's –and Earth's- destiny; and I wanted to warn my readers about how easily the best motives can be perverted, and the most honorable intentions corrupted. I have done so by imagining metaphorical characters, situations and events to shed light on reality.

1

Heading back to the White House in the back seat of USA1, and after first making sure that the ubiquitous cameras weren't trained on them, Barzhad shot an imploring look at Millie and said, "Shit! I need a cigarette. My presidency for a Marlboro!"

His wife's mood was still unpredictable, but his desperation, and the excessive turn of phrase he used, which he may have meant seriously, rewarded him with a burst of laughter: however, she smothered that at once. She gave him a Nicorette gum from the packet she had put into her coat pocket against just such an emergency, and he stuffed it into his mouth and began chomping greedily.

Honor guards in the full dress regalia of the various armed forces of the United States, accompanied by military bands playing well known and maddening, Scottish- and Irish-inflected, patriotic marches that alternately quickened or retarded their progress, were bound in the aggregate to prolong the trip. With Pennsylvania Avenue barred to other traffic, it shouldn't have taken longer than a single hot minute!

Finally at the White House Residence, still more delay stood between the newly inaugurated president and his last remaining drug of choice. His two young daughters, whom his mother-in-law had brought home ahead of them, ran past their mother and butted their respective heads really enthusiastically into his stomach and groin. Ouch, she winced: those were hard heads, however admirably the elite schooling was sculpting their insides. "The speech was greater than I expected," Marie, the more professional and discerning critic of the two, assured him, "the greatest." Sally, the younger, probably hadn't paid much attention to his oratory; she tugged his hand and insisted on his immediately accompanying her to her new bedroom. Millie's brother, his wife and their two children were staying until the following week, and so the whole extended family tagged along behind them. "Nice looking-out, Dad!" Sally said, introducing him to the space with a curtsey and a theatrical flourish. The domestic staff had left to one side her specifically personal belongings for her to arrange to her liking. "The !Mac goes here," she decided, "Dad, can you help me, puh-lease! Then, if you move the easel right over there, with those boxes of paints, I'd be much obliged. Thanks, you're the best, Dad, absolutely. If you start stacking the books, I can put Kermit and the Count and Curious George to bed for a nap. The excitement has exhausted them. In fact, I can tell E.T. is coming down with something!" Marie's room had to be inspected next; but as she was more of a private person than her sister, and fastidious, if not secretive, in her intimate preferences and appointments, they were hurried to Grandma's; and finally Auntie and Uncle's, and the cousins,' in the Lincoln and Blue Rooms respectively. Then, they returned to the dining room and sat down to supper. They hadn't thought about the food themselves, but the solicitous staff had; and they realized how ravenous the eventful day had made them only as they devoured it. Anyway, the paper-thin, *tandoori* roast mutton slices piled up on the crusty bread clamored for justice to be meted out to them. The new White House chef and his sous-chefs had crafted homemade condiments from fresh, select spices and herbs, which enhanced them to near-perfection. A pot of hot, Darjeeling tea was at hand for the adults, and the children had mugs of hot chocolate.

When he could reasonably excuse himself from the restorative, if hyperkinetic, family feeding frenzy, and was satisfied that Millie had more or less reclaimed her usual, even-tempered self, he strode to the Oval Office with longer legs than usual, retracing the route he'd memorized during the house-inspection tour the outgoing presidential couple had given them two weeks previously. Quickly inside, he double-locked the door securely behind him, stepped into the adjoining parlor, where Monica's green dress had been famously ruined, double-locked that, got out the Marlboros, lit up, and inhaled deeply and gratefully, nearly reaching Final Extinction as the smoke filtered slowly out of his nostrils. Thanks to the thoughtfully furnished interior layout, a thickly upholstered wing chair came between him and the floor as he barely consciously buckled downward.

His mother and father instantly materialized. His father, who never altered his attire –straw hat, white cotton suit, open neck bush shirt and tan loafers- was puffing his corncob pipe, which was also his unvarying practice. The blend in it varied over the years, and smelled this time like Cuban taboo-ed-in-America, with a whiff of island rum. His mother, Queen Makeda IX, was ever the more fashion-conscious and runway-resplendent: her golden coronation tiara, studded with yellow diamonds, blue sapphires, rubies and emeralds, each stone the size of a sparrow's egg, sat atop her elaborately coiffed hair; the state necklace of pearls and burnished fishbone ornaments was thrice wrapped around her neck; and her informal gown of off-white *esh* brocade opened out on the floor in a circle of a good three feet. The design embroidered on it was the gorgeous beetle from whose secretion of filaments the ultra-soft fabric was spun, and which thrived only in their original homeland. Her feet and footwear were hidden, as the traditions of the nobility in that ancient place demanded –although it had been eons since they had inhabited it, as it had imploded into a black star.

Without walking or other obvious locomotion, his parents arrived at the two identical chairs that were facing their son's and sat down. The volumes of smoke that came out of his father's pipe always flabbergasted Barzhad, and he hoped that the smoke alarms, which were sure to be around somewhere, were tolerant of the presidential indulgence, and especially his father's. They consumed their tobacco companionably for a while, under the Queen's affectionate regard, until Barzhad got up to find an ashtray, or some container in which he could discard his cigarette butt.

When he joined them again, with a ceramic bowl in case his father wanted to empty his pipe, his mother congratulated him, "How brilliantly you performed today! They loved you. Their acceptance of you is truly remarkable, and it's rare that our emissaries achieve that kind of rapport to such a considerable degree. I'm more confident than ever that you'll accomplish your mission."

The crosshatched planes in his father's face refracted the light from the chandelier. It played in the hollows of his dimples, above which his cheeks had the sheen of ripe, terrestrial black plums. Beams of illumination ricocheted from it onto the Queen, his fourth and favorite wife, and his twelfth son. He winked at the latter, and continued effortlessly to extract unimaginably voluminous billows of smoke from his pipe. "It's what they are made of in these environs," he observed, "Ether, air, fire, water, earth, vegetation and food. They can be played along that scale like musical instruments, and be brought down easily from any agitation into an amenable state. But concentration —now, that's going to be your challenge. Getting them to keep paying attention. After all, the notes go the other way too."

According to what he had been taught, his father had been at the Third Level of Ascension when this *saha* universe manifested, or well beyond the point where he might have been required to assume any of its forms. Now, at the Ninth, his disinclination was undoubtedly irrevocable. Both his parents were powerful beings, able to whizz through the fourteen –and counting- dimensions imperceptibly, shrinking to the size of a subatomic particle or ballooning out as large as Jupiter, as necessary; stopping rivers and relocating mountains; shifting axes and correcting orbits; but Barzhad knew they really couldn't wrap their heads around earth-bound specifics like "American," "Democrat," "Republican," "bipartisan," "economic recession," "currency manipulation," "stimulus package," or "terrorism," whether due to studied indifference or genuine perplexity. The problems that he was going to have to address on a daily basis, which Americans his daughters' age intuitively grasped, even if the majority, following unproven prejudices and herd instincts, frequently construed them erroneously and counterproductively, couldn't penetrate their intellects at all. As an American, he could get inside them like the rest; but why, as their son, hadn't he also inherited their powers, so that he could grapple with them as effectively as a Superhero could? Goodness knows he had mightily tried, again and again, but he hadn't been able to budge a millimeter up or down or sideways out of plain, unassuming –black- Clark Kent.

The Queen's unspecific encomiums were proof of his assessment of her inability to understand the nearly indigestible victuals that were lying on his plate. "Barzhad can lift them up," she asserted cheerily, "We mustn't underestimate him."

"Dad's right, Mom," Barzhad lectured. "Because of those same constitutional elements he described, individual persons here have their hands full dealing with their envy, anger, greed, and petty rivalries. Diacritics like race, ethnicity, class, region, age, gender, and sexual orientation bend them out of shape. Afflictions galore -lack of willpower, depression, laziness, addictions, mental disease, sexual obsessions, physical illnesses, and plain gullibility- shackle them like prisoners to their quacks, witches and witch doctors. With all of that going on, it's difficult for them to stay focused on the big picture."

He reined himself in, and looked expectantly at his mother. Whenever he revealed his insider's knowledge of the locals, it only encouraged her to be more unstinting in her admiration. "It was such a good idea to expose you to so many contrastive environments, situations and persons," she now said, "Black father, white mother, and a child and apprentice of all those different communities where you lived: and, of course, I know of no one in any of the worlds who could possibly rival your superlative observational or analytical skills. If anyone knows how to overcome any obstacles, it's surely you."

He thought ruefully that those very same observational or analytical skills, or participant observation, might have instead saddled him personally with said obstacles, rather than equipping him for their removal. He often had to struggle for the investigative distance and outsider's perspective that were supposed to be the methodology's rewards. Had he "gone native?"

"It's not as easy as you think, Mom," he said, "and the few gains I made wouldn't have been possible at all without your unflagging support, and Dad's timely counsel."

The light in his father's face suffered a sudden eclipse. "Well, it's difficult everywhere. Who knows what's going on in your universe, other than that it's troubling in the extreme, and needs critical intervention fast? Before coming here, we visited Eldest Wife on the sun. The energy loss there is really unbelievable and tragic. My oldest boy won the Solar Cup five times in a row for the high jump. He used to defy the Solar Laws of Levitation and Thermonuclear Fission going up and the Solar Laws of Gravity and Energy Displacement coming down. There wasn't anything more stunning in cosmic sports. Now he can't even attain half his record, and as for his younger competitors, forget it! They don't even come close to that. So, you mustn't beat yourself up if your attempts here don't ultimately bear fruit. All the previous ones failed anyway. After all, universes are just cosmic fast food –readily gobbled up, and pretty much empty calories in the end: easy come, easy go."

Barzhad could tell from his expression that, despite his ominous pronouncement, he was clearly very pleased by his cross-cultural expertise, and his familiarity with the local buzzwords.

His Blackberry rang out at his waist, and his parents vanished instantly. It was his wife. "The kids are breaking through the door and stripping the paneling. First day in residence, and they're already turning it into the 'hood. You can't be on the job today of all days. Open up!"

He was wearing his trademark easy smile when he let the troop in. "We are hitting the ground running tomorrow morning, 8am sharp," he said coolly, "just thought I'd jot down a rough schedule and some notes, is all."

Millie, who knew differently of course, smiled her Mona Lisa-with-a-tan smile. "Well, let's get through tonight first," she told him, "There are a bunch of events the grownups have to attend, which will mean we'll have been up nearly the full twenty-four hours. A few minutes quality time with the kids and to catch our breath before we change into evening wear will do us all a power of good."

Later, after dancing the night away at the events they had selected to attend, to the delight of the invited guests, the paparazzi and the television cameras, they were pleased, exhausted and relieved when they found themselves alone in their bedroom at 4am. Barzhad took up the house telephone and asked to be woken at six. Then, he took Millie in his arms, as he had done at all those ballrooms in the past eight hours. But this time, absent the public scrutiny, he was more spontaneous and affectionate.

"Thanks a lot for rallying around," he told her, "When I saw how out-of-sorts you still were coming into the grandstand, my heart sank. I thought, 'L-a-a-dies a-n-d Gent-le-men, the South Side of ....Chicago!'"

"Hey, welcome back, Mr. Nowhere Man!" she said, half jokingly and half in annoyance, "You've been 'Mr. First Credible African-American Candidate' and 'Mr. First African-American President' for so long, I clean forgot you were also Hawaiian, Tanzanian, Kuala Lumpuran and who knows what else besides. Anyway, please quit dissing the South Side already. When I was in Zen heaven on the South Side of Honolulu just a week ago, Native Hawaiians were expressing their bitter resentments against *haolis* in far more savage gutturals that the ones with which we articulated our kindred resentments in Chicago!"

Taking great care not to reignite the explosive topic, while at the same time acknowledging and respecting what was on her mind, Barzhad continued, "Anyways, maybe that's what the country really needs to bust it out of its rut: a First Family Reality Show Spat. If your predecessor had thrown open some of these doors for the American public to see the countless, honest reasons why she despised and detested her husband, and how much his know-nothingness and boorishness grated on her last nerve, we probably wouldn't be in Afghanistan or Iraq today. "

"Do we have to sleep in *their* bed?" she demanded, "I wish we'd brought our comfy Mr. Sleepy's from Chicago!"

The fervent remark prevented their first moments alone in their new home from frosting over, and Barzhad found an opening to appreciably advance the passionate moves he had started earlier.

"I'm sorry an' all," he murmured, holding her more tightly.

Relenting, she leaned in closer to him. God, she did love this man! "It really was my fault too. I guess I'm not yet accustomed to playing second fiddle. You know me as a person with independent and outspoken views, and that's how the rest of the family, my former employees and colleagues, our friends and people generally know me. I also happen to believe that maintaining that independence sets an important example for our little girls, given the gender wars that still haven't stopped wreaking havoc in the lives of women. And now it's, "Mr. President, this: Mr. President, that," and the whole bias towards homogenizing us and pasteurizing us as a two-headed, single beast! I guess I was scared I was losing my personality, my individuality."

He laughed, "Hey, you're The Perlmann! You know they were faking their performance, didn't you: it had been pre-recorded, because of the cold. Look, I value your advice above anybody else's. That was true when you were my first boss, and it's true today too. I'm getting just as exhausted and fed up as you with all the pageantry and heraldry. It'll soon end. Though I am really impressed by the sincere efforts everyone is making."

Here we go again! Millie disengaged herself as tenderly as she was able. "Sweetie, America keeps on escaping you, doesn't it?" she said, "It saddens me, and I don't know what else I can say or do to prevent it. Americans are *anything* but innocent and sincere, no matter how hard they pretend. There's always an ulterior motive!

"Do you remember how, during the campaign, voters were afraid of me –not you- because they thought I hated white people? That was back when we were still seen as having distinct, separate personalities, before we got mashed together in the one brand name, the Dream Team Solution to their every problem. Why do you think they had that opinion of me?"

Barzhad stopped helping her unzip her gown. He looked distracted. They'd been having this same discussion for their entire marriage. Yes, his mother's white, American family in Mississippi had raised him; and yes, although he'd never known his father, and had visited it only briefly for the first time at the late age of twenty-six, he'd nevertheless carried from infancy a subliminal feeling of greater connectedness to Tanzania, to its neat homes, banana groves and sociable cattle sheltering under the snow-capped southern slopes of Mt. Kilimanjaro, than to America. And yet, who knew the South Side of Chicago more intimately than him? Or New York and New Haven, where he'd gone for undergraduate and graduate studies? And didn't he regard himself spiritually as more a member of her mother's home than of his maternal grandmother's? America was a land of immigrants, they all assimilated more or less successfully, and who was more American than this President?

"Didn't everyone agree that some moronic Republican talk show host had taken a couple of your comments out of context?" he asked.

"I forgot how we resolved the issue," she said, "but it wasn't a mix-up or somebody's deliberate malice. There was a profound truth in it, a very accurate insight, or instinct, on their part. They were sure they'd get something out of you that they couldn't get out of me!"

Barzhad tried to show interest. "Which was?" he asked.

"I am still working it out in all its multiple ramifications," she answered, "We are talking about amazingly adept shape-shifters, morph specialists, the most skillful in the animal kingdom, you have to hand it to them! But certainly redemption; forgiveness for their sins; and a way to get out of the prison they've made out of their own white skins. They're so needy, and they knew you'd respond willingly to their needs. Just taking their vote gratefully and gracefully as a black man was an agreeable response, an absolution for them. But they figured I'd just say, 'stew in your own juice, burn in your self-inflicted hell, it serves you damn right!'"

Getting into her night shift, Millie studied the conflict of emotions being telegraphed onto his face, and knew exactly to the last letter the thoughts that were going through his mind. She'd been trying to get her point across for the same fourteen years he was likely reviewing at that moment. She couldn't help herself though. She said, with resignation, "Whatever else, the bottom line is: whites don't like us, honey. They can't, period. They look at us and they see who they really are -slavers, pirates, brigands, looters, rapists, pathological liars and genocidal monsters- and they recognize all the monumental bad karma they've accumulated over the centuries. Or they go into denial: we were such ineducable monkeys that they couldn't afford to spare the rod! The same alibis they use to duck Native Americans. And now it's just more vital than ever that you understand: if you don't deliver, and feed their need, they'll set you up to fail, so when the next black candidate comes along, they'll go ho-hum, been there, done that, and what a mess it was; there's no escaping the facts of nature; now back to business as usual."

He sat on the bed, bowed his head, and massaged the bridge of his nose between forefinger and thumb. She knew very well too what that gesture at this stage in the perennial altercation meant: he had tuned her out! And, despite her firmest resolve and her best efforts, she was aware that her anger was rising again, as it had earlier that morning. Her muscles were tightening and locking down into rigidity; the acrid , nauseous taste was filling her mouth; menace, negativity and profanity were prowling to force an entry into her vocabulary, although 'muthafucka,' 'niggah,' 'ho,' and 'cunt' had been expunged from it going on at least thirty-five years, when her mother had taken a short, electric cord to them on a memorable occasion; and Watts and Detroit, Oakland and Newark, and Scottsboro and Attica, were burning in her eyes, which were like live coals. She scrambled into bed, turned her back to him, and pulled the sheets over her head.

Re-emerging, she snarled, "Don't worry. When we wake up, the pictures on the front page of every newspaper in the world will assure us we are the world's happiest couple, the Dream*ing* First Family. We'll just take our cue from there."

And re-emerging again, "Talking about pictures: when I

saw that one of you and that disgusting rattlesnake, Gunther. in *The New York Times* on Monday, I thought the pair of you were auditioning for roles as Othello and Iago in an amateurish, sophomore, dramatic production. And now he's filled your head with all of this dumb China nonsense. No, the country isn't in this mess because shithead won't pay his goddamn income tax; or because his cousin 'made off' with $50 billion; or because the next-of-kin gave away $15 billion of their $25 billion government bailout in year-end bonuses to themselves and their chums; or because they just can't stop freakin' stealing and stealing and stealing, because after five hundred years, it's too deeply ingrained a habit to break. Or because they are too stupid to figure out how to teach a kid who's eager to learn, as the cane cutters in Cuba can. Or to provide adequate healthcare, again like the Cubans they spitefully blockaded. And on and on and on, like you said in your speech. No, it's the fault of the goddamn Chinese, manipulating the value of their two cents! They aren't making any goods for export anymore, and nobody can afford to buy them anyhow. So, what's the difference if they are charging fortune cookies or cow patties at half their usual rate?!"

On his side of the bed, Barzhad opened an eye. "I was the one talking about the Chinese as currency manipulators while I was a junior senator, Millie," he said tiredly.

"And I told you then you shouldn't base your opinions on international trade or foreign policy on your stupid dislike of perfectly good Chinese takeout!" she snapped. And turned off her bedside lamp. And shook: because now she was crying.

On his back, and straight as a ramrod in his place, Barzhad went into his twilight zone of semi-trance where he always repaired before finally falling asleep. Images of his parents' visit this afternoon flooded his mind. His mother thought unreservedly that he was one of them; Millie didn't think he was one of theirs; even the children had him tagged as a little weird, what with his barring ice cream, soda, cookies and potato chips from their diet; while he had thought of himself as the ecumenical nonpareil, with his several feet planted in all camps, one in each, like a Hindu god. How was that for the scenario of a major mix-up? He smiled miserably in the dark: people marveled how he kept so cool without wondering what he'd be like *if he weren't*!

Before sleep claimed him, he remembered his mother had congratulated him on his ethnographic detachment; and what his father had said about the constituent properties of humans, inviting to knowing fingers like the octave on a piano; and he wondered what they would have thought if they knew that he, their son, really, really, really dug thirtyish or fortyish, middle-class, white American boys!

2

Twenty minutes distant, at the Mayflower Hotel, Tommy Gunther hadn't yet, like the First Lady, forsworn profanity. He was ostensibly preparing for the second day of his confirmation hearing before the Senate the following morning. The president had nominated him to be Secretary of the Treasury. That worthy, with his wife, brother-in-law and sister-in-law, could now be seen on the hotel room's flat screen television arriving at the D.C. Neighborhood Inaugural Ball, the first of the ten such events that they would be attending that night. Tommy had turned off the volume to avoid hearing the cocky, Ivy League self-confidence in his prospective boss' voice.

Keeping his watery blue eyes nevertheless riveted to the screen, he told his companion in a peevish voice, "You know, Val, the shit really fucks with yours truly's brain! The black muthafucka actually makes you stand while he sits on his monkey ass. He sits right there in front of you, impudently staring up into your face. His mouth is level with where your dick is. Wait and see. One of these days, when I'm good and hard, see if I don't ram it right in!"

"Ooh," his companion said absently, "I'm sure he'd love that! I know I would." His companion was a thirtyish, pear-shaped, white woman who, like Tommy, wasn't wearing any clothes. She was preoccupied. She was kneeling beside the bed where Tommy-in-the-buff was lounging, using the bedside table as her work surface and absorbed in the chemistry she was performing. She had emptied about a teaspoon of cocaine into a cooking bottle, had carefully poured a little water into it from the pitcher on the table, and had added a pinch of baking soda from the Arm & Hammer box, which was beside the pitcher. She gently shook the bottle to combine the contents, and, rotating it slowly, applied at its bottom the flame of a Bic lighter, which was set at its lowest intensity. Chased by the heat, the mixture frothed up the sides of the bottle and then settled back down again; and at length, drawn by the steady, centripetal rotation, a quantity of cocaine alkaloid aggregated at the center of the surface of the water. Val continued mildly heating the bottle: then stopped; and removing its black cap, she slid in a small fragment of ice that she had fished out of the pitcher with a spoon, taking care not to break up the single globule of oil. The temperature of the water dropping, the oil solidified of a sudden as a cloudy ball, the texture of a piece of camphor and about the size of a hazelnut. *Voilà!* How magical, and so much more dramatic and realistic than the transubstantiation of the bread into flesh at Mass!

Tommy sat up in bed to witness the beatific finale. His breaths turned noticeably shorter and shallower, his eyebrows were deeply furrowed in furious concentration, and he was cocking his head from side to side for a better view, in an unwitting imitation of a bloodhound. When Val removed the freebase, or crack, from the cooking bottle with a metal dental probe and placed it on a china saucer to dry, he was passing the tip of his tongue across his upper lip, left to right, right to left, over and over again.

Val's were the sort of physique and general appearance that were evidently designed to arouse the libidos of a significant segment of Neo-Nazi males. Overall a muscular specimen, she had the de rigueur blonde hair and blue eyes, correspondingly a little scrappy and washed out in her particular case; barely prominent breasts; a wide, slightly concave stomach; and a breathtaking pelvic expanse, the very factory of the Fatherland's minions, keeping proportionate with which her buttocks also flared and swaggered out broadly, especially while she was kneeling, although they lacked depth. Her skin had a pale, somewhat brownish hue, and was covered with freckles, moles, blackheads, and other small, unidentified discolorations and blemishes of the same class. Her vivacity was her main attraction, and she was like a bee, unceasingly busying herself. The same liveliness, expressed in frequent smiles and other genial contortions, and especially enlisting the big mouth, saved an otherwise unappealing, rectangular face. Presently, she invested all these energies and their aforementioned manifestations to giving satisfaction to the well-nigh slavering Tommy.

First, she brought out of the closet a shopping bag containing a couple of boxes of Saran Wrap and, starting with his feet, began encasing Tommy in the clear plastic. She wasn't entirely clear how this ritual evolved between this particular client and her, except that it had originated from him; but it did leave her with a lot more freedom of action than him, at least in some physical aspects of the relationship, and she'd stopped wondering about it. The Saran Wrap crushed his hair against his skin, which acquired a corpse's pallor under the pressure. When she had bound both legs together, she worked upwards, back and front around the pelvic area and buttocks, and then the stomach, torso and each arm. She usually left binding the arms together for later, and the neck and head were optional.

Working quickly, she took up a small pair of grooming scissors next, and deftly liberated his genitals. The size of middling white onions, the testicles pushed free, and the penis tumbled out behind them and lolled groggily to the side. Val licked it good-naturedly with the tip of her tongue, and smiled vacantly as she noted that it bobbed briefly a couple of times, as though reviving. She surveyed her work, an eclectic mix of fetishes, including bondage and domination, and drawing on an understanding of the physiological circuitry of sensory perception and sexual arousal. Even for herself, for example, who had not invented the practice, there was some stimulation in the bound legs, which gave Tommy an almost feminine appeal, like a mermaid, or other large, albeit mythical, fish.

Finally, she fetched a small glass pipe and its parts from her pocket book, and after quarter-filling it with water, assembled them: fitting the rubber grommets into their appropriate holes; inserting the mouthpiece into one; and adjusting the stem in the other. The stem had been purposely broken, leaving the top a jagged piece of glass already charred black by several prior usages; but she placed a new, shiny, circular, brass-colored screen into it. Using a surgical scalpel that was lying on the bedside table, she separated the ball of crack into six chunks, each about as large as an orange pit. She placed one on the screen, and handed the works to Tommy, together with the Bic lighter. She reached into the shopping bag again, bringing out this time a flask of Courvoisier V.S.O.P. She measured out some cognac into the two glasses that the Mayflower had provided with the water pitcher.

Tommy suddenly slapped his palm to his forehead, and then held up a "Hold-on-a-sec-" forefinger. He took up his Blackberry and pushed a couple of keys in Speed Dial.

"Hi, sweetheart, I clean forgot to call," he said, his whining voice going from a little tremulous at first to more assertive, "I've been *so* hunched over these papers, I think it's thrown my back out."

He had also punched "Speaker" so as not to exclude Val. "Poor baby," a woman's voice came through clearly, "Please take care. You know what that back is! The kids wanted to phone, but we didn't want to disturb you. You're obviously the only man in the world who can do this job, so I don't know why they just don't give the approval and stop dragging you over the coals. So what if you prepared our tax return yourself!"

"Politics, darling," Tommy intoned, "Look, give my love to the kids, and let me get back to this shit! Will you be there in the morning?"

"Of course!" the voice emphatically replied.

"Okay," Tommy said, "the same place at eight sharp."

And, after disconnecting, to Val: "That'll keep the home fires burning," he said, "Let's see what we can do with this one. Not the Saran Wrap though!" They both laughed: self-consciously now, it seemed.

Tommy adjusted the lighter to the highest flame setting. He made a beak of his limp mouth, and put the mouthpiece into it. Then, he ignited the lighter; and the flame was beautiful to behold as, summoned by his in-breath, it curved into the stem of the pipe to find the sacrificial chunk of freebase, which made a sizzling-frying-crackling sound as it was impacted. A forceful stream of pure, white smoke immediately descended the stem, filled the pipe and mounted the mouthpiece with alacrity, disappearing in Tommy's mouth. The small world of the hotel room hung in empty space and absolute silence and stillness for a few seconds, but for the one or two wisps of smoke that escaped the corners of Tommy's mouth and nostrils. Beads of sweat swarmed his brow like a manic, in-vading army, and his eyelids fluttered involuntarily, in jerky, unsynchronized flickers revealing-concealing eyes that were pixilated and bloodshot.

He made vigorous gulping motions in his throat. Aston-ishingly, hardly any more smoke escaped from his nostrils or mouth. He passed the works to Val, who smoked the rest of his dosage. While she was playing the flame along the length of the stem in order to consume any oil that had dripped there before moving back to what remained of the crack on the screen, he knocked back the liquor in a single swig, and refilled the glass nearly to the brim.

They rested: but the stimulant properties of cocaine had kicked in, only a little tamed by alcohol. Restless, pent-up movement: glossolalia from both full throats: bravado from the prospective Treasury Secretary's.

"Those Republican cunts will be coming at me tomorrow," he boasted, "My taxes. Lehman Brothers. The A.I.G bailout. Bastards! Hypocrites! The worst thieves in the world! Worse than the Democrats, even! Boy, am I *re-a-d-y*! I can't wait to line them up and fuck them."

"Poor Tommy," Val commiserated, moving around here and there in the room, channel-surfing the television, and sipping her cognac, "they've already flogged the back taxes to death. I'm so scared of the I.R.S., I can't tell you how much. When I was working, in retail you know, H&R Block used to do my taxes. Did you know they give you an instant refund? You should have gone to them."

The president was on all the channels: replays of the in-auguration; the parade; Senator Kean's collapse; the couple strolling hand-in-hand on Pennsylvania Avenue; the presidential homecoming; and, in real time right then, the Youth Inaugural Ball.

There wasn't a percentage in being contemptuous of Val: after all, he wasn't hiring her for advice on taxes and taxation. "I could have laughed out loud when I dropped the China bombshell the other day," he said, "There was dead silence while this no-hitter from outfield sank into their friggin' thick skulls. If it's one thing they all like even more than ripping off mega-millions of the public's shekels, it's a good fight. War. Now, there's a stimulus bill for you! It would clear up the whole headache faster than an extra-strength Tylenol! You know chess?"

"Nah," Val replied, "Chinese checkers and 'Risk.' Hey! That's about war. You want to play? The front desk is sure to have them."

"No, I'm talking about the origin of the game," Tommy

explained patiently, "These fucking Hindu pederasts made it up, you know. Rajahs. They'd get their little servant boys to be the pieces -the pawns, bishops, knights, and king, and a transvestite cutie as queen. *Hijras*, they call'em. Our faggots on the Hill get the same thrill, sending the darkies and the Puerto Ricans to Iraq and Afghanistan as target practice for IED's and suicide bombers. You know what China would mean to them?"

"What's that word you said?" Val asked, "IED's?"

The future Treasury Secretary ignored the question. "Ah well, I guess a war with China is a long ways off yet," he muttered, "the more's the pity. But they'll be talking about this for weeks. We could slip the White House over to the muthafucka's home mud hut in Tanzania before they noticed a thing! The Chinese will huff and puff and threaten to blow the house down; the Europeans will spin around and around the Maypole; the liberal press here will be wringing their hands and earlocks; and it'll be weeks before anyone realizes that only two or three privately owned banks were left in the country. It could be called a kind of *de facto* nationalization, with heavy involvement from my selected representatives from the private sector."

"Weren't you against that?" Val asked.

As noted, Tommy had the expressions of a bloodhound, and he now shot her a surprised look, then quizzical, that would have been perfectly proper in that tortured, canine species. "That was for the Asians," he said, more soberly than before, "We can't have all the Asian governments looking over their businessmen's shoulders: those anal-retentive Chinese leaders are more than enough, thank you. Business would caulk up: how would we be able to cut a deal? To whom would we teach the fine arts of the touch? But if we are the U.S. government, and we run the show, and we decide who the private sector is, we can show up the rest of these bankers and investors for the penny-ante, three-card-Monte shysters they basically are. Can you imagine the scams a brain like Ruben's can dream up? Or Somerville's? Kid, you ain't seen nothin' yet!"

"Where'll that leave the little people like me?" Val wanted to know, plaintively.

"I'll take care of you, sweetie," he said unctuously, "you just take care of me." He was bouncing his penis up and down in his hand, causing the Saran Wrap to make perversely stimulating sounds.

Val sat on the bed moodily and took it from him. She bent over and put it into her mouth. She put it in and out, in and out, lingering over and prolonging each movement. Soon it was glistening with her saliva, had lengthened to a rigid six inches or so, and had darkened to a kind of pinkish-blue. As she continued these and similar ministrations, the tense cords that had been emerging in Tommy's face subsided, and he was able to smile more naturally again, which was to say with the usual smirk and curling upper lip.

"My favorite economist was a closet Darwinian," he explained, now in the more level tone of a schoolmaster coaching a so-so student, "Joseph Schumpeter. His key concept was 'creative destruction.' The idea was the economy progressed in cycles. It was as Darwinian as anything else, and natural selection predicated the cycles. It handed out punishments, not only rewards. The players left standing at the end of the day were the best equipped to carry the whole charade to another, higher stage. We are going to be entering a new cycle after a round of destruction sanitizes this mess. If they are very lucky and escape retribution, the rest of these private bankers and investors can go away to enjoy the peanuts they have amassed so far. But the field will be open once again to the brightest and the best. That's when we'll run up smack against the handful of tight-fisted old farts in Beijing, who'll by then have the whole of Asia in their grip. Of course, the downside of the gamble is that the whole thing could just disintegrate into a million little pieces like Humpty-Dumpty, or *Mad Max*, never to be put back together again. But before we get to either place, shall we go again?"

Val put another portion of crack into the pipe, but although her inveterate cheerfulness always acted as a cushion to keep her a-float at the most difficult times, she seemed to be sinking now ever more into dismay and despair. Her features sagged downward, and her brow stayed creased. She hesitated before handing him the pipe.

"Everybody's heard of Darwin," she said, "'survival of the fittest,' and all of that. But it doesn't seem to be true. It doesn't really seem to work that way. People look out for one another all the time. Are you saying charity and generosity are just illusions, or a waste of time?"

The freebase crackled again when Tommy put the flame to it, and he was too occupied swallowing and digesting the smoke, and trying to prevent a thread of it from escaping, to articulate an answer to the question at once. But he nodded his head up and down to indicate he'd heard, or that, yes, that's what he did mean. The effect of the drug was very different this time. It was immediate: there wasn't any sweat; instead, an onlooker might have thought that Tommy had been caught outdoors in the bitterest Arctic weather, and had frozen over. The freeze was visible through the Saran Wrap, palpable: and his penis, so game and self-assured only the second before, beat a miserable, shriveled retreat nearly all the way into his pelvis.

Charitable Val postponed her hit to un-thaw him. When he had knocked back some more Cognac, she eased him down on the bed with her hand and fell to work again on the disgraced member. It was more uphill labor than previously; but she was greatly aided by the tight body bandage in his lower body, which concentrated all the local sensation in the genitals. Still, her efforts took a long time to produce any result, and she was feeling the strain in her lips and jaw before the object of her attention stirred ever so slightly and peeped out, much in the manner of a terrified terrapin cautiously putting out its neck from its carapace. At that moment, an involuntary ejaculation produced a weak slick of watery semen on the glans. Generous Val persevered in her task, and gradually the death-grip of cold began to lift off her companion. He slid up on the pillows, and reached out for more liquor. At last, as his recovery proceeded, Val smoked her share of the drug in her characteristic careful and restrained manner. Compared with his, her reaction was unremarkable.

The news cameras of the world were dancing around the presidential party as it quitted the Western Inaugural Ball: some channels were broadcasting that exit; while others were replaying the many images of the presidential couple dancing together, or with other partners. While they watched, they smoked two of the remaining chunks, without any noteworthy consequence.

Their previous conversation had remained in Val's mind, for presently she returned to it. "The way you were talking," she began, "it sounded as if an economy was a battleground, from which a few would walk away with all the spoils, this time around the government bureaucrats here in Washington, and next time you or your rivals in Beijing. Is that what an economy is for? To make a few persons rich and impoverish all the rest?"

Tommy agreed with her assessment. "What else?" he demanded.

"Well, I think the earliest banks must have been a village's granaries or its storehouses for cured meats and fish," she suggested, "Oh, and stuff like fine cloths and blankets, or the masks and images of precious metals and gems they made for use in religious or state ceremonies. When those occasions arose, folks dragged them out. If a young man or woman needed to start off on their own on a farm, they could borrow the seeds or cuttings and the farm implements, to be returned when surpluses from their harvests allowed. No down payment; no interest rates period, let alone any resetting; and an unlimited term. And if the crops failed and a famine was looming, there'd be enough of everything for everyone to eat their fill. When did that model change?"

Tommy threw out his chest; he segued into philosophical mode; moreover, his penis, which had resumed its regular, un-aroused size and appearance, emboldened him. "Sheer romanticism!" he decreed, "As well as a complete misunderstanding of the Darwinian principle, which is very, very reverential towards the gift of life. You see, you're taking it for granted: it's been freely provided, so you aren't making a big deal of it. Truth is, life is very, very precarious. No species has a special claim to it, and it can be taken away at any time. Individuals lose it in the blink of an eye as a matter of course: the most anyone can hope for is that his genes get passed on to posterity, and eyes like mine or yours will still show up a few thousand years from now in one of our descendants. Well, of course, the best-paid medical researchers, who don't take Medicaid or Medicare, are trying to prolong the lifespan a bit. But all the same, since it's inevitably a struggle, in the end it means us against Beijing, and all other comers."

"Tommy, tell me truthfully, because I voted for the son of a bitch," Val was pleading, "Is Barzhad Osama in on this?"

"Well, he recruited us, didn't he?" he replied, "He got Ramsay "Rambo" Ezekiel to round up the posse, didn't he? Now, that's one scary guy! A businessman can't say 'Good morning' to "Rambo" without shedding millions into his private accounts. Well, "Rambo" went after us with a vengeance. He wouldn't take no for an answer. Baroness Orczy pointblank refused: but he badgered him and badgered him something awful, until he came on board. And he's agreed to help me get Petey Bowen appointed as my top aide. That'll help things along nicely, since my frank opinion is Petey really belongs in the mafia. The One won't like it, since he's passed an ethics rule to ban former lobbyists, but he lets me get away with anything I like. And "Rambo," as I said, will be lobbying for Petey too."

"Well, maybe he is Darth Vader, and keeps the president in the dark?" Val wondered hopefully.

"Who really knows?" Tommy told her, "it's not as if they pass out an agenda for these sorts of covert operations to Cabinet members or senior staffers. But another piece of the puzzle is party politics. While the Republicans were hauling off the loot during the last eight years, a small group of Democrats was vowing to rake it in and clean up if they ever got back in power."

"They?" she asked, with raised eyebrows.

"Hey, I haven't any party allegiance," he replied, "I'm like you, I go with whoever's paying."

He regretted the remark the moment it was out of his mouth, but as she didn't seem to take offense, he went on. "Come to think of it, "Rambo" *is* ringleader material, and a more avaricious man than you'd ever care to know personally, and both of those muthafuckas are from Illinois, whose sitting governor, as you well know, is anxious to prove that the state is the most corrupt in the Union, if not the whole world. As you also know, he's another Democrat. So, who knows whether or not there's a conspiracy?"

After Val finished playing the flame up and down the stem to catch any errant trickles of oil, she refueled it with another chunk, and they both smoked and drank again.

"Look, I'm just a career officer in finance, and not even a registered voter with either party," he said, when his power of speech was again restored, "So, what do I really know? I'll tell you, though: one thing the Hottentot Hottie has to his credit is IT-savvy. It's not simply that he's addicted to his Blackberry, or to Twittering and YouTubing and Facebooking and Ichatting and texting and emailing to everyone about everything. It's a powerful tool for mobilizing the faithful. Push come to shove, you could use it to bypass Congress and the judiciary altogether. It's a far more effective tool for making a dictatorship than anything that amateur Hitler possessed in his arsenal."

She looked so crestfallen that he took her in his arms and stroked her blonde hair, parted down the middle as on a distaff, kissed her mouth, and nuzzled her small breasts. The sole part of his lower body exposed to the feel of her, as to any other tactile sensory stimuli that might appear in the hotel room, such as a slight, random draft of air, his penis directly hardened. Experienced in the provision of these sorts of services, and aware also, and grateful, that he had been trying to mollify and please her, she mounted him, and rode him, the while bending forward so as to be kissed and nuzzled more, and sucked, and bitten.

A final effect of cocaine is that it is fatiguing, and eventually depletes its users' energies completely. It also makes the genitals numb, especially males.' After an hour or so, when he still hadn't finished, and remained as rock-hard as at the beginning of their embrace, she began to tire, and she tried abrupt, jerky moves to surprise him into climax, but to no avail.

"Fuck!" he exclaimed suddenly, "Look at the friggin' time! Get this shit offa me! I gotta get outta here!" And after she removed the Saran Wrap, she fell back on the bed and went to sleep at once, even beginning instantly to snore.

After he had showered and dressed in a dark suit, for which his boss-to-be apparently had a preference, he counted ten hundred-dollar bills out of his wallet and left them on the bedside table. In this kind of caper, he thought, you had to be careful not to short anyone, and he was convinced that, somewhere along the line, it was the stinginess of the former governor of New York that had led to his being 'formered.' Besides, he owed for the cognac and cocaine too; and anyway, he was sure he would figure out a way to get the outlay back by claiming it –or something equivalent- as a tax deduction.

He also wished he was surer about his proposed '*de facto* private-sector-assisted-nationalization' of the banks, which was mostly off-the-cuff swagger improvised on the spot to terrify the easily impressionable Val, or about any of the alternative plans to rescue the banking system. He needed to think them through some more. Truth was, nobody knew for sure what to do, and certainly not him; and it was unlikely that they would anytime soon. But he had many constituencies to please, and mostly his own bottom line; there wasn't anyone he could trust; and he'd have to play it very close to the chest —beginning in a little less than thirty minutes from now.

3

The macrocosm is the microcosm writ large, and the microcosm is the macrocosm pared down to the fine print. In light of this maxim, Robert was wondering whether the Dow Jones Industrial Average had fallen from its modest height of nearly 10,000 points in August 2008 to an abysmal low of nearly 7,000 -and still in rapid freefall- in January 2008 because the metric had become a metaphor for his personal failings, the same ones that he had been striving for so long and so hard to rectify. He was willing to wager the equivalent of a Big Three government bailout that many persons across the length and breadth of the country were scrutinizing their own histories for the same link between personal misbehavior and the global economy's collapse, in whichever direction the connection ran.

"I love you so very much," the email read, "and I can't wait to come back to show you just how much." Yesterday evening's message had burned into the monitor: "I think of you every waking minute, my darling, and I dream of you whenever I am asleep." That morning, it had been, "I wish you were here in my arms, which are empty and useless without you. I want to spend the rest of my life with you, building happy memories and having many children together." And so it had gone, two or more emails a day for the entire month that she had been away. Robert had been taken by surprise, and couldn't really say when the relationship had taken this passionate turn. After all, he was sixty-five, and she was twenty-six. The shock was compelling him to learn that, while meditation or a spiritual practice vouchsafed inner composure, which was surely equal to most of the trauma life might inflict, it was less certain as a protection against sexuality, even at his age, and at his fairly advanced stage of the practice. The difficulty wasn't really unforeseeable, if account was taken of sexuality as the central mechanism –a basic instinct- by which the world perpetuates its existence, with all its attendant frustrations, disappoint-ments and losses. It was easier to prune the tree, less so to cleanly deracinate it. Given the way, as he had discovered, that energies, qualities and events typically intersected in the universe, it was actually unsurprising that, just as he, in the course of his *sadhana*, and no doubt helped by approaching old age, was finally coming to grips with his sexuality, the body's last holdout, his path crossed with a beautiful young woman who was extremely conflicted about hers.

When she met him about two years ago, Awe had just ended the last of a series of abusive relationships with various males, this last having been egregiously harmful, when a so-called 'friend,' the week before his wedding, forced his way into her apartment and raped her. Her discomfiture had fogged up the tidy picture of his contemplative life! It had obliged him to revisit personal feelings of affection, empathy and caring that he would have preferred to superannuate or sublimate, and she to depend extraordinarily on them. She had gone to her hometown in Japan for the Christmas-New Year's vaca-tion, and had planned to return to New York on January 13, but had then postponed her flight to January 21, and he was expecting her to visit that day. In light of the troubling emails she had been sending, he had been analyzing her behavior and his during the course of their relationship for clues that would have located their origin, and whether, despite his better inclinations, he might not have encouraged the unsettling feelings they contained.

Their first meeting had taken place on a very warm evening in May 2007. Below the extraordinarily pretty, flower-like face, Awe had presented her comely figure in probably the skimpiest outfit Robert had recently seen. He liked to imagine his spiritual growth had, as of that date, already put him past flirting with women, and particularly with someone almost forty years his junior: but she did end up spending much more time in the store than the average customer, who merely intended to make a purchase. Had it started then, on that debut occasion?

After making her stunning, bare entry, she had looked around the store on her own for a few minutes before he approached her. Could he help? Was she looking for anything in particular? Candles? Incense? Perfumes? Essential oils? Soaps? They also carried yoga and mediation supplies, including books and CDs. He took down a dark blue candle and held up the bottom end for her to smell. When her little nose crinkled in slight recoil, he put it back and took another off the shelf.

Was that the sixty-five-year-old, soi-disant sage flirting with a twenty-six-year-old foreigner and visitor to our shores? She had appealed to him rather a lot, but he always had welcoming and kind words for all his customers, aside from the few who deliberately (and rudely) repudiated any interaction; and he always tried as hard as he could to relieve them of their cash, especially since sales had been plummeting for the past few years—the 'fundamentals of the economy' had actually begun weakening in 2000.

He asked what her name was, and she readily told him, "Awe." Her voice tasted like one of those dried, Asian fruits: sweet, salty, fruity, spicy, preserved, fleshy, leathery, dry, all-at-once. When he stumbled on its improbability while repeating it, she spelled it, "A-w-e. You know, like 'awe.' It's a common name in Japan."

But when he immediately informed her he was researching a book he was writing, and she was just the type of one of the main characters in it, and it would help him if he got to know something about her, she was guarded.

Now, why had he said that? Although it was *true: his spiritual preoccupation hadn't prevented him from being a careful observer of economic developments; truthfully, he had been anticipating the present crisis for some time; and his Plan B had been to produce a fiction, the sales from which would at least support him into his dotage. Besides that, it would have been a fulfilling accomplishment, a fitting culmination of his scholarly and writerly endeavors.*

"Is that how you write books?" she asked incredulously, "I mean, you just go up to people and ask them for their personal information? What if it's coming on to them? Like, you know, hitting on them? Or maybe worse?"

He said he didn't really know what the correct procedure was. A very long time ago, in high school, his creative writing teachers had told him he was good at fiction writing; then, he'd majored in literature at college; after graduate school, he'd taught creative writing in high school, and had published pieces –mostly critical essays- here and there in obscure literary journals; then he had stopped for many years; but since his boss didn't mind if he used the computer for his personal use, he'd decided to take it up again. Anyway, it helped pass the time. That's how other authors got started, and their books turned out to be bestsellers. He was sorry if she got the impression he was hitting on her.

Well, that was *the issue, right?*

She had been dismissive then, and maybe just a little curious. Perhaps she wanted to change direction, and have him tell her about himself, and not be under the microscope herself. Or she thought he was trying to hit on her, but was now reversing course, and it struck her as cowardly.

But, on her part, it was clear that she wasn't in any hurry to leave either. Of course, in light of what he subsequently learned about her, it might have been her conflicted sexuality responding to the sexual warmth he conceded he might have been emitting, unwittingly or not: as deer stand stock still in the beam of the headlights of the car that will render them road kill.

"Well, is it going to be a novel?" she asked.

He guessed.

She was relaxed and relentless. She lifted her delicate features in the barest smile. "So, what's it about?"

If she questioned his motives, why was she going on? He hadn't locked and bolted the door!

He thought it was shaping up to be about immigration, and becoming an American. He was from Trinidad, and, after putting it off for years, he'd only recently been naturalized, so he'd become interested whether a person's outlook and life-style changed with residence status, whether their employment prospects improved, especially nonwhites, and what it was like to trade in their native countries for American citizenship.

Why was he *going on?*

Her laughter, like the blast of noise large marine birds, ungainly at water's edge, made, cacophonous and sustained, bent her double. "And a main character is like *me-e-e-e*?" she hooted scathingly. Her lightly epicanthic eyes were unceasingly watchful and serious: her other exertions deepened their brown color.

Yes. She was an immigrant too, wasn't she? Robert impatiently returned the candle to the shelf and flung back behind the !Mac, where he had been sitting.

And that had been his cue for her to get out*! Really.* Go*!*

Successfully quieting down, she took the first candle he had shown her and brought it to the counter. "OK," she said. And, after he rang up the sale and gave it to her in a bag, she asked his name. Robert. Agitation, and the penchant for prolonging vowels, overtook her again. "*O-o-o-o-h-h-h*! Robert was my first boyfriend in the U.S." she said, "In Tennessee.

After my parents divorced, my mother sent me to boarding school there. We were the same age, fifteen. I cried and cried and cried when I met his family. I didn't know a family could be *so-o-o-o* sweet. I was crying for my own family, you know, because I didn't see my father again until last year. The father and mother were like brother and sister. They were the same with the children. There were five kids in all, including Robert. The father made a lot of money inventing kitchen aids and other household items, and their mother painted and gardened. She wore long dresses, and flowers in her hair. They were like hippies. They had a huge house surrounded by flower gardens, medicinal plants, vegetables and orchards. I loved staying there. Robert was very laidback; he wasn't the assertive, macho type; but after a couple of years we drifted apart. Then I got a scholarship to the Brooklyn Academy of Music and came to New York. But we remained very close friends. I still correspond with his mother."

The Brooklyn Academy of Music was famous. Everybody's heard of it. Was she a professional musician?

He was certainly in the clear here: he had been interested solely in the musical profession and the biographies of musicians. He had been a jazz aficionado, until his sadhana had preempted all such interests.

"My mother is a famous opera singer, and she was my earliest teacher, and I guess I am top rated as a vocalist," she answered, "A keyboardist too. But mainly I compose. My compositions combine Japanese elements with jazz, blues and classical music in an unusual, fresh, new style. I aim to support myself one day writing my own music full time. In a few months, I'll be recording my first CD, all my original material. But right now, to pay the rent, I work at a media firm. I write music for films the firm makes, mostly commercials. Right now, I'm working on a more interesting project -an installation for the re-opening of the Denver Museum of Science and Technology. It's an exhibition for kids about water. It will have six screens, and my part is to write a different music for each. It's opening in August, so that's another deadline. That's what I was planning to do tonight: go back home, light my candle and just write music the whole night. You think the candle will help?"

Its scent was for alertness. Tobacco leaves and bergamot. He wished he were like her. Creative. Productive.

He had felt affection and respect for her at that moment. A lot of affection and a lot of respect: both.

"Here is very good," she replied, looking around the store, "Very positive *feng shui.* What does the Japanese girl in your novel do?"

And she was growing more comfortable, more at-home, which pleased him. But were they already taking the feeling to an improper level —improper in terms of his spiritual goals, and the age difference?

She composed music. A Trini reggae singer liked her, but she already had a boyfriend, a white American. He played guitar in a rock band. He mainlined heroin. The Trini brother smoked ganja, since he was a dread, but marijuana wasn't really a drug.

"*A-w-w-w-w,* " Awe screamed, "you're just making all this up!" But after more carefully internalizing what she had heard, she evidently became ill at ease. Her mouth formed an "O," her eyes screwed several circles tinier, and her voice lowered half an octave and wavered when she asked, "Unless you are psychic?"

Japanese, he would learn, were all -to the last man, woman and toddler- extraordinarily superstitious.

He wasn't. Well, everything in a novel was made up, wasn't it? But this really was his original idea from the start, before meeting her. After all, Japanese girls had been going with white rock musicians since Yoko Ono went with John Lennon, and Lennon was a junkie, and many white rock musicians were also. But lately he had observed that a lot of blacks he knew were hooking up with Japanese or Southeast Asian girlfriends. They seemed to like black music and blacks a lot in return. So, that's the part about the 'Trini reggae singer.' Did she personally know Japanese women who went with, or were married to, black men? After all, why should Japanese like white Americans? Why should Iraqis, Iranians, or Arabs?

Looking back, he couldn't possibly bring himself to believe that the question was really about his *chances! But the longer she stayed, the more attractive she seemed. He hadn't really positioned himself to enjoy a conversation with a young woman for quite some time.*

She regained her composure after closing her eyes and breathing in and out deeply through her nostrils several times. She put fingers nearly as minute as a baby's to her temples. She sat down on the high bar stool beside the counter, causing her very short, white skirt to ride up to the level of her groin. She gained a more secure perch by crossing her stylish pale legs. She reflected, "Yes, you're right. Lots of Japanese women can't stand whites. I do personally know Japanese women who live in black neighborhoods like Harlem or Crown Heights; all their friends are either Japanese or black; and they date only blacks. But, like, for others, it's a power thing, you know. Whites have the power. Being more in white society gives them privilege or prestige, whatever."

Had he been downcast?

"Black guys *are* cute," she finally allowed, "Japanese girls are very stylish, especially my generation, and sure, they find blacks are definitely more stylish than whites. They take pride in what they wear, they have an eye for sharp clothes, and they wear them with flair. Black guys usually have a better attitude too. Like, you know, more friendly, and supportive and appreciative. That's the key. Japanese girls are brought up to nurture, to give. When a man is really grateful to receive that kind of attention, well, it's a perfect match, right?"

Had an idyll of perfect domesticity floated in front of him then? He had married and divorced twice, and even with the best will, could find nothing complimentary to say about either experience. Did infernal hope spring eternal, despite the indifference to romantic matters that he was trying to deliberately cultivate?

He nodded.

She continued, "The drugs are a bad situation," she said, "That's why you freaked me out, because it did happen as you said. The first boyfriend I had after coming to New York was a musician and a junkie. Mike. He played guitar in a rock band. He'd get so wasted before they played, he'd spend the whole time on stage with his back to the audience. He really had very low self-esteem, and the dope helped him deal with it. You have to know about his background to really understand. His mother brought him up in a trailer park in Boulder, Colorado, and everyday she smoked meth and drank bootleg until she passed out. I went there only once, but that was one time too many, thank you! She was a single mother, you understand. She had three other kids by three different fathers, and she never cooked, cleaned, or took them to doctors' appointments. Forget about school! The man she was with when I visited was a drifter, and when he was around, the mood in the trailer was like before a tornado. It crackled with violence. I'm always the mother, you see, that's my nature, and so, needy persons like Mike are my specialty. Naturally, I fell for him. On top of that, I'd been sexually abused as a child by a teacher at the school for the gifted that I attended; and later, by a man who'd been stalking my famous mother; and somehow the threat of abuse –or my reaction to the threat, which was to be compliant and complicit -always crept into any relationship I had."

Male and female were the two energies in the universe, and they were complementary. Accordingly, there couldn't be any fault in the solicitude and protectiveness he felt then towards her, could there? There was no way then for him to hurry her up, and send her packing, was there?

How did she meet him?

"At the Brooklyn Academy," she said, "The music world is like a small fishbowl. The audience gets to look in only from the outside, and sees exotic, colorful characters. Inside, it's the same few fish going around and around. At the Academy, it's classes, ensembles, rehearsals and concerts: the students are always crammed together; it's not like the vast undergraduate class in the sciences or general studies. After graduation, it's about us forming trios and quartets and quintets on our own: or using one another to find jobs, gigs, sign contracts, or just get noticed. Helping and preventing –both, unfortunately. Mike is really very talented. Of musicians our age, I'd say he's the one the general public will hear about first. I mean if dope –or his bad attitude- doesn't finish him off first."

Most talented musicians, pop or classical, seemed to have led tormented lives. Drug abuse was an occupational hazard. Jimi Hendricks. Beethoven. Kurt Cobain. Mary J. Blige. Billie Holiday. In Mike's case, his upbringing must have taken him readily from the Brooklyn Academy of Music to junk.

He had known the works of these musicians intimately.

"That certainly, but you also have to thank President Know Nothing too." she sneered, "Thank God, he's gone! He sent the biggest, most-organized and most efficient drug distribution organization in human history to Afghanistan, where poppies are grown and the stuff is manufactured. You don't see the stories as much in the media here, but in Japan they churn them out regularly. The minute the U.S. Army got there, production quintupled. Before, the Taliban had reduced it to zero, right?"

During the war against Vietnam, the military brought drugs stateside in body bags and in the pouches for top-secret, classified dispatches. There are plenty re-runs of those stories.

Whoa! Was he subtly undermining her preference for white, American boyfriends?

More, black thong reached him at eye-level as she re-crossed her legs for greater comfort and stability on the bar stool, and she continued, "Dope is wack, man. All of Mike's money went on it. His time too: it ate up all the time when he wasn't playing music -waiting to score, and being dope-sick and fit to be tied while he waited; the hassle of tracking down needle exchanges to get clean works; cooking up; injecting; booting. That's when you stick the needle in a vein and just keep drawing the blood in and out, in and out: he'd do that for hours at a time, like in a trance. He went from cooking up a bag, to a couple of bags, to ten bags at a time. Then there was speedball -boy and girl, the dope with coke. He'd go from manic to comatose, comatose to manic, everything-slowed-down to everything-fast-forward, and back again. Then he'd get a 'dope-dick,' when he'd just go on forever and forever and couldn't come. Let me tell you: not fun, to-be-seriously-avoided, especially if you're the unwilling, intimidated, exhausted partner. He wouldn't eat for days; or else he'd be eating everything in sight and then vomiting it up, like a river -effortlessly, everything, everywhere. They say that's a special effect of the U.S. Army Afghan dope. Again: not fun, especially if you're doing the cleaning up. He wouldn't shower for days, until he'd give in bad-temperedly to my nagging; and he kept wearing the same underwear and clothes the whole time. Finally, I'd get fed up and sneak them out to the Laundromat while he slept."

Did she ever try it?

"Never!" she exclaimed, "I like to be in control of my thoughts and emotions and behavior at all times. I don't drink alcohol, and I don't even drink coffee. In Japan, they teach kids *zazen* -to meditate- in kindergarten, and that's when I lose myself. But it's for more awareness, not less, you understand; and when you come out of it, you have even better control of how you think, feel and act."

He could have clapped his hands, he was that relieved on her account! He stored this nugget about Japanese pedagogy, and was happy they had something very significant in common.

Did she still keep up the practice?

She sighed noisily. "Would I be saying any of this if I did?" she asked, "I don't have to ask, I see you do. I should start again. But America isn't a supportive environment for it. Americans are very shallow, you know. Like Mike."

So, she ended the relationship?

"*He* ended it," she snapped, "or keeps ending it. The stop-go has been going on for four years now. Every year, when it starts getting colder, he'd start picking fights. He'd start resenting the care I was giving. The meals I cooked for him, the gifts I gave him, like to celebrate his birthday, or if the band got a new gig or venue. He'd never had that kind of attention from his mother growing up, so I guess it confused him. I was too possessive! I was stifling him! Then he'd start seeing other women and eventually he'd move out of my apartment. Always my apartment, which I paid for! Then, when spring comes, the telephone calls and emails start coming too. He misses me. He worries about me. He keeps thinking about how we were, when we'd been together. But this year I'm not going for it! I haven't answered the emails and the telephone calls so far."

This was one of the major things he was running from —the flesh, this worldly life, its transient pleasures that always ended in sorrow and pain, these disappointments, this deluded death-in-life!

Did she still love him?

"'What's love got to do with it?'" she said, "I miss him. I get lonely, and that's when I start thinking about him. But you want me to tell you the truth? Sometimes when I was lying in bed next to him, and he was asleep and usually snoring loudly, I'd feel *so-o-o-o* stupid! Like, duh! I mean, I'd feel I'd lost my intelligence or half of my brain, you know, that I'd grown dumber living with him. Just lying next to him was like a lobotomy! Like, I'd died! He's a great musician, but he isn't smart at all. No thoughts! No interests! No conversation! Forget books! The TV always on! Dope! Drinking beer in a bar with a bunch of male friends just like him! Picking up females!"

"I'm scared if I don't have a baby before I'm thirty, I won't ever have one!"

That was pure biology! And he had known girls in his time who had their hair done, painted their nails, spent hours on the telephone, read movie magazines, watched TV, and did little else. Since then, they'd be YouTubing and MySpacing and texting. He understood.

She paused a moment. "After we broke up this last time, one of those bastards came around claiming he had sent him to pick some of his equipment. Then he forced me to have sex with him."

He was speechless. But he was a bit of a caretaker, as she claimed to be, and knew that her disclosure would make it difficult for him to deny her anything she might ask of him.

"Are you going to put all of this into your novel?" she demanded. "I can't *be-lie-ve* how much I'm telling you! Let's talk about your novel instead!"

How were you supposed to proceed? The teaching was that the One Real Life shone forth from every creature, but they were unreal. She was unreal He was unreal! Yet they were One, the One Real Life. You had to live a paradox.

He wasn't sure how to proceed.

She gave that a thought. "Well, it's about musicians, right?" she suggested, "The details about the music scene will have to be authentic, isn't that important? You'll have to put in about the odd jobs, like waiting tables, second-hand clothes, walk-up apartments, and free food, whenever and wherever you can get it. Gorge or starve, like the Stone Age. Auditioning, the late night-early morning gigs, if you're lucky to play a well-known spot like *The Village Gate, Blue Note, Knitting Factory* or *Birdland*. Otherwise, you can take your pick of small hotels and bars and steakhouses. There are all those stifling school auditoriums and church basements in Jersey. Ditto in Europe, the Middle East, Japan, Southeast Asia and Australia. Dubai and Abu Dhabi are hot right now, because they're building all these skyscrapers, and they want American music in every room, on escalators, in the elevators and on sidewalks. The sheikhs pay well and they pay cash, U.S. currency, but you have to fight them for it. Then there's studio recording. That's even more boring and repetitive than a photo shoot or video, which you also have to do at one point or another. Getting back up, sidemen, technicians and sound engineers in one place at the same time is harder than drawing down the troops in Iraq! If you are a woman, add being sexual prey to all the other frustrations. Black guys *are* smoother! Come to think of it, there's this guy at the firm who really, really likes me, I can tell, but he's *so-o-o-o* cool about it. Desmond's his name. He just looks out for me, you know?"

Was he a musician?

"Not at the firm," she said, "but I think he plays in a soca or reggae band here in Brooklyn. In fact, I remember he'd put the idea to me about coming out with him to Prospect Park on a Sunday, to listen to the drumming. Seems drummers have been gathering there for over thirty years on Sundays during summer, and a lot of vendors also come out to sell food and handicrafts. Lots of Asian women go, so I'd fit right in. You sound a lot like him, so maybe he's a Trini. *Stra-a-a-a-nge!*"

It was one of the larger islands, and, consequently, the immigration to the U.S. was substantial.

Presently she asked, "Are you married, or with anyone?"

Why had she asked?

He wasn't married or seeing anyone.

"Why not?" she wanted to know, "You have this dignified manner, and you're easy to get along with. Here I am, pouring out my heart to you, and I've just barely met you! You don't act gay. Are you?"

Because I'm old enough to be your grandfather, that's why!

41

At my age, I should be preparing for what comes after this life, if anything. Were birth and death real?

He wasn't.

"I never dated a black guy," she said, "there weren't many in Tennessee, and only a few at the Academy. They kept to themselves. I sort of got caught up with the white crowd."

There was the Trini at her office.

"Oh, Desmond. He's *so-o-o-o* sweet," she agreed, "Very mild-mannered and polite. Very quiet and serene. Never raises his voice. He'd be in the same room with you, and you'd never notice! *Aw-w-w*, wouldn't that be just the thing for you? If I went out with him, that would be your novel, wouldn't it? Whole and complete!"

She would have to keep an accurate record and report to him regularly. A novel about a black-Japanese love interest would make a realistic departure from "Sayonara" and "The Mikado." *Guess Who's Coming to Dinner?* -the Japanese version.

She added, "The Black-Japanese babies I've seen are *so-o-o-o* cute! Aren't Barzhad's daughters adorable? The talk about black fathers is all nonsense!"

Yes and no. Income, education, and community expectations have a lot to do with it. Slavery hadn't been the best parental-training school, especially for fathers, and the rate of incarceration of black males contributed to absenteeism, divorce or abandonment. Mothers were left to take on parental responsibility singlehandedly.

She looked at her watch. "*Aw-w-w-w,* " she exclaimed, "look how long you've kept me! I should have been working! I'll be back when I've finished the candle. Best of luck with your novel!"

Afterwards, their relationship had kept on strengthening. Awe visited daily: and sometimes, because he no longer knew what to do with himself in a restaurant, they'd order in and share a meal; and although many of his customers liked and respected him, he never took up their invitations to visit them at their homes, offices or places of business, but a couple of times, he'd accepted hers to have tea at her apartment. On a few occasions, she'd visited his apartment, which she had immediately commenced cleaning, that occupation apparently being a sort of national hobby among Japanese women of all ages. In the course of these exchanges, they had shared all their secrets candidly with each other, and grown as close as two persons could become, without being lovers. About graduating to that status, there'd never been any overt move, although it did remain in the background as low-level 'white' noise; and there had certainly been no discussion or indication about 'having babies' or living together as a married couple, the two most worrisome topics of the recent emails.

So, there it was, as completely as he could recollect it. Where were the inducements that had led to the emails? They were the difficulty her anticipated visit was causing, for he feared the crescendo of those messages would then be reached; and he would be put in the tricky situation of having to explain matters about himself that hadn't been appropriate previously, avoid causing hurt and embarrassment, and make some firm decisions regarding the two of them.

Robert washed his face and hands and feet in preparation for *sadhana*. He remembered how difficult it had been to do this when he first started, but, after five years of practice, it was growing so much easier. Now, the problems with Awe and the Dow Jones Industrial Average had already vanished by the time he was seated on his meditation pillow. Of his five senses, only smell remained functional, and that was as he had intended: and when the jasmine scent of the incense had succeeded in carrying him very nearly inside the sought-after, empty, odorless space, it tapered off, and it too vanished. Thereupon, his feelings started beginning not to stick, even the very one that noted they weren't. However, he did still experience his mind briefly –but as an inert companion, a sort of slumbering house pet, without any perception, cognition, reasoning, or thought disturbing it, until it was momentarily aroused by the memory of a Zen koan. That riddle went: new to the Master's monastery, a monk asked for instruction of the Way. The Master asked. "Have you eaten your breakfast gruel?" The monk replied, "Yes." The Master told him, "Go and wash your bowl." And the monk had an insight. And he slipped Robert right in behind him too!

See. Know. Enjoy. One. Lofting him to that blissful state occasionally, for longer or shorter periods of time, his *sadhana* had proven the best defense against anxiety, worry, confusion, haste, impatience, annoyance, anger, greed, lust, and impulsiveness. It was still in its infancy, even after the five years of application, and he understood accordingly that even greater insights and blessings were surely ahead. And so, it would be upon oceanic waves of gladness and gratitude that he would ride back into the quotidian. He found he required practicing at least twice a day, morning and night, this cleansing of his total disposition, just as his body required daily showers, or the ritual ablutions immediately before he began.

At the end of an hour or so, his mentality began striking scattered forays at the edges of the infinity in which he was wandering. Forms. Names. He kept being pulled away from connecting with them, as a powerful undertow in the ocean keeps dragging a swimmer back into the deep. Finally, a sense of equanimity helped him meet these invaders. He was an ordinary citizen, after all, with the obligations that came with the status; and a taxpayer, and had a job to go to.

Robert was the sole employee at the retail store in Brooklyn where Awe had discovered him. It was the ideal job. His boss was the most agreeable person a boss could be, a handsome, carefree, fun loving, great-hearted, Burkharian Jew of twenty-eight years of age. He would turn up at the store once or twice a month merely because he happened to be in the neighborhood and wanted to take the opportunity to throw some encouraging compliments and good wishes Robert's way: otherwise, he left every aspect of the business – opening and closing, ordering goods, maintaining inventory, serving customers, keeping records, deducting his very generous paycheck and payroll taxes, filing sales and corporation taxes, banking deposits, and making withdrawals- entirely to him. As a consequence, Robert was spared the mutual distrust and adversarial standoffishness that soured so many employer-employee relationships, and instead, after five years of service, he had developed a strong proprietary interest in the store.

But these were only some of the benefits the job afforded. For example, the pursuit of his *sadhana* would have been impossible, or very problematic, without the indispensable practical and emotional prerequisites of an excellent, steady paycheck and the harmoniousness of the workplace. Moreover, the job often left him with lots of leisure time during working hours, which he had put to good use in reading, studying and writing. He had also grown fond of the neighborhood where the store was located, a quiet, leafy block in Park Slope, down the hill from magnificent Prospect Park, which was by itself a tremendous resource, affording strolls and walking meditations in the early mornings and evenings along its secluded, tree-lined paths and trails. Some of his neighbors had gone out of their way to be considerate and friendly, further augmenting the pleasure of being there.

Another benefit was the substantial stature he had achieved in the composite roles of counselor, personal trainer and advisor in the field of alternative healing. As his *sadhana* intensified, a refreshing coolness of affect, respectfulness and benign regard automatically wafted off him towards his customers, browsers and other visitors to the store. They told him they felt becalmed and surer of themselves in the store and in his presence. Yoga, daily workouts and a sensible diet had improved his complexion, toned his muscles, moderated his speech, and sweetened his breath; and he radiated an aura of simultaneously occurring relaxation and alertness. As he was single, even if of an advanced age, he attracted the amorous attention of a significant number of females: but his deft, suave avoidance of that type of connection, and of sexual banter or innuendo, only won him additional kudos.

Consequently, it was not long before customers began to enquire about his "secret," and to solicit his advice how to overcome the circumstances and behaviors that were preventing them from achieving what they clearly perceived as his enviable state. Sexual relationships were an area of considerable conflict and unhappiness to most of them; dissatisfaction in their jobs, fear of dismissal, or tense, workplace relations were equally as commonplace; debt and money worries were ubiquitous; some had problems with drugs and alcohol or other obsessive behaviors; and ill health, stress and depression laid rough, heavy and unfriendly hands on the rest. After his advice had scored some really noteworthy successes, he discovered that he was being extensively recommended by word of mouth as a person to be petitioned for consultations. Kind and charitable, he was nevertheless conscious that his employment depended on the profits the store made; and while he refused to take payment for any counsel he dispensed, which was pretty much to describe in impersonal or general terms what he was doing, or to tailor it to a specific need, and recommend that his interlocutor should follow his example, he built up a brisk trade in yoga supplies, meditation pillows, books on these topics, religious statues and other devotional items, and the incense, candles and essential oils that he thought were beneficial for a particular person, in her or his introduction to *sadhana*, or in the specific trouble from which they wanted relief. Overall, he took care not to usurp the expertise of medical personnel, or other certified service providers; but the character of the store gradually changed to cater more to those he did offer.

In the five years of his employ, therefore, he had made a name for himself, if not primarily in his immediate neighborhood, which was predominantly white and affluent, then certainly in the outlying sections, such as Flatbush, Crown Heights, Prospect Heights, Bedford Stuyvesant, and Sunset Park, where immigrants from the Caribbean and the Spanish-speaking Circum-Caribbean had settled in dense communities, and where the folk-religious and -healthcare beliefs and practices of their native lands continued to exert a powerful influence. At length, he could claim as his own a permanent caseload of many clients and petitioners.

It turned out that he would greatly need all his own reserves on that stressful day in January 2009, not only because of Awe's impending visit and the romantic heat he was expecting it to generate, but also because a lightning bolt from the world's tanking economies had chosen to score a direct hit right in his own backyard. His boss arrived soon after he opened the store. But pale, drawn, unkempt and carelessly dressed, he brought bad news: he had lost every dime of a substantial fortune in an infamous Ponzi scheme operated by one of his late father's closest friends, was scrambling to avoid personal bankruptcy and homelessness, and could see no way out of giving up the store forthwith. As of next week, therefore, Robert should add himself to the 200,000 workers who had been laid off so far in the first three weeks of the year. His boss wished him luck finding another position: but as many more layoffs were expected in the final week of January, he didn't think his prospects were promising. He wished he could say he at least had some severance pay to offer, but he didn't. He was flat broke! Robert would learn from him by the end of the day the arrangements he was making for transferring inventory into storage and, of course, he would be paid while he supervised the clearance. There wouldn't even be time for a "Going Out of Business" sale, but Robert was authorized to sell off whatever goods he could at steep discounts. Sell them to your friends: he didn't care! He left abruptly to attend to other related, grim business.

At his age, Robert found the news harsh in the extreme. His boss was of course right about the outlook for finding another position, even without the age discrimination with which doubtlessly he would also have to contend. He had once worked for the New York Board of Education, but not long enough to earn a pension; and his 401(k) accumulation from that job had already dropped by about 50% in the *annus horribilis* just ended, with further losses already mounting in the current year. Looking at the brighter side, such as it was, he'd get a few months' unemployment, perhaps destined for an extension from the stimulus bill then being debated in Congress: and his age now entitled him to both Social Security benefits and Medicare. But it was axiomatic that he would no longer be able to afford his apartment beyond the next month at most. So, like his boss, he was also facing homelessness. Then, would he also lose the clientele for his counseling services? On hearing his boss' bad news, he had thought at once that his consultations could serve as an alternative source of income: but he didn't have the means to rent an office, or send out advertisements to his clients; and he wasn't even sure he'd continue to be able to afford an Internet connection. It said something about the benefits of meditation that he remained remarkably dispassionate as he examined the staggeringly awful bill of misfortunes he'd been handed. He guessed he should get used to the inevitable and start planning to shut the place down, first of all by gathering packing supplies.

Of course, the loss of his job had at least forced an unexpected resolution to his quandary regarding Awe. Did he any longer have the luxury of investigating what his real intentions, or hers, had been, or were? Or of concerning himself with what the future of their relationship would be? The recession -or Great Depression- of 2008-9 —or whatever name it would be assigned, and whenever the end date would turn out to be- hadn't any patience with romance, or the lack thereof, did it? How many in the U.S. and across the globe were engaged at that moment in a similar re-prioritizing? Foremost now among his worries —and theirs- was where he would lay his head when night came, and how to find food the following morning, and shelter from inclement weather. Right behind those questions was whether Barzhad Osama and his new administration in Washington could cobble together a recovery plan -and follow through on it- that could save him, and others in the same predicament, from an undue, prolongation of their pain, which would result in epidemics of ill health, and physical and emotional debilitation the longer it persisted; and whether they would be spared an old age and death, the epitaph of which would be only disappointment, the frustration of cherished goals, and the loss of their best beliefs and ideals. If his intentions towards Awe had really been pure, meant only to provide a young distressed girl far away from home with grandfatherly and mentor-ly support that she could clearly use, then the great recession would have to take the rap for his inability to deliver. But then, wouldn't something very rare and precious have disappeared from the world's store of blessings? And if it were not, well, it was just as well the recession had stepped in, wasn't it?

Said recession, however, applied a surprising twist to the tale that afternoon! He was just preoccupying himself with these thoughts when here she was indeed in person, flinging herself through the door and into his arms, clinging to him as if she didn't intend to ever let go, and murmuring exactly what he had expected to hear, "I love you. I love you so much!" And she reached up, and for the first time, put her soft, wet, hungry lips squarely on his.

After they somewhat disjointedly disengaged, Awe settled in the papasan, a bright red addition to the store since she had last visited. It was large enough to completely enclose her, once she had removed her shoes and had curled up in it with her stockinged feet tucked in.

Robert sat down behind his !Mac, his "driver's seat." Attempting to end a silence that had only lasted a second so far, but was already beginning to seem too embarrassingly long, Robert said, "That chair with you in the center has turned into a hibiscus. The chair would be the five-lobed petals, and you'd be the stamen and pistils: in Trinidad, we schoolboys used to lick the pollen off them, right off the flower where it was growing, which was usually on somebody's hedge. I guess we were imitating the humming birds and blue jays."

"It must be a beautiful island, your Trinidad, "she said, smiling as if to imitate the pretty hibiscus, "I hope there'll be a chapter in which I am your guest there."

"I hope so. But not for a while, I'm afraid," he replied grimly, "I just lost my job. The owner is closing down the store. I'm looking at homelessness, among other horrors."

She cringed into the papasan, and now looked less like a flower than a small animal burrowing underground to escape an awful fate. "How terrible!" she shrieked, "Robert. I'm so sorry, darling!"

"Well, it's not just me," he told her, to lighten her distress on his behalf, "Were you following the news stateside? While you were away, the crisis just got worse and worse. Banks and big companies closing. Profits drying up. Everyday, more layoffs. A couple of laid-off workers murdering their families, and then killing themselves. Or refusing to vacate the workplace."

She said, "Yes, the Japanese newspapers are full of America's woes. The outlook there is just as grim, and we were only just recovering from our meltdown of the 1990's. That was the reason for the delay in my returning. My father's real estate business went bankrupt, and because my mother still had money invested in it, they started bickering. They'd already gotten used to bad economic news, and to being frugal to the point of penny-pinching, but I guess a further reduction in their standard of living panicked them. I couldn't leave in the middle of the fight. But a huge stimulus plan is in the works there too. How's your writing coming along? Are you working on the same, best-selling black-Japanese 'Sayonara?'"

He told her, "It's coming along. I'm collecting information about recent immigration from China, Japan and Southeast Asia. You know: like Korea, Tibet, Thailand, Vietnam, Laos and Cambodia. You keep seeing many more immigrants from those countries living in black neighborhoods, and I got sidetracked a little."

"I know you're doing your best," she said, "but if you got published, that would save the day, wouldn't it? Japanese publishers might also take an interest. They snap up features and stories about Japanese in America."

He agreed, "That's my goal, to finish and get published," he said, "but publishing is reportedly one of the hardest-hit industries. "

She got out of the papasan and came over to where he was sitting. "My poor sweetheart," she said, "I missed you a lot in Japan, and thought about you a lot. We've known each other for over two years, and my feeling for you was growing the whole time, and I sensed yours for me was too. You can't know the extent to which I admire you. How you've quietly made your life an adventure: and I want mine to be a part of it. The time is right for us. We'll have many, happy, future years of building memories in common."

By the end of this declaration, she was rubbing her crotch into his upper arm, and now she bent over and again glued her lips to his.

Freed at length of the tasty embrace, Robert blinked hard, as though to reaffirm the reality of what was happening. "I really hadn't suspected you felt quite this way," he demurred, "although I wondered about some of your emails."

She went around the counter and hoisted herself onto the barstool.

"Things weren't quite right for me in Japan," she said, "they never are for the children of an ugly divorce anywhere in the world. My mom resented my closeness to my dad, from whom she had separated me for so long, and he in turn resented her persistent hostility and coldness. She's very haughty and set in her ways, and he's milder-mannered but quite passive-aggressive. It's draining to be caught in the middle. And then, on top of that, there was the crisis his bankruptcy caused. My mother put the entire blame on him, on his failings as a person in her eyes, when of course it was the national, or global, economic crisis that was the problem. By the end of my visit, I came to the conclusion that I was grown up, and I should give up being involved in their fight, which will go on until their deaths, and concentrate separately on my own happiness. That's when I seriously began to think of what kind of life I really wanted, and you started figuring very prominently in that."

"But I'm so very much older than you," he protested.

"You're fitter and more vital than persons much younger than you," she replied, "Look, I know we enjoy each other's company a lot, and we both respect working hard and self-improvement. Furthermore, I have an apartment and a job, and consequently, you don't have to be homeless and penniless. What choice do you have?"

They both laughed long and heartily at her audacious announcement, which amazed them the more the longer they were amused by it: but it loosened them up to be more freely affectionate and flirtatious, and lobbed their discussion to more practical ground, where they could examine the issues more soberly.

"You're right. We have evidently grown to enjoy each other's company, and I am beginning to feel as warmly about us together as you," he said, "and of course it's very flattering, and completely stops the anxiety I was having about my housing situation. However, there are still several, stubborn facts about a relationship between a sixty-five-year-old man and a twenty-six-year-old young woman, especially one as exceptionally beautiful as you, which need saying.

"Obviously, compatibility and propriety come up first. On aesthetic grounds alone, I'd say as a general rule that young people look better together, rather than a much older man and a much younger woman. You shouldn't forget either that aging picks up steam rapidly as it progresses. As a result, emotional exploitation can easily –or is that inevitably?- creep into the relationship, as well as unequal power games. And then there's the sexual quid pro quo: you're sure to be giving more pleasure than you'll be getting. Speaking of my case, I wasn't more than modestly effective in this regard to begin with, and age would have whittled away even that competency. Besides, I've been celibate for more than ten years!"

She said, "Boy, you're still standing on your own two legs! I'm confident you can pony up enough libido to sire a child. That's my main concern: to eventually have your kid."

"That's a whole other bunch of complications," he replied, "How do you know whether a child would like a geriatric for a parent? But seriously, it partly relates to being celibate, and for now we should finish dealing with that. My point was that the lack of practice would probably have diminished my sexual performance quite a bit more than age only. And the second thing is –after all this time, do I want to give celibacy up?'"

An uncomprehending look wrinkled her brow and pushed out her lower lip. Her confusion brought a self-conscious smile around his mouth.

"I hadn't planned on it," he said quietly, "you read about the requirement in religious or spiritual books, but it didn't seem to apply in this modern day and age, not even for the clergy, let alone if you were merely an amateur contempla-tive. Then, you begin dieting and exercising, which promotes self-control and impulse management, no matter what your calling or sexual preference is: and doing yoga and meditation, which are about being mindful and identifying with your in-ner states; and you find you're gradually being left without a stake in 'the other.' I have to say I did experience a little panic when I got there: but I seemed to remain fully functional, in case I ever chose to be –a bit of macho reassurance, I suppose– and so I just let the matter drop."

"Well, it's like composing music," she agreed, "or like writing fiction, I'm sure. Both point in the direction of a solitary existence, and meditation does make you self-sufficient. But I am twenty-six, and I am really ready to have a baby. I remember what you said when I brought up the topic before; it must be a biological imperative! Suddenly, everywhere I look I see mothers and their babies, and I'd have this compulsion. Otherwise, as you know, relationships haven't benefited me much. If it weren't for this thing about babies, I'd just as soon not bother. So, you, you don't have to think a sexual marathon is required of you!"

"This is hard!" he exclaimed, "I do like you, it's mad to turn down a proposition from such a beautiful person, something the rah-rah boys only dream about, and I need a place to live and a woman my granddaughter's age –if I had one- to support me financially. So, I guess that clinches it!"

She slid from the high stool, around the counter, and into his lap in a blur of effortless movements. Now they kissed more naturally, and for a much longer time.

He then remarked, but very tenderly, and still holding her against his body, "But shouldn't we also discuss the mixed feelings you have about relationships generally, and your sexuality? I keep going back to thinking this is much too much of a good thing for me, but what about you?"

She looked at him sadly, and remained silent for a while. Then she said, "When the plane took off from Narita International, I felt I'd never see Tokyo or Japan again. I told you: I'd written off my parents, and I don't have any other family. Then, I cheered up quite a bit, because I thought, 'Hey, of course, I'm coming back –with Robert, to show him around this city and country I love so much!' I guess I *am* only twenty-six, I felt orphaned, and I was expecting you to take the place of a parent, although I do think of you very much as a potential lover too. Very much! Oh, it *is* mixed up!"

She began weeping quietly, and, for such a tiny person, so many tears rolled down her cheeks that he thought she was at risk of drowning. He gently guided her back into his lap. "Look, sweetheart," he said, "we should just go about this very carefully and very thoughtfully, and come out of it stronger individually, and better friends –inseparable friends, even if we do end up being man and wife, or lovers, whatever; because friendships between men and their wives, or lovers, are very, very rare, an entirely endangered species. And look here, the bottom line is I need a place to live and more pocket change that I get from Social Security, and you promised!"

It was stirring to see on Awe's face the mirth breaking through the tears, like the sun through the clouds after a rainy morning. "You're the kindest person I've ever met, darling," she managed to say, "I really am an orphan now, and I need kindness very badly."

"Sweetheart, you'll always have my love unconditionally," he assured her.

"Then, as you said, we'll proceed with caution," she said, "your *sadhana*, your celibacy, your writing, my composing, having a baby, my relationship with my parents, and a thousand and one other things that are sure to come up. I don't know the timetable you have, but I'm going to start arranging things in my apartment from today, so when you have to give yours up, you can move in smoothly and immediately. And I don't know how it will eventually turn out, but it'll be wonderful sharing with you!"

Robert said, "I guess it's an ill wind that blows no one any good after all, as the saying puts it. I'm also sure living together will work out well for us, and that for me it will be a great improvement to living alone. It's a relief not to have to try my luck on the streets and in the subways and in the parks. Millions of others have already drawn that bad card, and I suspect many millions more will before this nightmare is over. I thank my Maker, He'll show us the right way; and I thank you; and I hope I never let either of you down."

Mopping her face with Kleenex and smiling innocently again, she added, "You'll also have really authentic, first-hand material to put into your book!"

4

E vents following the inauguration didn't lighten the depression that had threatened to incapacitate Millie on that day. Her feeling that Barzhad was caving in to the centrist and even reactionary wishes of his infelicitous appointees grew even more strongly. Although she wasn't very good generally at hiding displeasure, she put on a brave face in this exceptional situation, and tried to make compensations that would balance her increasing sense of failure, defeat, despair and anger.

She was adamant, for example, in insisting that appointments to the household staff would be her sole prerogative. She was particularly concerned about the children's upbringing; and especially after personally experiencing, at PTA meetings she had attended, the unapologetically privileged and white ambience of their new school, was determined that the home environment at the White House Residence would be a bastion of contrarian views, which would encourage the girls to be more appreciative and proud of their specifically black history, culture and legacy. She'd raise their consciousness regarding these matters, even if she couldn't improve that of the nation.

Accordingly, overriding her husband's occasional objections, which tended to be along the lines of being careful "not to offend mainstream sensibilities," and "manifesting a nondiscriminatory policy in hiring," she made sure that the household staff primarily comprised African Americans, Caribbean Africans, Hispanics and Africans. She chose many naturalized Haitians, Martiniquans, Guadeloupeans, and Senegalese, because she wanted the children –and her too- to acquire fluency, not only in the French of white Parisians, which their school taught, but also in the dialects of the former Francophone colonies and the immigrant quarters of French cities; Puerto Ricans, Mexicans and persons from the Dominican Republic, because of similar ambitions regarding fluency in Spanish; English speakers from the former British West Indies, because of their familiarity with black self-government and their deeply ingrained resistance to the least vestige of white supremacy; and, of course, many African Americans. The chef was the poster boy of her hiring strategy: he was a twenty-nine-year-old Trinidadian of Indian, Chinese and African ancestry, who had trained in Guadeloupe, the epicenter of *haute* Caribbean cuisine: and his way of combining the culinary styles of the five continents was both poetry and seduction.

It was the salaries of these personnel that were principally affected by the pay freeze for White House staff, which Barzhad announced on his first day in office, thereby immeasurably infuriating his wife: the salaries of the millionaires in Congress and in his Cabinet hadn't even been considered for inclusion in the hypocritical show of governmental frugality!

She allowed her resentments to boil in private for the first couple of weeks, before letting them spill out into the open. The children had been packed off to school rather earlier that Tuesday morning for a special, campus-wide event their school had organized, and the presidential couple had a few extra minutes at breakfast for a second cup of coffee, before he strolled over to the Oval Office.

She started off banteringly, but the rawness of the South Side projects was already shot through her voice, like twisted cables of thick steel, "Looks like you're picking these guys from the Wanted list down at the precinct," she joked, "any of them also running a "Happy Bunny" farm?"

"Hah-hah, very, very funny! Nah, but we've got this pretty sophisticated, smuggling thing going on. Thai boys! Diplomatic pouches! Go figure!" her husband responded, "'Fly you to the moon, Alice!' So what's been on your mind of late, dear? We know you haven't been the happiest camper. The children, your staff, me –we've all been feeling the chill. So, what's the scoop?"

"What?! Trouble in history's Happiest, Amos n' Andy First Family? You kiddin' me?' No way, José!" his wife said, "Oh dear! Oops, sorry! I sure hadn't meant to conjure a Hispanic immigrant! More like 'Tommy' or 'Rambo' or 'Fred' or other American red meat. Strike 'José.'"

"Sweetie, we've been through this before," he said, "blacks and Hispanics aren't the only constituencies, and they aren't the biggest. Our win was actually very precarious: largely on account of the fact that the Republican alternative was so comical, the electorate really didn't have much of a choice. God, let's not go over these elementary statistics again!"

"I'm not talking about the black or Hispanic constituencies, Barzhad," Millie said, with exaggerated patience, "I've never said you were elected to represent them. I'm saying you were elected to represent a black state of mind, by whites as well as blacks and Hispanics. That's different!"

"Oh-ho! But we've been working overtime putting more research and analytical sophistication into those earlier formulations, haven't we?" he said, "'The black state of mind.' I like it. It's a redoubtable rhetoric, no doubt. Does it also mean something?"

"Yes, my views have evolved," she asserted, "Isn't that a normal function of growth and learning? And maybe the worsening crisis we're finding ourselves in has educated whites too, and their views have also evolved. Perhaps it's not just absolution and redemption of sins they want from you, or a pass saying that since they elected you, it means they've transcended their bloody past. I've often thought those were their reasons, and I still do strongly believe they are, but now I am putting more emphasis on another conviction: that they also want to survive; and as the sky falls in on top of our heads, they realize it's not your forgiveness that will save their skins, or any of the tired, old parameters of racial discourse in this country, who did what to whom; but only a brand new way, one that goes completely beyond them. So, yes, I do put a high value on growing and thinking, and yes, I have refined how I look at our predicament and the solutions to it, and the most promising of those is what I'm calling the black state of mind.

"Which leaves you, the great spokesman of change: only your hidebound predispositions and attitudes haven't changed. For example, I see Freddie Dachshund was in the news today. Seems as if he couldn't afford an accountant either, like his buddy, Gunther, and consequently neglected to fork up $182,000 in taxes. Usually the presumption is: if you can afford one and don't use an accountant, you're trying to cheat the federal government."

"People make stupid mistakes all the time," Barzhad said lightly, "filing your taxes isn't exactly the most intellectually rewarding or pleasurable sort of exercise."

"That's why there are accountants," his wife snapped, "They love the drudgery. There's my boring cousin in the South Side who did my taxes when I used to have a job. Care to recommend him to your buddies as a fair, honest, detail-oriented, certified accountant? Unless, of course, you're going to stick to your guns against nepotism when it concerns my relatives?"

The president drained his cup of coffee. "I'll pass along the information," he said, "don't forget, though, that Freddie Dachshund was the first to support my run, and he's a close personal friend, not only to me, but also to the whole family. Guess I'd better be going."

"I think you'd better have another cup," Millie said, "We need to talk. Or I do. About certain so-called friendships, among other things."

Barzhad looked resigned, "Then by all means, let's. Do let the minor business of affairs of state wait. Let's also throw our insulin levels off by OD'ing on as much coffee as we can."

"Chances are you mightn't need coffee," she said, menacingly, the bleak Chicago projects and their desolate grounds much more discernible now, "but you *sure* don't need a messy White House divorce or separation, complete with raised voices the neighbors can hear, and the carpentry made by slaves being shattered into little bits from doors slamming and such. My mother, me *and* the kids calling up car service to take us to the airport, en route for home. It'll be what they deserve for letting you-know-who move into the neighborhood!"

"Hey!" he said, with a great show of cheerfulness, and slurping hot coffee, "we're *talking*!"

"According to the newspapers, your friend Dachshund makes $5m annually, all from peddling his position as a lawmaker. Will you be doing that too eventually, when your term ends? He gets $2 million in consulting fees from a private equity firm; consulting fees from a student loan company and health insurance firms that receive government reimbursements; $2 million as a partner at a law firm that lobbies for health insurance firms; over $500,000 for speeches on behalf of these same companies; and he picks up a little something moonlighting as a college professor. The health insurance firms hire his law firm to lobby on their behalf, making him a lobbyist. I thought lobbyists were banned from office in your administration. And when he becomes Secretary of Health and Human Services, with oversight over the health insurance firms that were paying him, wouldn't there be a major conflict of interest?"

"There's a legal definition of what a lobbyist is," he offered.

She pounced on that. "He is *de facto*, if not *de jure*, a god-damn lobbyist!" she said, "He influences his former colleagues on the Hill on behalf of his clients, doesn't he? And he also instructs those clients the best way to influence them."

"As a Harvard trained lawyer, you know well there's the little matter of evidence, or proof," he countered, quite pomp-ously, "all of it calculable in the actual dollars and cents of a measurable loss or damage."

His wife ignored the objection, "He owes $182, 000 in taxes because he didn't report as income the costs of transpor-tation and a chauffeur provided by one of his employers," she continued, "OK, he makes what you've labeled this 'stupid mistake,' cozies up to the health insurance industry he'll be regulating, and you really aren't hesitating to hand him a good portion of that $789 billion stimulus package for spending on healthcare initiatives. Lovely so far: but his charitable dona-tions really burn me up! Our family friend the creep claims he gave Salvation Army tons of clothes, City Harvest tons of food, and cash handouts to all the wounded military returning from Iraq, but forgot to get receipts! How low can you get? Why can't you plainly see this sonofabitch is a corrupt, lying, thiev-ing, Washington insider –change you *don't want* to believe in?! God! What's wrong with you?"

"Look, they're still investigating this," he said urgently, "if there's a hint of any wrongdoing, he's out."

"My Caribbean nanny network is always in the know," she added, "I guess you haven't listened in on that grapevine, have you? Seems that, come June, the Romeo of the Dakotas is planning to divorce his wife and marry, in a lavish ceremony, the prettiest of his blonde undergraduates, an infant some forty years his junior, and younger than his own grown children! Does 'lavish' strike you as a little steep, given the economic fix the nation is in, and the mounting job losses and home fore-closures? Never mind the business of your pals not being able to keep their hands off girls their granddaughters' age!"

"It is foolish," he conceded, "regrettable, both things."

Detecting his rueful attitude, Millie pressed her case forward less aggressively. "If he had the least bit of decency, or any regard for you personally, or more generally for what your presidency stands for, he'd just withdraw."

"Maybe he should," he admitted, "and maybe he will. I just feel badly having to ask him to do it."

"*He* should have felt badly not disclosing these knee-slapping little peccadilloes the minute you said you were thinking of nominating him," she insisted, "'Hullo! Me vs. the I.R.S is a blood sport.' But that brings us back to the 'black state of mind,' because I am warning you again: you're misreading white people and what they really want from you –what we all want from you, blacks, Hispanics and the world. Sure, your opponents were a joke, and it was a feel-good opportunity for whites to vote for a black man since they really couldn't do otherwise any way: but it wasn't only to get away from the dynamic duo that you won; the whites who voted for you really wanted you, a black man. They know their weakness, that they can't easily admit wrongdoing: but they realize that we'll keep on losing jobs, more homes will go into foreclosure, credit will be remain frozen, and we'll be stuck in these doldrums forever if they don't. So, they needed a sacrificial lamb to do it for them. Wasn't your mother their precursor, your very first white vote?"

Did she actually bring up his mother? Ill at ease, the president started fidgeting. Rubbing his chin, massaging his nose, flexing and un-flexing his fists, getting up abruptly and stretching his limbs, sitting down again. He got up, bent over and touched his toes. He performed these and similar maneuvers whenever they discussed his mother or his maternal family. He got up and poured them their fourth cup of coffee. He took out a cigarette, but didn't light it.

She went on, "She was white, and although she married twice, it wasn't to a white man either time. She was an anthropologist, and apparently took the study of human evolution very seriously, so much so that she not only wanted her children to be familiar with human variation, but also for them to *embody* it. It was evidently her way of repudiating the white ethnocentricity on which she had been nurtured in Mississippi at your grandparents' home. Lots of whites are as intelligent as she was, but most aren't as brave, and can't come right out with it, and just say no; or, what's more pitiful, they end up unable to help themselves, and they just keep on taking the unfair advantages, and close their eyes to all the wrongheadedness and wrongdoing, and go into denial. They cover up and make believe all their lives. But those bad faith options are becoming less and less tenable at this historical juncture; the chickens are flocking home to roost; and so, they needed you to lean on –a black man- to get them out of their predicament.

"For God's sake, can you really, finally, make an effort to be a black man, Barzhad? The "black state of mind" comes naturally and spontaneously to us as African Americans –and now you're tempting me to say genetically too, certainly culturally, because it seems you have to be a native-born African American to really get this, it's a black *thang*, and having any old black skin doesn't just *hand* it to you. And another thing: it just can't be repressed, once you have it.

"So, what is it? Well, it radicalizes your white mother's intuitive stance to the max! Going much, much further than hers, it's the blanket, across-the-board, no-exceptions-barred opposition that we have always had against anything whites, however innocent-seeming, no matter how friendly they are to the family, think, say, feel or do. Cuba, Vietnam, the Dominican Republic, Iran, Grenada, Afghanistan, Iraq -you can't find a single, solitary black who really supported those aggressions, even if they also happened to be uniformed, active-duty, five-star generals. Opposition, skepticism, disbelief, distrust, disdain, disavowal, disengagement: it could be the constitution, the beatification of the founding fathers, democracy and the free market, Emancipation, Abraham Lincoln, the Civil War, foreign wars, the Civil Rights Acts, universal suffrage, taxation, the budget, even the First Black President –what have they got up their sleeves, what's the scam, where's the catch? There's *has* to be one! There always *is* one!

"All of this relates to the economic crisis. I doubt there ever was an African American who wouldn't have preferred to keep his paycheck in his mattress rather than in a white bank! And how right he would have turned out to be."

"Look, Millie," Barzhad said, "all this may be true, but it's also ancient history. We have a sophisticated modern banking system, a global banking system; it's in a mess today; and we have got to fix it. It's no good wishing for a time when we had forty acres and a mule!"

"Is it, now?" his wife swiftly responded, "Something noteworthy is the way Gunther, Ruben and Somerville keep talking about the regrettable greed of their white former colleagues and acolytes, as if they weren't personally just as guilty, and as though it was just a matter of bad taste in the office décor, or something of that order; but when it comes to assigning the actual blame, the greed had nothing to do with it; why, it's China of course; or Negroes who took loans they knew they couldn't repay — by the way, a trifling debt Warren Buffet could dissolve with a single, personal check! What was rotten was the banking system itself, or where Gunther, Ruben, Somerville and friends had taken it! If we're going to fix the mess, we're going to have to replace it, root and branch."

"With what?" Barzhad demanded hotly, "nationalization?"

"Eek! Praetorian Guards! The Marines! Did I actually hear you say that forbidden word in the sanctity of the White House Residential Dining Room, within earshot of my Barbadian housekeeper?" Millie asked, with mock incredulity, "The scrambled *ackee* does bring on disoriented thinking and impaired speech if it's not properly prepared. I'll speak to cook about it."

"Try to be serious, Millie," he went on impatiently, "as you said, five or six million workers –the number increases geometrically by the day- are going to be thrown out of their jobs. It's no time for indulging ideological daydreams."

She laughed out aloud. "That's what *I*'m talking about, Mr. President," she said, "Russia gave up communism, China modified theirs, and it's high time we gave up our stupid, cold war, ideological talking points and propaganda too. What are private enterprise and the free market? Somerville, Gunther, Homespun, Ruben, Fuld, Thain, Lewis, Wilson and Madoff? Anything associated with them is as valuable as a plugged nickel! Those guys haven't the IQ of a newt, or the morals of a viper! Homespun used to read the trashy novels of a third-rate novelist and pass it on as economic advice from the Delphic oracle to three presidents! Pure *whiteness* put them where they were, or are! Who's daydreaming?"

"This is an awfully complex set of issues, Millie," he began, "you…..

"You *go*, Mr. President." she said sarcastically. "'This is an awfully complex set of issues,' and women aren't equipped to discuss them? Right? Didn't that obnoxious, unspeakably conceited, racist, white, male chauvinist pig, Somerville, brief you on the topic of uppity women -and blacks- who are out of their league? Brings me to another matter, your blind reliance on the Ivy League. As if you and I personally hadn't had our fill of assholes and incompetents at Yale and Harvard, among both faculty and fellow students!"

"Did Lenin or Stalin have Yale or Harvard degrees when they lifted Russia out of the Stone Age and into putting a Sputnik into space in a mere fifty years flat, and ten years before we could? A little later, it took Chairman Mao and Deng Xiaoping the same fifty years to do the same thing in China. What couldn't Fidel and Ché have done, if spiteful Ivy Leaguers hadn't put a sky-high blockade around the island, to keep out trade, goods, services, science and technology? You should get white boy Dunstan to drop all this sterile quarreling about teachers' pay and tenure and accountability, and telephone Fidel before he dies, and find out how Cubans raised the literacy rate from zero to 99.9% in under twenty years —in spite of the embargo. You've been in office longer than a week, why hasn't that egregious remnant of cold-war malice been lifted already?"

"I don't think the American people are too sanguine about collectivization and forced relocations of whole populations," he intoned, "nor are they happy with Fidel's gulag."

"We did have the Trail of Tears, remember," she retorted, "and 'Grapes of Wrath' emptied and relocated the whole of Oklahoma and the Dakotas. That's how Susan Paltry and her tribe landed up in Alaska, wasn't it? Fidel's gulag mightn't have existed if U.S. hostility hadn't fostered xenophobia on the island, and our gulag population is a shocking four and half million, mostly blacks and minorities. But my point was not to recommend any particular methods. What I meant was that you really don't need an advanced Ivy League degree to get potatoes into people's stomachs and roofs over their heads. You need those credentials only when you're planning to be malicious, or to steal."

"Progress is being made," Barzhad said reassuringly, "Gunther has promised a detailed plan in a few weeks….

"Gunther is not, -I repeat, *not*- going to have anything anytime ever," Millie snarled, "because he's a very dumb, super-dumb, weak minded, super-rich muthafucka! Has he, or Somerville, or Ruben, or any of the other chuckleheads told you anything already that your barber couldn't? 'It's gotta be swift, it's gotta be targeted to the low- and middle-income strata, and it's gotta be paid back.' Who said, 'take your time, don't pay it back' and actually, *they*'re going to give it all to the bankers and the shareholders all over again, minus the cut they slip into their own pockets without the I.R.S. noticing. Not a penny is going to be left to employ a single, part-time, low- and middle-income worker to fill a single goddamn shallow pothole!"

Barzhad looked at his watch, fumbled with his unlit cigarette and got up. "Thanks, sweetie, but I really have to go to the job," he said, "I'll give what you said some thought."

"Try to get it, 'Mr. Cool,'" she shouted angrily at his departing back, "Pure whiteness got us into this mess, and only pure blackness is going to get us out. White people didn't put you in there to tolerate Dachshund. Ditto Gunther. Ditto all the rest. He's them, and that's who they know they need to get rid of. So they elected you to help them do it, because they can't do it on their own, it would be too much like suicide. That's why they turned to you –for that black state of mind! Can't you search around in there and see whether you can't find it somewhere?"

He lit the cigarette the second he was out in open air. Truth was, he did feel put upon by Freddie Dachshund, and a little less than awed by the performances so far of Gunther, Somerville, Volkswagon and the others; but he wasn't too sure what he could do about it. Although the blogosphere was ablaze with commentary against them as negative as Millie's, he was still afraid he'd be branded 'Emperor Jones,' or 'Idi Amin Dada,' if he started firing staff right and left. It wasn't as if he was blind to racial prejudice, as Millie's carrying-on sometimes seemed to suggest!

He was also ready to concede that his strategy, or the secret side of it that he had kept to himself, may have been so successful that it backfired: he had done a little 'setting up' too, and had made some of the appointments knowing that their incumbents would fail; that way, he could claim the prizes for generosity or bipartisanship or colorblindness, as the particular case may have been, without really having to endure them for long; but he hadn't realized how quickly they would crumble, and that replacements would be needed so soon; and he had none ready. He acknowledged he was being transformed into a hardened, calculating schemer, and was sorry for himself. What was he going to be like after four more years of this, or maybe eight? He thought that question too was at the bottom of Millie's malaise, together with all her other fears. How deluded those people were, who actually thought being the president was such an exceptionally fine achievement, on which innocent, young children should be encouraged to set their sights! Unless, of course, they had taken his predecessor as their example!

He realized it was going to be a long day, when upon entering the Oval Office, he found his father sitting at his desk with pipe in hand, although, deferential to the house rule for a change, he wasn't smoking it. He was dressed as usual in open neck shirt, jacket and slacks. Although Barzhad genuinely enjoyed his father's company, a visit usually meant that another effort of profound introspection would be required of him. He brought his palms together in greeting and bowed deeply, then went out and gave instructions to the Marine Honor Guard that he was not to be disturbed for any reason whatsoever. Then he went in and sat down in a visitor's chair, respectfully facing his father.

"The origin of the cosmos is between your wife's legs," his father told him, "Take heed. Without the female, males are less than useless, they're plain destructive. Like that ruffian. We're so sorry for what he did. I believe it's behind these questionable appointments you're making. You have to put it behind you. It's been so many years."

"I'm trying, Dad," he said, plaintively, "Honest. But it's difficult, so difficult. Mind, body, feelings, soul: they all go in separate, opposing directions all at once."

"It's really not accidental that you have a personal moral dilemma to resolve while you are helping to preside over a universe that has to evolve morally in order to survive," his father said, "it was important for you to feel how they feel, and contingency, what happens out of blue, that's a big part of their lives. All the same, I wish we could have prevented your suffering, or helped you more to reconcile with it."

"I should hate them," he said, bitterly, "yet I bend over backward to be conciliatory. Isn't that a victory, or a milestone on the way to virtue?"

"It depends," his father replied, "If you've truly forgiven the thug and bear no grudges, it is. If you are merely resigned to being the victim of whites, you know the answer: no, it isn't."

"However we decide that, it does give me a better understanding how they tick," he said, "And as I struggle with this, I understand how ordinary people have to struggle too, to make good judgments, and lead responsible lives, and assume responsibility for their fate. I've been meaning to start meditating again."

"This is the do-or-die moment for this universe, and teachers are arising," his father said, "Someone exceptional will soon appear to teach you how. Meanwhile, you'll be relieved to know that Dachshund will withdraw from contention later today. It will revive your popularity with the public."

"I really don't know what it is with their taxes," he said, "As educated men earning millions of dollar a year, you'd think they'd be above stealing peanuts. You'd think they could afford to hire accountants. What makes it more galling is that as earners in the top income brackets, they are beneficiaries of some of the most unfair tax cuts in decades!"

"You should reinstitute progressive taxation in your forthcoming budget," his father replied, "So, that leaves Gunther. Let's see how he measures up. It's no accident that it's your banking system where most of the malfunctioning is. Gunther is dishonest, and the only way he can succeed in fixing it is by succeeding in fixing himself. "

"What's your idea?" he asked humbly.

His father answered, "I can't tell you everything, Barzhad. Those are the rules. Humans –you- have to work out their evolution on their own. They are already lucky to have you, and me advising you as much as I am allowed, but the idea is for you –them- to measure up. What's the use of putting someone unprepared in a situation where the preparation is critical? It would be contradictory, self-defeating. I can tell you to watch your back, but *you* have to watch your back, I can't watch it for you.

"The cosmos is young and still evolving. Universes are coming and going out of existence with a volatility and violence that human brains and imaginations are unable to comprehend. This universe is not an exception. As I told you, the evolutionary stage you are striving for here is crucial to your survival, and it is precisely to go beyond the sort of petty thievery and duplicity Gunther and Dachshund exhibited and arrive at greater trustworthiness and cooperation. It's a personal, communal and global evolution that's necessary. A trifecta."

Barzhad noticed the glee with which his father mouthed the indigenous word. "And the banking system is the key?" he wanted to know.

"Millie was right about it," his father said, "The only reason Gunther and his friends are so keen to pour the $700 billion –or whatever the figure will be at the end of the game- back into the banking system is because they expect that when their days in office have ended, the bankers will reward them with fat sinecures. If they can overcome their greed, they'll readily see the banking system for the rotten apple it is, and just let it crumble.

"Don't let them allocate a penny there. You want to create twelve million jobs in the U.S.? Of course, hire workers and start repairing and making brand new those bridges, roads, levees and clean water supply systems at once –you should have already completed a bunch of those in the last ten days! But I'll tell you another way to do it fast: create twelve million jobs abroad. Hire six million Americans and send them to Africa; for each American hire, hire two Africans; by March 2009, the Sahara and the Kalahari and every space in between will be covered with windmills or solar energy installations, manufacturers of batteries to store the energy, soybeans, artificial lakes for fish farming, other industry, whatever; build up the infrastructure –roads, bridges, electricity, clean water, hospitals and clinics, the lot; clear the slums and put in affordable homes; and by June, the Africans will be demanding Apple computers, broadband access, computerized health records, air conditioners, G.E. refrigerators, kitchen appliances, battery-powered automobiles, lawnmowers, even McDonald's and Starbucks. Those companies will have to take on an additional six million workers in the U.S. to meet the demand. There you have it on a plate: twelve million jobs created in America!

"Initially, you pay the salaries of the first six million Americans and twelve million Africans out of the $789 billion of stimulus money through a national bank. After that, the enterprises themselves will pay, and pay back the initial expense. Then, on to Southeast Asia. The Caribbean. And bring Europe, China, India and Russia in on the scheme. There are enough lands in those countries, and in the U.S. as well, that are still underdeveloped, underutilized and unproductive. The oceans and seas are two-thirds of your total surface area, and apart from sporadic hunting and gathering, not used prudently and systematically."

"Our anthropologists and evolutionary biologists tell us that human interests, loyalties and attention span are shallow," Barzhad said sorrowfully, "the immediate concerns of what to eat and what clothes to wear and where to live; a few generations backwards and forwards; a tight little circle of contemporary friends and relatives around ego; that's all we can handle. A world community and a world government –I don't know whether anybody can sell a big idea like that. Americans can barely get the hang of universal heath care in the U.S., let alone clean drinking water for all the peoples of the earth. As for Gunther…."

"I know," his father said, clucking sympathetically, "he won't even pay his taxes to maintain the bridges in this country in the state of near-collapse they're in! Let's hope the scientists are wrong, though. Let's hope psychology has a few surprises. Otherwise, it's over!"

"Dad, I'd scheduled a thousand meetings," Barzhad started to say: but his father had already gone.

When the president opened the door, his chief of staff, "Rambo" Ezekiel, was waiting impatiently and foul-temperedly outside, "That dumb fucker Dachshund didn't have what it takes," he screeched. "He just copped out! He wants to withdraw."

His wife and father's warning stoked the president's rising temper, which he struggled manfully to contain. "He figures correctly that he can't win against the disgust he's generated," he said, "and he's dragged me down with him as well. He should have paid his taxes. Taxation in the U.S. is mostly about voluntary compliance, and he set a very, very poor example. And I'm getting a little fed up having to talk to you repeatedly about your potty mouth! This isn't a bar-and-brothel we are kicking back in."

The two men went into the Cabinet Room, where Cabinet members and the most senior staffers had assembled. The president strode across to his chair and sat down. His somber mood was so transparent that complete silence overtook the room.

"The Freddie Dachshund debacle should come as an object lesson to the rest of us," he declared, "there are ideals we said we stood for, and we shouldn't be compromising them before two weeks of this administration are out. It's not as if personal sacrifice is entirely unheard of in politics. Gandhi, Nkrumah, Nyerere, Kenyatta and Mandela set us a good example of sticking to high ideals, never mind their other failings. None died a millionaire. They had to pass a collection plate in the Indian

Parliament when the Gandhian Prime Minister, Lal Bahadur Shastri, died, in order to scrape up a pension for his wife and children, because he refused to take a salary for his public service, although he came from a poor family to start with. Here, our guys are all acting like the Shah, Marcos, Bokassa, Mobutu and Mugabe!"

Still chafing from the reprimand he had received earlier, "Rambo" Ezekiel started cracking his knuckles, making reports that echoed loudly in the silent room. He knew the habit annoyed his boss, who in fact frowned in his direction. "My guess is that Dachshund probably had more nasty secrets up his sleeve," the president continued, "and if I were him, I certainly wouldn't have wanted a closer examination of how I made $5million a year from the mere circumstance of having been a lawmaker, and chiefly from the health insurance industry he would have been regulating as Secretary of Health and Human Services. What's your feelings about turning the electorate's support in the elections into a payload of millions of dollars from special interests, Mr. Ezekiel?"

Ramsay "Rambo" Ezekiel was far more notorious than Freddie Dachshund for his talent of turning public office into a private gold mine. He had already amassed a personal fortune of several millions of dollars as an investment banker on Wall Street when he began adding exponentially to it during his twenty years as a lawmaker.

"How the fuck should I know?" he asked, "I was thinking of enrolling in the food stamps program, now that it's a free-for-all!" He turned a smirking face towards his colleagues around the table, expecting the support of sly smiles, if not a guffaw or two. But he was staring into an unbroken phalanx of seriously dismayed, pale faces.

"Mr. Ezekiel, you will be asked to leave the room, and eventually to resign your position in my administration, if your profanities in the halls of government do not immediately stop. I was at a public charter school yesterday morning in a very depressed area of this city where children are disciplined for saying 'damn!' And here we go again with the double standards: one for Mr. Dachshund and you, and another for everybody else. It won't do! I've also spoken to you about disrupting these meetings with knuckle noises. What on earth do you think this is –a zoo or an animal farm?"

"Rambo" opened his mouth to make a hot comeback; but apparently thinking better of it, remained silent, if not exactly contrite.

"I'm considering a cap on the compensation of persons in this room, myself included," the president said, "I'd first like all of you to update your income and tax records and present them to me, accurate and free of error, by the end of next week. This includes income from all sources. Your accountant must certify your submission; if you don't already have one, hire one. We'll talk about the cap after I review them. "

He looked around for any comments; but as there was none, he continued, "These events have of course distracted us from the plight of over four million of our fellow Americans, who are wondering today where their next meal is coming from. And our domestic woes are multiplied untold times abroad, affecting many more millions of humans. It's time we returned our focus to where it truly belongs. How are we getting on with the recovery plan for the banking system, Mr. Gunther?"

Like the others in the room, Tommy Gunther was unprepared for Barzhad's new attitude, so much like a very irate schoolmaster's, and rather than risking his neck on the half-baked, get-personally-rich schemes that were sloshing around in his brain as solutions he might offer for the public crises, he cautiously decided to stick to the neutral, accepted nostrums on these matters instead. "Well, sir, we're thinking pretty much that we should put the banks' toxic assets in a 'bad' bank and free them up to operate with a clean balance sheet."

Somerville and the other economists in the room, particularly Rover and Glucksbee, nodded their heads vigorously like schoolchildren who wanted their agreement to be noted, so as to avoid being individually questioned. The president's new tone had shaken their self-confidence as well as Gunther's, whose consternation they had noticed, and begun to feel.

However, Glucksbee, who had a reputation for jesting, foolhardiness and derring-do to maintain, ventured, "The problem is how 'bad' the proposed bank is going to be. We are having difficulty figuring out how much we should pay for those toxic assets, how many we should buy outright, and how many we should simply guarantee, without a purchase."

But the president was hounding them for greater clarity and reason, "And once you have determined the value of these toxic assets and removed them from the banks' balance sheets, what then?"

Inwardly cursing Glucksbee, Gunther looked around for support, as "Rambo" had done, with the same zero success, "Well then, sir, the banks can start lending again."

"Is there a guarantee they will? Why can't we start lending right now?" the president pressed him, "I mean, we –the government? The bankers and their shareholders will step aside, we'll put out the money for the public works we envisioned, and *we*'ll put up the money to the businesses and individuals who are seeking it. And private investors can get a reasonable return for their money supporting us by buying government bonds and similar government-backed instruments, instead of unrealistically chasing instant riches, as they had done previously, when 'anything goes' was the rule."

Already having difficulty accurately gauging the president's mood, and being clearer about what he was actually thinking, Gunther aimed to be noncommittal, and not to give his game away. "Why, sir," he blurted out disingenuously, "that's nationalization! And we'd be leaving the banks to fail and disappear."

The president was amused, "So? I thought we were all

unswerving Darwinists –or is that only when it is a matter of the 'undeserving' poor? The banks weren't the fittest, so they got buried and joined the fossil record."

Taken aback, Gunther decided he should take the high ground, just to be safe. "Sir," he began, in a pontificating manner, "our financial system is run by private shareholders and managed by private institutions, and I'm sure the American people would like to keep it that way."

Somerville took heart from Gunther's pluck and quickly added, "Governments make poor bank managers."

"Right," the president agreed, "then why are we giving them a gift of $700 billion in public funds, no equity demanded, no strings attached? And it isn't the first time. Maybe we should also ask to review everyone's educational credentials, because it sure seems as though some of us need refresher courses in Basic English comprehension and logic! Furthermore, we wouldn't be having this discussion in the first place if the performance of private bankers had been so stellar."

Secretary of State Hilda Brunton had been carrying herself with the most composure and poise of all throughout the proceedings thus far. She cleared her throat, and her colleagues turned to her expectantly. She commanded a lot of respect, and not a few regretted at that moment that she hadn't won the Democratic Party's presidential nomination the previous year. "I'm surprised Mr. Somerville's grasp of history is so tenuous and inaccurate," she said "Perhaps men aren't genetically good at history? Government, or government- and church-run companies were responsible for the Pyramids; the Taj Mahal; the Great Wall of China; the imperial buildings, roadways and aqueducts that still remain as mementoes of the Roman Empire; all the great cathedrals and other medieval public monuments of Europe, and its universities, such as the Sorbonne, Cambridge and Oxford; and they funded the philosophical and scientific breakthroughs that allowed the Enlightenment to flourish. Back then, only piracy, slave trading and similar enterprises were truly in private hands. As they arguably still are! In the U.S., add the Erie Canal, the transcontinental railroad and the highway system.

"A more recent example is the Japanese automotive industry, which actually remains profitable, and is obviously surviving the downturn far better than the Big Three. In Japan, the Japanese Ministry of International Trade and Industry was charged in the 1970's and the 1980's to bring creditors, the unions, the shareholders and automobile companies' management together to decide policy, assign responsibilities, and distribute risks and liabilities. The Ministry encouraged companies to consolidate, and even told each what it could and couldn't make. Soichiro Honda, for example, was told Honda had to make motorcycles only. As Honda manufactures many other vehicles, the ministry was evidently not an unbending dictatorship: there was plenty of room for disagreement, compromise and private initiative. But the point is: the Japanese government took a leading role in management, which is still having fantastic results. The U.S. government is playing copycat in our automotive industry today, but unfortunately the private managers of the Big Three keep getting out of the cage and getting in the way!"

The other participants in the room seemed to have suddenly found their voices; they began talking among themselves; and Ramsay "Rambo" Ezekiel wondered whether he could get away with cracking his knuckles again, and declaiming, "Fuck this shit!" as he would have dearly loved doing.

The newly appointed commerce secretary, Grover "Groggy" Budd, Republican of New Hampshire, bawled, "We aren't Japanese! I won't put up with this stealth attack on our values! Big government is un-American. The founding fathers must be turning in their graves!"

"I hope I won't have to flick the lights on and off to signal time out," the president said, in a menacingly quiet tone, "what are the rest of your views on all of this, Secretary Brunton?"

"First of all, Mr. President," she said, "I'm delighted and relieved you're determined to regain the higher moral ground that you spelled out during the campaign. It was unconscionable of so-called colleagues and friends to have brought the risk of dishonoring your administration and all of us in public service so much by cheating on their taxes. Please add me to the effort to remove the stain, and I'll gladly forward to you my financial records by the deadline. And I'd be willing to comply with a cap on my personal income while in office. Of course, as everyone knows, I'm deeply in debt.

"Regarding the stimulus plan, as secretary of state, I'm puzzled that my colleagues haven't emphasized that this is an international crisis. I see it as an unprecedented opportunity, not only for all the nations of the world to work together to solve it, but also to solve other longstanding problems, such as world poverty or eradicable diseases, that had always required a united effort; and also, to lay a firm, unyielding foundation for the future for a more unified world in every respect. I have already taken up with the Treasury Secretary his reckless bid to antagonize China, and I hope I don't run foul of the Chief of Staff if I say that an immediate improvement of the situation in Gaza is imperative, as also in our relations with Iran; and those diplomatic improvements correspond identically with the economic relief that should be in the stimulus plan. The stimulus can be doubly effective if it is not confined to this country."

"Rambo" Ezekiel yelled, "I don't understand why I'm being singled out. I'm not the only one who happens to think that nationalization is a lousy idea!"

Secretary Brunton replied calmly, "I wasn't referring to that this time. I was referring to your father's unfortunate opinion, which he stated to a newspaper in Tel Aviv, that Arabs were only good for sweeping the floors at the White House. Frankly, if I were an Arab, I'd feel like lobbing a missile or two in the direction of the source of such an egregiously virulent, racist insult. And I defy anyone here to tell me my feeling would be wrong!"

For the first time that day, the president smiled again in the happy, easygoing manner that had variously won him the appellations of "Mr. Cool" and "Mr. Zen Hawaii;" and which had endeared him to the electorate during the campaign. "I seemed to have heard similar sentiments of late," he said, and his dark brown eyes were twinkling, "Would you care to elaborate, Ms. Secretary?"

"Well, sir, I'm inclined to agree with you that no additional money should go to the banks," she said, "I'm very hardcore Darwinist on that point, if not on any other. The money we didn't waste on them could go into emergency international development. The rebuilding of Gaza should begin tomorrow if it were possible, and a few hundred thousand Americans should be employed at once and dispatched to begin or assist in that effort."

Somerville burst out, "The chief argument against government managers is that they will be driven by politics when making their decisions. How are you going to avoid that? You are already taking sides in the Middle East situation, and putting men and money behind your political choice!"

"I don't know which is a better thing," Secretary Brunton replied, "political preference or the personal greed and self-aggrandizement that private bankers pursued, which have brought us all to the abyss. At least, there are institutionalized checks against the former. The Justice Department and the Department of the Interior during the last administration illustrate my point. In the first, appointments were made following a Republican, neo-conservative political agenda; in the second, government officers were literally in bed sharing sex and cocaine with the people they were supposed to regulate in order to protect endangered species and the environment. How were they found out? Well, the courts, litigation, oversight panels of the House and Senate, their own accountability committees, and principled whistleblowers did a very commendable job. The same will apply here. Moreover, in this administration, we are hoping to gradually build a culture of responsibility that will ensure that each one polices herself or himself."

"Mr. Gunther, please take notes," the president interrupted, "we'll want to put into the recovery plan the elements Secretary Brunton is outlining. I'm sorry, my dear. Please continue."

"As it was cheap Chinese imports that actually helped us to beat inflation in the 1990's," Ms. Brunton said, "and as it was Chinese money that kept our banks solvent and flush with cash in the 2000's, I think we should acknowledge our multiple indebtedness to the Chinese, and invite them to partner with us, not only to bring about our joint recoveries, but also in international development. They had been doing a significant amount of the latter on their own in Africa before the downturn, and we should join forces going forward."

"Groggy" Budd couldn't be contained any longer; his face had turned beet red, the jaw jutted out, the jaw muscles flexing, and the veins were throbbing at the temples. "Lie in bed with the yellas all you like, but Republicans will fight this socialist evil in the House and the Senate tooth and nail," he vowed," Tooth and nail! No holds barred! And I resign the position of Commerce Secretary. You won't get my bipartisan support for the undermining of my beloved country's most cherished values." And knocking over his chair, he stormed out of the Cabinet Room.

The other staffers all started talking at once again, but before the chaos escalated, the president said forcefully, "Mr. Gunther, please work with Secretary Brunton on her ideas for the recovery. And Mr. Fibbs, please repress your outsize talent for prevarication this time, and try to give a more honest account of our discussion, when you meet with the press. We'll adjourn for today."

5

From a good mile away, the repellent efflorescence of 'digs-for-aging-frat-boys' indicated the townhouse off Dupont Circle as the in-term residence of the six Republican lawmakers. Inside, the pileup of grunge -unwashed china, coffee cups, soda and beer empties, wine and liquor bottles, week-old cartons of takeout Chinese with stale food still in some, discarded pizza boxes, dirty laundry strewn everywhere, unmade beds and mountains of daily newspapers and magazines- returned the verdict of a positive identification.

Two large Domino pizzas with extra toppings of cheese, sausage, and pepperoni had been delivered, and the six men, all at home together for a change, were sitting around in the kitchen —at the dining table, at the counter- preparing to eat their dinner. Bottles of California reds and six-packs of cold, bottled beers were at hand. Representative Steven Wolf, Republican of North Carolina, who liked to walk around naked, had graduated to white briefs and T-shirt for the occasion; Elvis Singer, Republican of Virginia, remained in the sweaty outfit he'd been wearing at the gym; Senator Jack Coin, Republican of Texas, wore striped pajamas; while Senator Tony Cockburn, Republican of Oklahoma, Representative Jack Wimp, Republican of Tennessee, and Representative Spender

Bach, Republican of Alabama, were wearing slacks and short sleeves. The men were at the same time watching television interviews of the president, the secretary of state, the press secretary and other participants about the fateful meeting in the Cabinet Room.

The telephone rang and Tony Cockburn picked up and listened to a voice at the other end. Then, almost instantly, the doorbell rang, and again Tony Cockburn was the one who answered it. And in trooped Grover "Groggy" Budd, Ramsay "Rambo" Ezekiel and Tommy Gunther. Tony Cockburn raised the beer bottle in his hand, "Welcome, and here's to bipartisanship," he toasted, "such as The One hadn't foreseen. Make yourself comfortable, grab something to drink, and I'll order more pizza. All the toppings, right? Groggy, you could have given us more than a minute's notice."

"Go read *The Secret Agent*," Groggy replied, "Conrad will instruct you how this sort of thing is done. That black bastard likes to come off as the Second Coming of Our Lord, but he probably has bugs planted all over Washington by now. You have chairs a person can sit on?"

His listeners looked around them warily, focusing particularly on the light fixtures and the smoke alarm. 'Dirty tricks' in American politics was not a novel concept to them.

Breaking the uneasy immobility in which the room had frozen, Elvis Singer and Steven Wolf dashed up the stairs and returned with four chairs; then repeated the operation, yielding two more. Those completed the seating of their visitors.

"Groggy" addressed the company, "The U.S. is about to become a socialist state with an internationalist agenda, like the former U.S.S.R., "Weak brains and the wretched of the world, unite! You never had anything to lose anyway." *Aux barricades, mes amis*. Otherwise, we're going to be in the tumbrels, and it's our necks that will be fed to the guillotine."

The three visitors quickly summarized their first-hand, uncensored, not-made-for-television accounts of the afternoon's stormy session in the Cabinet Room. "That fucking big-arse bitch was all over the Negro," "Rambo" said, wrapping up their presentation, "Our Tommy here has been ordered to collaborate with her in finding the most efficacious way to suck Chinese dick. Go, Tommy! The day is soon coming when gooks and other friggin' slant-eyes are going to be sitting where you are on Capitol Hill. Unless we do something to stop the creeping horror."

Wolf said, "The blogosphere has certainly gone off the deep end, and it does look like the makes of a new Civil War, socialism vs. American values. It's tipping on the side of the former, but that's because half of these jokers are illegal immigrants who should have been rounded up, locked in fiercely managed immigration prisons to cool off, and then deported to the caves whence they had come- long before they could have afforded a broadband connection."

"That muthafucka insulted me three times," "Rambo" complained, "the cock has to crow for his black arse, or crucify me instead. "Groggy" says you guys are ninja Republicans, and we need a war strategy. That's why we're here."

The doorbell rang again, and this time it was Spender Bach who brought in two more boxes of pizza. The men concentrated on wolfing down the food until there were only smudges of cold tomato sauce left in the boxes, and then kicked back with the drinks.

Jackie Coin said, "The internationalist thing caught right on with the bloggers. A lot of Whole-Earthers, Trekkies, drug addicts and other space cadets out there soil their continence briefs when they think of the United Milky Way Federation, and The One was The Universe's gift to them. With him aboard the starship, with Sulu the Jap and Chang the Chink at the controls, and big-butt Lieutenant Uhura ready to teleport, they're off where no man has gone before."

"Now you're talking," Tony Cockburn said, "never to return. This whole thing is really about reparations for slavery, without using the word. In the end, it'll make white people feel just as guilty as if they had."

Wolf said, "We'll really have a Civil War on our hands if we move against him openly. His numbers dipped over the weekend behind Dachshund's nomination, but now that he's gone, they've gone way back up again. And climbing: as Jackie boy said, all these illegal immigrants and the other darkies think he's the New Age Messiah, because he's sucking up to the chinks and the sand-niggers."

"That cunt even insulted my poor dad," "Rambo" remembered. And he recounted the exchange with the Secretary of State. He got up and turned off the volume of the television, where said female adversary was being pictured.

"I was Brutus when we did 'Julius Caesar' in tenth grade," "Groggy" said, "so you might say I have a bit of experience in this sort of thing. And the Ides of March are less than five weeks away."

Elvis Singer said he always liked "Othello" better, which they read in his grade school, but hadn't had the opportunity to act in it. They said he didn't have the aptitude for acting. Otherwise, he would have liked to be Iago, and bring down a knows-all, black usurper who didn't know his place.

Tommy Gunther was exploding his head with laughter, and was having such a good time after the humiliations of the day that he almost wished he had brought along some crack. He was certain the company would either have indulged, or wouldn't have minded if he did. But, hearing mention of two of Shakespeare's plays in which bloody regicide was the major theme, he thought he should rein in his companions before the discussion slipped out of control. The examples of Abraham Lincoln, John F. Kennedy, Bobby Kennedy, Martin Luther King, Jnr., and Malcolm X came to mind –Americans weren't necessarily bashful when it was a matter of assassinations.

"Guys," he said, "the touchstone is the recovery plan. If we can derail it, his supporters will do the knife job for us, and our hands will be clean. The plan rests on repairing three things: the banking system; the subprime mortgages and the housing values situation; and the broader economic collapse, which the stimulus spending is to fix. So, instead of talking murder, which, of course, could still be a last resort, as long as neither "Groggy" nor Elvis insist on doing it in Roman or Moroccan drag, we could start off with sabotage. Any ideas how?"

Spender Bach had majored in political science for his undergraduate degree at Arkansas State and regarded himself as a major gift to the discipline. "Like Jackie, I was surprised by the support socialist ideas are getting on the blogosphere," he observed, "There's a really huge populist wave the common folk are riding!"

"Millions of ideas are coming out," Jackie Coin added, "and some of them are going to catch Osama and Brunton's eyes. One blogger gave a detailed structure, complete with diagrams and all, of what a national bank would look like. I suppose it has a superficial, populist appeal. It's catchy, and the kinks can ultimately be ironed out."

Bach said, "There are several ideas like the one Jackie described, and others which push the idea onto the international stage. I saw a blog from our old friend Qaddafi, who's just become head of the Organization of African States. If a national bank is set up in the U.S., he wants an African wing to it; and he's willing to put in all of Libya's wealth. Right at this moment, he's pressing African heads of state to turn the continent into one centrally governed federation, with one federal banking system, to be better able to allocate development funds throughout the continent to the greatest advantage. Chinese and Japanese bloggers are also pouring in much gusto and concrete elaborations of the idea. How do you propose to stop this huge socialist tsunami, Tommy?"

Tommy had an answer ready. "Let's start first with the banking system," he said, "Where do we want to end up with that? Jackie was right to draw our attention to the huge groundswell of support that's building for nationalization. You heard the president today, right? He's in the same execution squad too. Rage at the bankers is all it is, a demand for the proverbial –or Shakespearean- pound of flesh. Other than that, I'm not sure that all those bloggers, or Golliwog, for that matter, have a single, coherent notion what nationalization is, and that's OK, because it can be whatever we want it to be. The F.D.I.C. routinely takes over a couple of smaller banks a day, cleans them up, and re-privatizes them: that's nationalization, and it goes on hidden in plain sight under the title of capitalism as usual. Besides, "Groggy," we're going to have to accept that not every bank and every shareholder and every private investor is going to come out of this thing whole. In fact, the truth is, the majority just can't be saved! And the truth is also that the majority aren't the ones who have your back or mine or anybody else's in this room. So it's inevitable, and also in the best interests of the people in this room, to just let the majority of them sink. Really, the important thing is what the fallout will be when the curtain falls on the final scene.

"My point is: we have to make sure that the banks that have our backs aren't the ones that are going to fall; and when the others have, they are going to be fewer, and much, much, stronger, and in a better position than any time previously to do what we want –watch our backs, and take care of us. I mean even if the bush baby's government took over all the banks, they'd have to re-privatize eventually –and what we have to do, is make sure our boys are the ones left standing when they do."

Elvis Singer was puzzled. "What do you mean, 'our boys?' You keep saying that."

"Elvis, you're not back in Arkansas in Sunday School!" "Rambo" snapped, "You should know nobody does anything for free in this town. You have to look out for Numero Uno! Always!"

Jackie Coin grumbled, "Some things you shouldn't have

to explain, Elvis. No wonder they didn't pick you for 'Iago!' Didn't they teach you that in drama? Context, right?"

Elvis Singer appeared to be satisfied.

Peeling his scathing glance away from Elvis with as much difficulty as if it were attached with Velcro, Tommy continued, "Naturally, any plan to nationalize –or they might call it something more palatable, like 'temporary receivership,' or something dumb like that- is going to have to pass through the House and Senate, and of course, you guys will fight it tooth and nail, as "Groggy" already promised the boss to his face today. Following me there, Elvis old boy? And so will Democrats, and yours truly, because on this particular issue, I'm going to have to leave myself with a lot of wiggle room. I am going to have to ask Elvis for a set, and next I'll twirl The Man around the ballroom, but Elvis is now sure for whom I'll be saving the last dance. So, that's going to gum it up for weeks, if not months, even if popular support for the idea continues to build. But the delay is critical in other necessary ways. We can wreak havoc in the meanwhile, which will allow us to completely cover our tracks. Yes we can, right, Elvis?

"Fibbs will be giving a press conference at noon tomorrow, and the Massa has warned him to be candid, so it's going to be all over the news that the government is 'toying' with the idea. Left on their own, the bankers will oppose the idea; but at the same time, our boys –the eventual survivors- should be figuring out how to cut their losses and maximize their remaining assets, by throwing those toxic assets in with the government. But in addition, we have to get them all to act ugly the minute the news is official, or starting tomorrow. That'll give us a big head start, and we can create serious mischief and a panic! Sorry, can't cash your paycheck. No money in the ATMs. No withdrawals, period. No credit. Claim a really bottom-of-the-barrel, liquidity crisis and say they can't resume unless there are immediate injections of billions of dollars. The One can't act on nationalization without legislative authorization, so he'll have to concede and go through the existing channels, i.e. the banks, or face riots in the streets.

"Once the billions have gone into the banks, what can the populists do? Very little, unless they are willing to print money and risk stagflation big time: no growth, no job creation, but prices skyrocketing. Or, without new money, the alternative would deflation and stagnation: still no growth, still no job creation, and the even more frightening prospect of prices falling and remaining at rock bottom for the foreseeable future. I saw that happen in Japan, and it wasn't pretty. So our boys will have lots of time to consolidate their positions, and be in place to be the eventual winners. And for our hard labor, Elvis, we get a cut, naturally!

"Next, what to do about the stimulus plan? The idea was to boost employment and productivity. It has two parts: the tax cuts, which taxpayers are supposed to spend on their own mini-stimuli, such as expanding their businesses, and taking on new employees; and secondly, the actual cash disbursements from the Treasury for spending on infrastructure, education, health, Medicaid, enhanced unemployment benefits, food stamps, green energy, science and technology, communications and so on.

"The first part is easy: if the citizenry had been willing to riot in the streets yesterday, would you, as a businessman, put in new plate glass windows or new machinery today? Hell, no! You'd put your money under a mattress, get ready to board up the place, stock up for an emergency, and buy guns and ammo. I've already taken those precautions, and I guess you have too. I spent my $34,000 wisely, you betcha; and I'm sure Freddie Dachshund did as well with his tax cut. Well, before we had to pay the damn thing back! An obvious strategy, therefore, is to negotiate in the House and Senate to account more of the money as tax cuts, and have less going out to the second part, or the actual disbursements.

"As for that part, which we should strategize therefore to

shrink to next to nothing, like cutting into aid to the states and education, a good portion will be spent over several years, like broadband connections, and computerizing health records, and won't immediately affect employment or productivity. As for what's left, which could conceivably have immediate effects, there'll be such a squabble in the House and Senate, and among the states, in the states' governments and with the contractors who will be doing the actual work that a little effort on our part can bring it to a total standstill. Does this mean that our state will have to continue these benefits as a regular practice in the future? Will we have to permanently rewrite our legislation? Are the feds usurping states' rights? Where's the constitutional backing for this? Does this meet our unions' guidelines? Is adequate care being taken to protect the American worker from foreign competition? Is protectionism a good idea now? Was it ever? Is this provision threatening religious freedom? Is this one blurring the boundary between church and state? Endangered Species Act! And we can work with state legislatures and the contractors to throw many more spanners in the works.

"The mortgages and housing values are the easiest. With all the rest going on, the homeowner who gets a bailout will be reviled like the bankers who got one today. Why him, and not me? As foreclosures climb to eight million or so, which is where we realistically think they are heading, housing values will tumble more, greatly aggravating all the strains I've already described.

"Meantime, while the circus is in full cry, the job losses are mounting, production has ground to a complete halt, retail has evaporated, credit card debt in the trillions has been written off, and even his supporters are wondering whether blacks are genetically equipped to govern.

"Do I get an A-plus?"

Steven Wolf clapped his hands politely, and the others joined in. "We each have a lot of telephone calls to make," he said.

"No friggin' calls!" "Rambo" screamed, catapulting out of his chair, "Cocksucker, what are you, fuckin' crazy?! Go in fuckin' person! Make sure you're not followed! Choose public places to meet, where it's harder for the dicks to eavesdrop! Be fuckin' smart and discreet, hear? *Fuckin'*A!"

6

L iving together in her apartment was working out rather well for Awe and Robert. Musicians and writers are a natural pairing, with phrases of songs, instrumental music, poetry, and passages of arresting prose permanently exalting and enlivening their living space, even in the dead corners and under beds. It was a spacious two-bedroom walkup on the second floor of a scrupulously managed building on Prospect Park West that comfortably accommodated two private persons. She went out several times a week to the media company or her recording studio, he was often either at his gym or the library, and writing music and fiction respectively for much of the remaining time kept them from being in each other's way. Days went by without them having the opportunity to even share a meal. Meditating, which did occur at times when they were at home together, had been difficult at first for him, as he had to learn getting used to having another person in the room; but she had learned how not to be a distraction during *zazen* instruction at her school in Japan; and eventually he grew comfortable with it. In fact, their combined practice actually increased the benefits each received: the absence of mind persons who meditate needed now felt to them more palpably like the presence of the hyperconsciousness they sought, and they returned from it more enriched and elevated, as if they had been physically staying for a vacation at some warm, luxury resort of the spirit. Afterwards, they were sure to engage in their mundane activities more unhesitatingly and sure-footedly, as if they had all been transcendentally pre-scripted, and they were confidently following the direction they'd been handed and already rehearsed.

One Friday morning, for example, Robert was moved to visit former customers and acquaintances he knew in the Bedford-Stuyvesant section of Brooklyn and, dressing up in some freshly laundered clothes for the occasion, set out walking briskly: he planned to drop in on an art gallery owner on Nostrand Avenue, a funeral parlor owner on Jefferson Avenue, and the pastor of a Baptist church on Herkheimer. He knew from past experience that there were always opportunities hidden under the radar in the ghetto that might provide him with part-time or even full-time employment: grant writing; keeping written records, such as the various types of progress reports that funding agencies required from their non-profit grantees; teaching or counseling at these same non-profits; private tutoring; and even in retail. At the store, he had gotten to know many wholesalers, and he reckoned he could now perform as an intermediary between them and a different client pool. Even his knowledge of the city's geography as a long time resident, for example, which enabled him to locate where hard-to-find Chinese, Tibetan, Indian, African, Eastern European or other ethnic goods could be found, had proved lucrative in the past.

The art gallery was located among a strip of small stores and ethnic Caribbean restaurants at the western end of Nostrand Avenue. A shiny brass plaque, "Benjamin Robinson, Esq.," distinguished it from the other storefronts, as did the exhibition of Haitian sculptures, all made of recycled materials, which were currently on display. Indeed, the towering figure of Oshun, the Yoruba god of war, and an important *orisha* in New World African folk-religions, stopped every passerby dead in her or his tracks each time, no matter how often they saw it: the corrugated zinc and rusty iron nails that had gone into its construction gave it an immediacy and potency that they couldn't ignore. The owner of the gallery, said Benjamin Robinson, Esq., was an African American of formidable girth, whose huge leonine head bore an astonishingly close resemblance to Frederick Douglass,' the famous black leader, orator and abolitionist during Abraham Lincoln's presidency. He could be espied behind a desk at the back of the gallery, where his black-and-white Yoruba gown blended in with the shadows. Needless to say, it was a *basso profundo* that called out a genial welcome to his guest. "What a pleasure to see your face of glory and wisdom, my brother!" it boomed, "I thought you never left the safety of the white people's enclave of Park Slope. You aren't any the worse for risking the trip, are you?"

The men laughed over this pleasantry, which was really a jibe at Robert's well known solitary habits, who nevertheless reminded the gallery owner, whom he called Benjie, that he was no stranger to the neighborhood; and work had kept him away, was all. He then explained that he had more than enough leisure time at his disposal, now that the store had closed, and he was looking for a gig, any kind of employment that would drum up a little extra income on top of the pittance he received from Social Security.

"Another casualty of the white boys' greed, huh?" Benjie commented. "I'm feeling the pain like everyone else, and I don't know how much longer I can hold out. You mightn't have noticed, as you haven't been visiting frequently, that the number of men, young and old, who are stamping their feet in the cold outside are about four times the number you would have seen during last summer, when the hot weather obliged them to be outdoors. Nothing unusual in that, of course: the white boys screw everything up on Wall Street and in Washington, and here in Bed-Stuy, the coloreds and the immigrants take the hit directly on the nose."

Robert nodded: his walk had taken him through the gradually gentrifying streets and avenues of Prospect Heights; but, after crossing into Bed-Stuy proper, he had begun noticing the unusual number of persons, mostly males, milling about, despite the temperature, which was in the teens that day, and had been saddened by the troubled or hostile expressions on their faces and their general, woebegone appearance -overcoats torn, shabby and dirty; sneakers worn down at the heels. Benjie filled an electric kettle with water and plugged it in to boil; and he put a couple of herbal tea bags in a teapot. "It was like Carnival on Nostrand Avenue the night of November 4," he said, shaking his head sorrowfully, "we knew by eight o'clock the jig was up for the great white hopes, and people started pouring out of their homes. Dozens of drummers set up on the sidewalks, and it was like the investiture of a great African chief –dancing in the streets, women wailing salutations, children running between the adults' legs; and mountains and oceans of food and beer just appeared out of nowhere. Folks must have been busy all day in anticipation, frying flocks of chickens, barbecuing racks of ribs of an untold number of beasts, baking thousands of macaroni pies and peach cobblers, and boiling acres of collard and mustard greens. They dragged television sets outside to watch the acceptance speech in Chicago, and the party went on long past that ended, into early morning. Police cruisers came and had to leave: they didn't dare declare the gathering illegal, as there were no disturbances to give them the excuse; it was peacefulness and joyfulness and gratitude all around. Did you by chance see a single happy face today? The honeymoon is already over, and it hasn't been two weeks!"

"It really doesn't look promising." Robert said, "The job losses just keep mounting day after day, foreclosures have reached five million and are climbing towards an expected thirteen million, and you can't get clarity on any details of the stimulus bill, or when it will be approved, or implemented, and when people will start working again. The only reliable news is about another rip off, another scam, and Ponzi schemes that had seemed to have sprouted like mushrooms while the Republicans had been in power."

"But you're a different story," Benjie declared, "your talents are just tailor made for these rough times. With that white beard and all! Boy, ain't I been telling you for the longest while to get yourself a matching white robe, white turban, and a long rope of big, brown prayer beads? Oxford shirts and denims don't cut it! When you really channel your inner angels, you're deadly! People would trip over one another to pay for your advice. My sister swears up and down the Bible that you put her back in the driver's seat as far as her diabetes was concerned, and I hear other stories about you all the time, how depression, and can't-find-a-job, and the-neighbor-working-obeah-on-me, and I-can't seem-to-get-ahead are small potatoes for you, they just don't stand a chance! If you're not making a mint of money by now, you got to take my advice this time and stop hiding that light under a bushel."

"My," Robert joked, "what a demonstration of the eclectic auto-didact!"

"Joke all you want," Benjie rejoined, "take my advice, do some good, and make some money too. I mean, big time: not the chump change you've been pocketing all this while."

To placate him, and to change the subject too, Robert said, "You know more than enough to know this much: you teach when you get called to teach, and not before. I'm just being patient, is all, and if people gain something in the meantime from what I feel able to tell them, it's from my being a humble apprentice. You know what I'd do if I had the ability? I really wish I could say something useful to that first black president we elected!"

"Yeah, you could start by telling him about that born-to-fail economic team he's assembled," Benjie said, grumpily taking the bait, "How are we going to get 'change we can believe in' out of the same people who got us into this mess in the first place. Now it's turning out that every last one of them is a thief, who won't pay their taxes even when they're being forced!"

Robert wondered whether economists were really the right kind of experts to take on these problems in the first place. He observed, "After all, back in August or even September last year, none of them had the least inkling that, by October, banks would be failing, credit would freeze up, those homes would be foreclosed, and unemployment would have climbed above nine percent – and they had no notion these effects would be global, international."

Benjie agreed, "You're absolutely right about economists! They aren't up to this challenge! These problems aren't about an erroneous value given to some factor in some econometric model, like productivity, the interest rate, the supply of money, the level of investment, marginal utility, the GDP, or other 'fundamentals' like those. This is about the three trillion and three dysfunctional, maladaptive ways in which we Americans sense, emote, perceive, cognize, reason, decide, and behave!"

Robert threw up his hands in a theatrical gesture. "When we really need them, where oh where are the intellectuals?" he asked, "We don't need technocrats, we need real intellectuals. Where are our postmodernists, our deconstructionists, our post-structuralists, our rational humanists, our utilitarians, our behavior modificationists, our molecular biologists, our philosophers, our evolutionary psychologists, our neuroscientists, our physicists, our cosmologists, our psychological anthropologists and our evolutionary psychologists? Aren't they going to tell us what all this means about the nature of reality, matter, consciousness, human nature and the prospects of the human race for the future?"

"And how we are going to get out of the soup! Come up with a couple of really novel ideas about concrete solutions to the problems!" Benjie added, "And you don't have to look for these intellectuals only at the universities. Some of the brightest people you can hope to meet live, or are homeless, less than a hundred yards from this gallery!"

"That's just it!" Robert exclaimed, "The biggest failing in Osama's team is that there's just no diversity whatsoever. Where's the 'change?' It's the one and the same old mindset, period! Take Volkswagon. He's to head up the Economic Advisory Committee. He's the one who brought the economy to a standstill in the 1980's under Reagan. Knocked it out cold by raising the interest rates sky high and drying up money and jobs. But prices didn't go up because the Chinese were flooding us with cheap, lead-tainted goods and the Colombians with cheap cocaine, so *he* walks off with the credit on his résumé for controlling inflation.

"That's something they're really wonderful at!" Benjie said, "Taking the credit for other peoples' ideas and inventions! They've been doing it down through the ages."

"Skip to the next decade," Robert continued, "By then, the Chinese and Colombians have earned trillions of dollars from the sale of those cheap, lead-tainted goods and crack cocaine and have parked them in U.S. banks and financial institutions, the Arabs and Japanese have parked a few trillions more, and the eyes of Homespun, Volkswagon, Somerville and Rubens are just popping out of their heads. How to get their hands on all that loot?

"Well, tax cuts! Deregulation! C.D.O.'s and C.D.S.'s and securitization and all those "exotic financial instruments" they couldn't remember the details of the minute after they had dreamed them up. Only a tad more complicated than the garden-variety lies you told the teacher and your parents about the homework. Was it grandpa that died this time, or did I say grandma? And they'd sell this worthless paper throughout the world, raking in trillions more. And then *they* walked away with the credit of raising the GNP by creating the tiny class of the American super-rich and their outsize compensation.

"Now, they could have given these foreign depositors a good return on their investment by instituting universal healthcare, improving our schools, rebuilding the infrastructure, and by expanding and revitalizing retail, industry and agriculture –just as we are preparing to do now, hopefully. But no, thievery was uppermost in their minds, and they ended up with billions each. But we ended up with the meltdown, and I ended up with no customers, no store, no savings, no health insurance, mounting debts, homelessness and no prospect of work anytime soon.

"And now they are Osama's team! Brings you to tears, right? What can he be thinking?"

"You're forgetting they voted for him," Benjie remarked. "And if he doesn't do as they say, well, just remember what happened to JFK, Bobbie, and Dr. King!"

"The pressures must be immense," Robert agreed, "So, what do we do? Give it up as all a pipe dream?"

Benjie said, "Well, if you won't become a maharishi and you are looking for work, that's not a problem at all! There's always something for the likes of us. There's crime. And sales of heroin, cocaine, meth, Ecstasy and marijuana are booming, just booming, a real growth industry: just take another, closer look outside. You come up with a novelty, something really new to add to that dope menu I gave you, and you'll be the king of Bed-Stuy, Crown Heights, Flatbush and Harlem. You'll have franchises all over the tri-state area, if not the nation!"

"You know, I take a little time each day to write down these opinions and email them to Change.gov. or White House. gov.," Robert said.

"Me too!" Benjie bellowed, "Absolutely! I've never missed a day. You think somebody reads our contributions?"

"In one of my entries, I wrote about an outbreak of crimes, drug use and violence, and that the nation's first African-American president could well end up presiding over a doubling of its prison population. I also applied for a job." Robert confided.

"You, me and 300,000 others!" Benjie told him. "It's just a drop in the bucket, but if we all got hired, that'll bring down the unemployment rate by at least 0.00001 or so. It's something!"

"They did say it would take awhile," Robert said, without too much optimism in his demeanor, "maybe it's too early to give up hope completely."

"Ain't that something, my brother?" Benjie continued, "We were there for him during the campaign and the elections to put him in office, and I'll let you in on a dreadful, dark secret: I am convinced a lot of white people voted for him because they were scared witless what we would do if he didn't win, especially since he was running against an opposition comprising a polar bear assassin and a long-deceased mummy! And now that he's won, there isn't a single yardie in the whole line up! Apart from the White House domestic staff his wife apparently took on, not a single homeboy or home girl! As if we had nothing, not a damn thing, to contribute to the recovery and wellbeing of this great U.S. of A! Just a pack of ignorant, chattering monkeys, the same as we always were, the whole pack of us!"

"I bet I could write a speech," Robert opined, "or at least a few paragraphs for a press release. I wouldn't of course aspire to be the Press Secretary!"

"Well, *I* could misinform the press as well as Fibbs," Benjie asserted, "If I was sure Moms wasn't listening in or watching!"

"Guess I'm too old to be a page," Robert said ruefully.

Benjie's laughter pealed out like the bass notes of the organ in a cathedral, "I'm too wide," he spluttered.

Wristwatches were consulted, the overcast skies were noted, and the men got up and embraced. Robert bundled up and went out into the frigid street. The winter was more severe this year than several previous ones had been, and the deep freeze seemed to have arrived to harden into permanence, for future ages to review, the hard knocks and disappointments that kept coming, one tripping over the heels of the other. As he exited the avenue, he was more observant of the ashen faces and the deteriorating buildings he saw, and alerted by Benjie, noted the clandestine transactions that indicated the thriving drug trade. A plaintive reggae by Bob Marley skanked out of the door of a Rastafarian music store he passed and weaved its mournful path of regrets, sorrows and unfulfilled dreams among the forlorn tenements. When would the Abyssinians in exile ever get their deliverance? When would Jah turn the sufferers' night to day? When would it arrive, that change that was so long in coming, of which their prophets, *griots* and balladeers had been singing for five hundred years?

After his discussion with Benjie, it seemed pointless to go on looking for work, but Bed-Stuy, really one of the city's most beautiful sections, despite the ravages its current poverty had wrought on its appearance, was fascinating Robert anew, after having stayed away for so long, and he headed towards Jefferson Avenue, where the funeral parlor was located, adjusting his coat more tightly around him against the forbidding cold. His route went past Masjid Al-Taqwa, one of the largest mosques in Brooklyn. It was still early afternoon, and prayers had just let out. The good thousand or more worshippers who had attended were thronging the sidewalks and the intersection of Fulton and Bedford Avenues. How delightful it was to be caught up in the midst of ubiquitous bouquets of wide-open smiles and cheerful cries of greeting! The day suddenly seemed warmer by several degrees Fahrenheit! He was reminded that the Prophet Muhammad had set aside Friday not only for prayers, but also as the happiest day of the week. The faithful represented every corner of the globe: Senegal, Côte d'Ivoire, Mali, Burkina Faso, Sierra Leone, Nigeria, Niger, Chad, the Cameroons, Somalia, Yemen, and Sudan; Indonesia, Pakistan, and India; and Trinidad, Guyana and Jamaica. There were Arabs; African Americans; Europeans, and a few Chinese. Clean and sparkling in their most resplendent clothes, smelling sweetly of aromatic oils and perfumes, they were going in and out of the myriad, small stores where the aromatic oils and perfumes, as well as incense, books, clothes, and religious items were sold. The Senegalese and Côte d'Ivoirian restaurants were packed with families and friends feasting and partying, and new arrivals helping themselves from the laden steam tables. The esprit of interethnic *umma* and joyousness was contagious, and the sun was setting when Robert thought reluctantly to separate from it. Then, it took him at least another hour to exchange fond farewells –and telephone numbers, addresses and emails- with all the new acquaintances and potential business partners he had made. In all, he was made to feel that the pessimism and perils of the recession were a million miles away –*accàn*, in America!

7

The governor of Alaska, Susan Paltry, was snuggling up to her husband, Hunky Hank, in bed. It was an *idée fixe* of hers, not that she cared for the French, who had dissed the former president and the Republicans over the war against Iraq and sucked up to the One, that her *derrière* improved in appearance after her husband serviced her, and went abroad after the deed rounder, rosier, and heftier. Seeking these effects for display later that Sunday morning, when her family attended the matins at their church, she roused him with tickling fingers and a hot, breathy appeal in his ear, "drill, baby, drill!" Awakening, and throwing her legs over his shoulders, as he knew she liked him to have unimpeded access to her innermost pleasure centers, Hunky set about the task to which he had been summoned. An instant after he had stuffed himself into her, the governor commenced a long trail of repetitions, "drill, baby, drill! drill, baby, drill! drill, baby, drill!" which ulululated hysterically and unevenly towards the end; it was rounded by a series of grunts, rather like those of an exhausted, young, adult seal; then heavy breathing. Hunky was relieved at that, as customarily his was a quiet demeanor.

Later, she admired her butt in the mirror and with her hands as they dressed for church. It *had* benefitted from the

Ansley Hamid

morning's efforts, and was even better for the black Vera Wang skirt in which she sheathed it. The clothing was booty she had carried off from a campaign stop in New York during her unsuccessful run for office the previous year. Before leaving their bedroom, the governor carefully ticked off the date on a wildlife calendar on the wall. She kept count of the nights she spent in her house and billed the state for them for as official lodgings, reasoning that her stay was about governmental, rather than private business. And, as she once explained to Hunky, in apparent defiance of linear logic, nobody could deny that his "business" was "official."

At the Friendship Church, the sermon that morning concerned the Large Hadron Collider, which rather puzzled the congregants, although Pastor Joey Flake's flock was used to his eccentric and erratic animus, which had let fly over time at UFO's, hip-hop, Angelina Jolie, molecular biology, genetically engineered foods, and naturally, evolution. He was evidently very incensed against this latest irritant, the LHC. At any rate, fearing he would completely lose them, he halted himself in full cry and retraced his steps in order to acquaint his listeners with details about the offender *du jour*.

"The Large Hadron Collider, or LHC as they call it for short, is the largest scientific instrument ever built, just as the Tower of Babel was in its day. It's buried seventeen miles under the Swiss Alps, near Geneva, Switzerland. The scientists behind it are mostly Europeans, but they get most of their money from your taxes, or in other words, through the U.S. Government. These scientists are going to accelerate protons in the LHC close to the speed of light, or as close as possible to the speeds attained during the big bang, or what they say was the beginning of Creation. Can you already see the hand of the Devil in this, my brothers and sisters in Christ?

"They are looking for what they call 'the God particle!' *The God particle*! Listen up, my brothers and sisters in Christ: *The God particle*! God is not our help in the hour of our need:

He's a particle hiding out in the LHC! You see, their theory is, when you accelerate particles at those speeds, they turn into all sorts of other, totally unlike particles. It's as if I were to throw you a fastball real, real fast: it would turn into a piece of fried moose cheek by the time it got to you. So, if they accelerated a known particle in the LHC, it might come out as the God particle, which, according to them, gives other particles mass and quality, and that right there in a nutshell, according to these idolaters, that mass and quality, is the world and us.

"I can't tell you whether they want us to fall down and worship this thing, if they find it. But go deeper, God's children, go deeper into this blasphemy for our times. If, as they say, we were created in a big bang that generated, or was the result of, incredible speeds, faster than anything you or I can imagine, speeds with destructive as well as creative potential, what's going to happen when they recreate these speeds in Switzerland, and use them to hurl projectiles under the Alps? Why, according to their own sinful theories, a big bang! Whole worlds flying apart at incredible speeds! How could we possibly survive that?

"When you're going to do a scientific experiment on that scale, you have to let the authorities know that you've looked into it carefully, and you're satisfied it's not going to cause any harm to the environment or living creatures. That's why they are stopping our great and beloved governor here –Hi, Susan- from bringing much needed jobs to the state, because further exploration for oil might harm a couple of old polar bears, although it's OK for certain hunters to kill them to preserve their so-called traditional way of life.

"The LHC was scheduled to begin operating on September 10, 2008. Before they threw the switch, however, a couple of concerned scientists, brothers in Christ, tried to stop them. They filed a complaint before the Federal District Court in Honolulu, Hawaii, saying that these European scientists hadn't done their homework, couldn't guarantee that their experiment wouldn't destroy the world and the lot of us, and the U.S government should take back our taxpayer money -I'm talking billions, my friends, going abroad for this doomsday threat as over four million Americans have lost their jobs in the last four months- and insist that the Europeans cease and desist immediately.

"Well, the axis of evil quickly went to work to discredit those two good Christians, questioning their intelligence, their credentials and their motives, instead of talking about the violations of the law they had brought to light, which were really the points at issue. And they succeeded in their wicked work.

"But, my friends, the Lord our God, the Living Jehovah, will not be mocked. When they threw the switch on September 10, 2008, guess what? Nothing happened! They'd built a doomsday machine, but they weren't smart enough –the Devil wasn't smart enough -to build it so that it would work! It just wouldn't work, no matter what they did! And so, by the Grace of God, we were spared the Armageddon they and their evil lord had prepared for us.

"In their pride and wickedness, however, they want to try again on July 25, 2009. Now, God put out His hand and spared us last year; this year, He wants *us* to stand up and be counted. It's no accident there's so much suffering in the land today. It's a sign we have to turn away from our evildoing and obey His laws again."

"Let us pray.

"Almighty God, in whom we trust, we thank you for all your many blessings. Guide our steps towards the path of righteousness this coming week. Many of our brothers and sisters are desperate, as they lose their jobs, their homes and their savings. The evil in the world is multiplying its forces, causing distress everywhere. Help us to rally ours for the battle, so that in the end victory will be Thine and ours. Protect your planet, this home you have given us, from those who deny your holy presence. In the name of our blessed Lord Jesus, amen."

Pastor Joey was more explicit in a conversation with Governor Paltry, as he bade her family and her farewell until Thursday evening, when they would meet again for the regular, mid-week prayer meeting. "That LHC is something we have to fight, Governor. The children of Ham hijacked our high places and set their seed upon our throne, which rightfully belonged to you. You can be sure the usurper will be all for this evil. But that's how Our Lord ordained it: *this* was really the battle you were meant to fight, my dear, and you won't lose it."

The governor often found the pastor's pronouncements a little melodramatic, even to her taste, and consequently paid little heed to this revelation. Indeed, the family forgot about the sermon almost entirely almost immediately, but for the detail that, on their luncheon table that day, fried moose cheeks and tongue were appearing as a side dish.

Susan remembered the following day, however, when her staff, in a state of near panic, summoned her out of her office to view from the balcony a rather frightening spectacle a block away, in front of the Bank of Alaska. A mob had gathered; shouts, yells and rifle shots were ringing out ear-splittingly in the frigid air; and among the multiple, confused movements, there was the arresting centerpiece of men and women hurling garbage cans and bricks and whatever else they could lay their hands upon into the bank and against its façade. The bank doors were hastily shut; and now the men and women were dousing them with petrol, which others must have brought, and flames began immediately to devour the thick pine, giving off dense clouds of Mr. Clean-smelling smoke, soured by the petrol fumes. The governor and her staff heard sirens; and police cars, fire engines and ambulances, all their flashing lights greatly aggravating the nightmarish aspect of the proceedings, rounded into the street in a sudden heap. Police helicopters swooped overhead. It was then that Susan recalled the battle of good vs. evil, and the part —at that moment struggling to better define itself in her head- that the Large Hadron Collider in Switzerland was playing in it.

Thanks to the large federal handouts and earmarks on which Alaska had subsisted for the past several years, the ratio of uniformed Alaskans to plainclothes civilians was higher than elsewhere in the nation, and the disturbance was quickly brought under control, and the mob dispersed. Causes were readily forthcoming: the bank had been telling customers that it had run out of cash and couldn't honor withdrawals or pay out against checks; the word had spread; and the riot had been the result.

Back in her office, ensconced on the grizzly bear skin sprawled over the sofa, Susan turned on the television and wasn't entirely surprised to learn that similar riots had been occurring across the nation since afternoon. After weeks of uncertainty concerning the options available to rescue the banks, which wavered among the TARP strategy, or buying off their toxic mortgage-related assets in exchange for government equity; buying the assets off, parking them in a so-called "bad" bank, and leaving the banks "clean" and capable of conducting business as usual; and persuading private investors to buy them, with the government providing a guarantee against any losses, the White House appeared to have settled on abandoning the banks to an inglorious demise in their own sweet time, and itself assuming the tasks of accumulating capital, selecting areas for investment, and making loans. The banks had retaliated by immediately turning into ice, freezing out all comers. The latter, or irate ordinary Americans stuck without the cash to make essential purchases, had reacted with varying degrees of violence. The threat of a more general breakdown of law and order loomed.

Susan was under considerable pressure at that time. Like other state administrations, hers was faced with the problems the recession had deposited at their door, such as the lack of cash and credit, rising unemployment, falling productivity, an increase in poverty, and the demand for social safety-net provisions. Additionally, however, she was still suffering the aftermath of her much-lampooned run in the presidential elections; and only that week, had become the target of a horde of animal rights advocates. They were roundly condemning the license hunters were given in Alaska to kill moose, caribou, wolves and bears as they pleased, often with high-powered weapons fired from helicopters or other aircraft. And now an unwieldy thought, yoking together many possibly incongruent elements –moose, caribou and polar bear kills, the hypocrisy and inconsistency of the animal defenders, the prospect of the nationalization of banks, the global economic crisis itself, the rioting, and the LHC- was jostling in her brain to achieve some kind of coherent, recognizable form; and a conviction was simultaneously emerging that, once she got it, it would vindicate her against all her tormentors, especially the immediate animal-loving ones. Was it an Act of God, a Sign from on High, that the telephone rang at just that moment, with the print and other media requesting interviews with her to learn her opinions about the national outbreak of rioting?

Susan chose to give a single press conference for the massed journalists of Alaska in the kitchen of her home, as she could then bill the government for another night of putting it to public use, and quite a bit more for providing dinner and refreshments to the more than fifty persons she had invited, including her neighbors, congregants and officials of her church, high school classmates and government staff -the four types of identity usually coincident in the one person. The refreshments consisted of piles of pasta with the governor's special, homemade moose-ball sauce; lots of beer and soda; and a small regiment of cakes. Her parents had taught the governor that plying persons with food and drink invariably caused any ill will they harbored to evaporate.

When she finally faced the cameras, she had these prepared remarks for Americans:

"See, the Washington insiders, and the media intelligentsia out east, and the Hollywood elite –it makes them want to spit when they see how tight Alaskans and me are. I mean you can just look around this kitchen to see how tight we are! It bothers the gotcha-journalists when they can't figure a thing out; and I'd be bothered too, you betcha! Because this time around it's is *so-o-o-* easy. Because, my friends, what's the tie? You know it in your bones an' mine: it's we're folks, me and my Hunky and the kids and grandkids, and you're folks, who work with our hands. Yes, work with our hands. So, who has time for the *non*-sense?

"Now I'm talking about this siren of the silver screen who is down on you and me and the other law-abiding, peace-loving citizens of this great state of Alaska, which is the mother of all solutions to the energy problem, and the one always standing up to the Red Peril, which we can see with our own eyes even on cloudy days, because we prune our herds of wild animals, and harvest the critters. And if we fly over the herds and shoot at them from on high, why, that girl should leave her bikini and swimming pool and palm trees and we'll see whether she can manage the subzero temperatures we live with day in and day out all year round. Think she'll put on shorts and a halter-top and go out there on foot to make nice to a caribou? No way, you betcha!

"See, me and you are hunting and farming people from way back when in Europe and in the Dakotas. You've got to prune and harvest the plants and the animals, not only because they make that powerful satisfying spaghetti 'n moose-balls we had awhile aback, but otherwise they'll overpopulate and kill one another out -but *good*. So what we really do is conservation, and preservation of species that don't know any better than to extinct theirselves.

"Now I wonder how these same people feel about the LHC. That's short for, I got it written down here, if you will excuse me, it says the Large *Hay*-dron Collider. Now this thing is really the Tower of Babel in our times, and if you put a moose-ball in it, and accelerate the speeds inside there, whoa! well, if it ain't a bunch of expensive Chiquita bananas down at the supermarket that comes flying out the other side. Up here, we call that the Devil's work; but the Washington insiders, and the media intelligentsia out east, and the Hollywood elite call it an instrument of science, and they say it will help them find a particle –that's a very, very, tiny, bitsy, atom- *that's really God*! Now, straight up, that's what they are saying! This particle, the itsy-bitsy atom, is really God –the God particle! Well, do you think Our Lord Jehovah is going to just sit up there in the sky and allow this mockery of His Holy name to go on? A thousand times, *no*! Like the Tower of Babel, He'll make it strike them down in their sinful pride! Uh-huh, you betcha!

"Seems as though some good Christians tried to stop this blasphemy in September last year when they first tried to start up this doomsday machine, but God struck it down, and they had a problem with the ignition. So, now they're hoping to start it up again in July this year. But now, Jehovah wants *us* to do the right thing, and it's our turn to turn off that key.

"Now, my friends and fellow lovers of our great state, I hope you dig what the rioting we witnessed today is all about. All these threats to ruin the economy and nationalize the banks and destroy our freedoms and the free market and respect for the individual and our way of life is to distract us from the real iniquity that they have up their sleeves. And what's that, folks? This plaything from the Devil, the LHC! And I say we have to fight the whole package and not give up the fight until we prevail. Otherwise, unemployment will just keep going up and up, there'll be no money in the banks, good people won't be able to buy food in the supermarket or bullets to go shoot it themselves, no homes, and then in the end they'll mop us up with their LHC.

"Now, I'm not saying that the rioting I saw today is the way we are to go. It's unlawful, and the state troopers have instructions to shoot on sight anyone they see rioting and looting But, you see, when they come in their shorts and halter-tops to heckle us for pruning and harvesting the herds, to conserve and preserve them, why aren't they out there fighting the real fight, that will save jobs and stimulate the economy and save the planet and our beloved Alaska from destruction?"

"Well, that's all for now, folks. Come to Pastor Joey's prayer meeting on Thursday, and bring a dish for potluck dinner. See y'all there!"

She called Hunky and all the children up on stage for Alaska, the nation and the whole world to see; but when she took him in her arms, her three-month-old grandson peed on her gleaming red, Karl Lagerfeld designer dress; and all her neighbors, friends, fellow congregants of Pastor Joey's church, old high school buddies and staff –who were the same persons counted five times- swiftly worked their way in front of the cameras, and the interview abruptly ended.

Pastor Rocky Walrus was moping in his McMansion in Lake Forest, California, as was his habit since the inauguration. He had been out-of-sorts because the crowds on the Mall on that historic occasion had paid him, as he was invoking the blessings of Jehovah on their behalf, even less attention than they spared the departing Butcher of Baghdad. Now, there was a low blow from which recovery was understandably difficult! Innuendo, indirection and a pretended intimacy with the Maker were his stock-in-trade, while the occasion had called for honest, well-chosen, weighty, resounding and substantial words; and so, he had failed to spark an interest even in the most impressionable breast. Worse, sales of his formerly bestselling book had taken a steep dive after the event; viewership of his nationally televised broadcasts had also fallen; and weekly attendance at his church had declined noticeably.

He was watching the news and listening listlessly as Governor Paltry was addressing the Alaska end of the national scourge of bank trashing, vandalism and rioting that had broken out that day. Although it had been her candidacy and her running mate's that he had initially endorsed and had continued to tacitly support throughout the previous year's campaign, and despite her feminine allure, which he experienced rather acutely, as was the way with televangelists nowadays, he wasn't moved by her trademark, rambling discourse, characterized by the usual rising peaks of confusion and inarticulacy, on economics, banking, wildlife harvesting, preservationists and God's will, until she zeroed in on this strange animal, the LHC. That galvanized him, and he listened more intently. When the interview ended, he went over to his computer and searched "LHC." He came up with a trove of information: reams of self-congratulatory material submitted by scientists at CERN, or the European Organization for Nuclear Research, who had built the instrument; descriptions of it; details about the international team of scientists, including Americans, who would conduct experiments, and collect and analyze findings; the expected results; details of the complaint brought by two Americans living in Hawaii before that state's District Court; an account of the ensuing legal proceedings; and a report of what happened on September, 10, 2008, when the instrument was first "turned on." He was distracted from his depressed mood on completing his research, opened a new document in his "public addresses" file, and soon produced a text for his upcoming televised sermon:

"Brothers and sisters in Christ, Jesua, Jesu, Issa, Jehovah's blessing on us all. I will keep my comments brief today. Our economy is in shambles, many livelihoods have been demolished, and the horsemen of poverty, starvation, disease, and violence are stalking our beloved land. No one has escaped being affected, and each of us knows in our own hearts the deeply sincere words that she or he has to offer the Divine Fount of Mercy, which relate to the particular pain each one is feeling.

"But remember, O Israel, that not everyone comes into the public square with the pure hearts of the community of saints, the beloved of Jehovah. Those there are for whom this hour of our distress is their time of opportunity, to sew dissension and confusion among the faithful, to bring assaults upon our parapets, and humble this shining city that He has put on high, as a light to the heathens.

"I remember the boasts of those ancient enemies of God when I hear of the plans afoot nowadays to take away the banks from their lawful owners and investors, and to reward evildoers with the spoils taken from hardworking, honest businessmen. And now it has come to light, thanks to that ever-vigilant public servant, Governor Susan Paltry of Alaska, that their plan all along was to give a lot of it to the sorcerers' apprentices, working in the bowels of the earth, whose vain hope is to become a rival to their Creator. I am speaking of the Large Hadron Collider, or the LHC, in which they believe their evil lord is hiding, and their intention is to free him, and with his help gain dominion over the world. Otherwise, the doomsday machine will just destroy everything.

"Brothers and sisters in Christ, our duty is clear: we must fight them!

"Let us pray:

"Almighty God, thou shalt smite them asunder from on high, those who dirst oppose the Omnipotent to arms, thou shalt bind them in adamantine chains and burn them in penal fire; and forever after the New Jerusalem shall be that Shining City on the Hill. Amen."

And leaving John Milton, who had jealously husbanded his royalties, to spin furiously in his grave, he smiled crookedly at the viewers who still tuned into his show. True, he was still off his peak form: but his boundless faith in people's credulity persuaded him that he would make up the deficit.

8

arely three weeks into his presidency, Barzhad was explaining to any sympathetic audience he could find, such as first graders at a public charter school in one of north-east Washington's shabbiest neighborhoods, that Millie and he "were already sick and tired of the White House and the job." The front pages of the newspapers, and 24-hour television programming were chock full of nothing else than news and pictures of the rioting. Violence had by then broken out in trouble spots in several states, and copycat developments were occurring around the globe.

The biggest trouble was pinpointing exactly what was causing the violence. The causes evidently varied by the affected region, its ethnic composition, whether it was Democrat or Republican or in a 'swing' state, whether mostly workers or the unemployed had taken to the streets, religious affiliation, age, gender and many similar factors. Perhaps Alaska best demonstrated the heterogeneity of these factors: many had disregarded Governor's Paltry's stern warning against rioting as mere made-for-television, pro forma statesmanship, and the disturbances had spread from the principal cities of Anchorage, Juneau, and Fairbanks and were infecting smaller towns and villages throughout the state, including Wasilla and Prudhoe

Bay, strongholds of the Paltry clan and its supporters. Fore-closures, falling house values, and recent job losses were the specific causes of much bitterness, but church-going, working class Alaskans, and especially those employed in the oil and petrochemical industries, also embraced their governor's characterization of the LHC as a diabolical doomsday machine and a weapon of the anti-Christ; Pastor Rocky Walrus' broadcast had given her view more authority in their eyes; and there was much sloganeering along those lines as their sports-loving teenage and young adult sons and daughters, warmed by beer, liquor, crystal meth and Ecstasy, clogged the downtown streets of the cities and the main streets of towns, occasionally join-ing in the looting and burning, but constantly preventing the police and fire departments from getting their jobs done. It should be noted that in those latter ranks, there were already much disaffection and rebelliousness, which were compromis-ing the seriousness with which the officers performed their work anyway.

Hunters, trappers and fishermen, burning and looting stores, banks and government property, and stripping liquor stores of their goods before putting them to the torch, were releasing the rage that had been building ever since the elec-tions, which had put Democrats in Congress and a black man in the White House. Caricatures of the rugged, American out-doorsman, they were unanimously opposed to nationalization; yet, injecting a vitriolic element of class and regional warfare into their normally unquestioning faith in individualism, they also believed that fat cats on the East Coast had hijacked the banking system, turned it into a personal fiefdom, and, while siphoning off for themselves wealth and luxuries Middle East-ern oil sheikhs and potentates would have envied, had used it as a weapon against hardworking men and women like themselves, denying business credit and home improvement loans. Additionally, the spreading lawlessness permitted per-sonal animosities and age-old feuds to resurface which bore no relation whatsoever to any of the topical issues, and old grudges were being settled at last by ambushes, shotgun shootouts and murder. Beyond this potent mix, alcohol subsequently became a cause of unrest in its own right.

Inuit, engaged for centuries in fighting the white outsiders who had been incrementally encroaching on their traditional ways of life, and long humbled by unemployment, high rates of alcoholism, and social and political marginalization, were burning trading depots and terrorizing the mainly white representatives of the state government, such as state troopers, police, the courts and court officers, corrections facilities and social workers. It could be fairly said that they'd seen a free-for-all and had taken advantage of it to vent their own very particular grievances.

Rage at the East Coast fat cats, and the equation of nationalization with godless socialism inflamed cities, towns and villages in wide swaths of Alabama, Kentucky, North and South Carolina, Virginia, Kansas, Missouri, Mississippi, Louisiana, northeast Florida, central Texas, Arkansas, the southern parts of Nebraska, Ohio and Indiana, Cedar Rapids, Michigan, Colorado Springs, Colorado and Orange County, southern California, where born-again Christians, evangelicals, social conservatives and Baptists had been going *mano-a-mano* with the Devil for decades. For them, mostly white, and rural in outlook, the doomsday LHC symbolized the full roar of hellfire, to which, in the culture wars of preceding years, abortion, contraception, same-sex marriage, euthanasia, the teaching of evolution, embryonic stem cell research, genetic engineering, genetically modified foods, the banning of prayer from schools and public buildings, the denial of tax-exempt status to religious charities and social work organizations, legislative attempts to control the sale and ownership of firearms, as well as the persecution of clergy, on trumped-up sex, corruption and drug-abuse charges, had already contributed long, lashing tongues of flame. For them, therefore, some of the highest rates of foreclosures and unemployment in the nation were not indications of an ailing economy, but signs of the Almighty's wrath, foretelling even greater retribution to come in the afterlife. It didn't help that a 'Negro' was the face of the federal government as these resentments infected an increasingly disaffected population. In Greenville, South Carolina, home to Bob Jones University, mobs burned federal facilities to the ground; in Dallas-Forth Worth, Texas, bands of armed men and women demolished banks, raided liquor stores, burned cars and police cruisers, and took occupation of the streets. From Charlotte, North Carolina, heart of Billy Graham's ministry, bus- and truckloads of armed men traveled to Durham, where they rampaged through the Schools of Science, Biomedical Research, and Engineering of Duke University, destroying computers and other equipment, eviscerating all the laboratories, freeing animals used in research, and shooting at point blank range five campus police officers who had offered them resistance; in Lynchburg, Virginia, where Jerry Falwell had been the veritable 'voice of God,' a synagogue and a mosque were gutted and burned, and a rabbi shot to death; and in Elkland, Indiana, there was a prison breakout, with the prisoners overrunning the local hospital, terrorizing patients, robbing them and the medical personnel, and making off with foods, drugs, medicines and medical equipment and supplies.

On the east coast, in New York City, where the weather had again turned unseasonably mild, mobs entrained at subway stations in Harlem and Washington Heights, Manhattan; Bedford-Stuyvesant, Bushwick, Brownsville, Sunset Park, Crown Heights and Flatbush, Brooklyn; and converged on Park Avenue, Battery Park City and Sutton Place, Manhattan, where the Masters of the Universe resided in luxury townhouses and supersized apartments. Two transit ticket collectors who stood in their way were the first of the many local fatalities and casualties of the night of horrors that followed. Here, however, religious fundamentalism played a less important role; it was all about the banks, their CEOs, their grossly inflated compensation, the outrageous risks they had taken with other people's money, the dwindling likelihood they would be called to account, the trillions of dollars of being set aside to bail them out, and their lackeys, such as Tommy Gunther, Somerville and Rubens; and as these were also persons Barzhad Osama had unfortunately appointed to high positions in his administration, he too was the target of some condemnation, although for the most part it was subdued. Incensed men and women went from doorman building to doorman building, from townhouse to townhouse, assaulting staff, breaking into homes, driving residents out into the streets in their nightclothes, dragging out furniture and other heavy, household items, and making bonfires of them in the streets. Large quantities of fine wines and liquors had been retrieved from the pillaged homes, and now fueled the start of an outdoors party.

However, the ferocity of the resistance on the part of the homeowners, once they had gotten over the initial shock of being besieged, fairly rapidly brought the invaders of their homes to a standstill. The Masters of the Universe, who usually appeared as feckless gourmands and sybarites, and as physically powerless as grubs, had evidently provisioned their homes with sophisticated arsenals –semiautomatic handguns, pistols, revolvers, derringers, assault rifles, shotguns, and machine guns-and lots of ammunition. They started emptying out their weapons in the crowd. Meanwhile, the first wave of policemen, who had been standing around petrified with fear as their cruisers were overturned and torched, took heart with the arrival of reinforcements from the other boroughs, and also opened fire. Sandwiched thus between two fronts offering sure annihilation, the rioters slunk through basements and service entrances and melted into the side streets of the city, en route for their points of origin. They left behind twenty-three dead and many wounded, who, with homeowners and their family members that had been manhandled, badly beaten, bruised and wounded, had to be evacuated by ambulance to nearby hospitals, like Lenox Hill Hospital and New York University Medical Center.

By daybreak, the most serious rioting had substantially abated, although isolated flare-ups were still occurring, and police, firemen and ambulances found themselves in possession of deserted streets, eerily haunted by the specters of the disintegrated social order, which wouldn't be made whole anytime soon. As the day wore on, it was apparent that New York City had effectively closed down –no throngs of workers heading to their jobs, shops remaining shuttered, buses few and far between – as though a major snowstorm or other extreme weather, and a national holiday, and, of course, a major social catastrophe had landed one on top the other, leaving it inoperative.

In Oakland, California, the rioters were mostly after the police themselves, and the situation teetered more on a razor's edge. Unemployment was sky high among young black adults locally; the foreclosures were turning whole blocks into habitations for ghosts and squatters; anger against the banks and bankers ran high; but the police –*they* were the real culprits! In previous weeks, there had been several incidents of police brutality, the most recent being the shooting of an unharmed, black male in an Oakland subway station, which had been videotaped and photographed by bystanders. Shown on YouTube, MySpace and other Internet outlets, the shooting of the young man in the head by the police officer, as he was laying spread eagled on the ground and held inert by the officer's backup, provoked the pent-up rage of local residents. Seeing the violence being enacted elsewhere in the nation on their television screens and streaming onto the monitors of their computers and hand-held devices, young black men and women swarmed the streets, ready to exact revenge. The police also came out in force, in riot gear and with stun guns, water hoses, tear gas, and dogs; but their opponents were beyond caring for their personal safety and stood them down. As night came, they were the kings and queens of the streets; police cruisers and other vehicles were being consumed by roaring flames; and, free to do as they pleased, the rioters began methodically to smash the windows of stores. Widespread looting followed.

And so it went. Overseas, in Lagos, Nigeria, sectarian strife between Muslims and Christians was piled onto the more general, familiar causes for disturbance; in Colombo, Sri Lanka, the economic crisis gave the Tamil Tigers a fresh opportunity in their decades' long career of wreaking havoc and destruction on their ethnic rivals; in Phnom Penh, Cambodia, shortages of rice, flour, cooking oil and other foodstuffs fed into the ongoing clashes between Buddhists monks and the military; in Sydney, Australia, Indigenous Australians protested both the current hardships and their historical second-class status by setting fires that were continuing unabated, as the death toll mounted to an astonishing 200; the Taliban killed 20 in an attack in Kabul, Afghanistan; and in Gaza, Palestine Hamas lobbed a few rockets into Sderot, Israel, without causing any casualties or much damage.

Going against his gut, but responding to the very real fear that the disturbances would escalate into an even broader, more intransigent breakdown of law and order, nationally and internationally, Barzhad had to divert attention and funds from the recovery plan, which therefore remained up in the air, and rush aid to the states to beef up their police, corrections and security forces. He remained on alert throughout the day, receiving and responding to governors and mayors, who were calling in to report the deteriorating situation in their cities and states.

He found the LHC hysteria truly insufferable! With everything else on his plate, it was maddening to have to deal with what he regarded as a non-issue. However, the mobs that had taken to the streets in London, Dublin, Madrid, Paris,

Berlin and Amsterdam, who were mainly drawn from the Muslim immigrant communities in those cities, whose civic and political incorporation was still incomplete and problematic, might have stayed at home despite the additional hardships caused by tanking economies; but the LHC proved to be a provocation they couldn't ignore. Their grievance was perhaps best expressed by the stinging comments made by the Hamas leader in Gaza, who said on Al-Jazheera television: "The U.S. president is prepared to contribute to the spending of billions of dollars on a doomsday machine, but has offered not a penny for the relief of hundreds of thousands of destitute Palestinians in Gaza, where more than a thousand of his fellow Muslims were massacred by the army of occupation, as he remained silent."

Trying to resolve the controversy was like trying to handle a balloon filled with hot water: if he squeezed it here, it poked out there. If he came out against the LHC to appease Christians in America, he offended Christians in Europe, and vice versa. In his telephone conversations during the day with European leaders, Barzhad had been frustrated by their intransigence. Their scientists were at CERN, like the U.S., they had invested money in the program, and they would be damned if they backed down! It scandalized him that a major cause of their intransigence was that their Muslim minorities opposed it, but he could do nothing about it, and had to be careful to choose his words carefully when he broached that topic. Indeed, reacting to Barzhad's suggestion that they consider a postponement of resuming the program at least until all the world's economies had somewhat stabilized, the Europeans had responded that, to the contrary, they were thinking of moving up the date from July 25 to March or April. The fundamentalist Christians in American with whom he had consulted were eager to delay the program, but, if he tried changing their minds to please the Europeans, it went against him that the American Muslim community, which comprised a higher percentage of professionals, including physicists and nuclear scientists, than in Europe, was scoffing, after some initial support for the delay, at the backwardness of backwoods American Christians. And so, the controversy over the LHC continued to build without any effective checks throughout the nation and the world.

In the midst of the turmoil and all the persisting violence and controversy, a delegation of scientists and intellectuals, calling him on his incontrovertible support of science during the campaign, insisted on a meeting in the White House to press the case against his succumbing to what they labeled 'the forces of darkness.' For his part, Barzhad was as usual reluctant to give offense by refusing the request, and, more positively, rather welcomed the occasion to converse with sensible and rational men, as he deemed scientists and intellectuals to be; accordingly, he had expected their visit to create a temporary oasis of calm and civility in the Oval Office, which was being besieged, as he saw it, by runaway passions, inflamed emotions, one-sided thinking, and extreme behavior. However, he hadn't fully taken into account that they also happened to be outspoken atheists, and believed that science was incompatible with a belief in God.

The head of the delegation was a tweedy, British academic well known for his vaulting ambition and sybaritic lifestyle, whose scholarly writings were marbled with lengthy descriptions of the sumptuous feasts he had enjoyed, the expensive liquors and wines that had washed them into his alimentary system, and his bisexual romantic engagements. His atheism wasn't actually based in any solicitude for philosophy and science. Rather, he was an intolerant holdover of the British Raj, who would have been content to co-exist with the tepid, religious protestations of the Church of England, but for the rabid Islamophobia that consumed him, and the dread that any concession to faith would have likely been construed as encouragement by the Muslim hordes, whose footprint on England's "fair and green," sacred soil was growing steadily larger, and in his opinion, uglier. Another Englishman, a novelist known best -and actually only- in his native land, had been introduced to drugs and sex by a dissolute wreck of an aristocratic father in early childhood; and his atheism had evidently resulted from the psychological and moral trauma he had undergone. However, he too was an unrepentant racist, who had recently gone on record with the policy recommendation that the Muslim community in England should be "visited with an unrelenting campaign of deportations, detentions, house arrests, imprisonments, heavy fines, restrictions, denial of rights and privileges, and other onerous encumbrances until they learned to be more compliant subjects of Her Majesty, the Queen." Yet another Englishman was a naturalized American, resident in New York, who freelanced for literary journals; but he figured more prominently in the gossip pages of the tabloids, where he had chalked up unrivaled infamy for drunkenness and debauchery; and arguably, his atheism merely proceeded from his rarely being sober. Of the two American members of the delegation, one was a dissembling professor of the philosophy of science, whose idea of an intellectual discussion resembled a round of three-card Monte on the sidewalk of a disreputable neighborhood; and the other was a doctoral candidate in neuroscience, whose prior academic qualifications did not prognosticate the publicity he would garner when he came out as an atheist.

The delegation began their defense of the Large Hadron Collider on strictly scientific grounds, attempting to show an earnestly attentive Barzhad that the experimental conditions and events that were to be recreated in the instrument occurred naturally and repeatedly in the universe on any given day, without posing a danger to anything, let alone life on this planet. But they were unable to answer cogently whether the same benign results, which took place in the vastness of the universe where any effects were naturally diffused and diluted, could be also guaranteed in the tiny, tight, confined space of a manmade scientific instrument under a few hundred square feet of the Swiss Alps. They then tried to argue for the indispensability of the experiments, both for the advancement of theory in physics, astrophysics, and cosmology, and also the practical applications of findings in the development of new technology. Reasonably enough, these could not be exhaustively specified in advance.

But then Barshad's patience began to fray when they focused more and more on their atheistic viewpoints.

The young, aspiring neuroscientist and anti-religious pamphleteer, who apparently enjoyed the status of a sort of mascot in the group, blurted out. "Sir, religious belief has a way of undermining even the best scientific training. Please don't overlook the fact that the terrorist attackers in New York, London and Madrid were all highly educated, middle class men; they can't hide their acts behind a lack of education and poverty; and, of course, the Pakistani responsible for nuclear proliferation in the pro-terrorist Muslim states is, well, an expert nuclear physicist."

"The best research shows that religious belief is like a bug in your computer system, causing a persistent misfiring of connections, the production of maladaptive mental processes, and has zero –or less than zero, actually: negative- evolutionary value," Tweedy declaimed.

"Tell me," the president asked, "do you think a belief in God is also responsible for the frightening recession we're in, or the rioting that has erupted here and around the globe?"

The American philosopher laughed uneasily, "Well sir, we aren't economists or political scientists, you know. Such matters are a little bit difficult for the lay man to understand."

"Nor was Adam Smith an economist!" the president shot back, "he was the Chair of the Department of Logic and Moral Philosophy at Glasgow University, in other words, a person in your field. There wasn't an economics department, or economics for that matter, until he thought of them. In fact, he derided his contemporaries who were the forebears of our current blight of economists who gave us the duplicitous CDOs and CDSs.

"I am tempted to revert to my old role of a professor, as your comment indicates that you are woefully ignorant about the history and philosophy of the sciences, which you nevertheless profess to teach. Economics was in a tiny saucepan on the smallest backburner way in back of Professor Adam Smith's stove of many pots. On the front burners were things like the bloody English, feudal social arrangements, jurisprudence, rhetoric, Greek drama, historiography and, above all, "the motions of the human mind," or motives, cognition, perception, memory, feelings, the imagination, the heart, manners –in a word, evolving human nature. Aren't those matters that directly concern you, as evolutionary biologists, philosophers, neuroscientists, novelists, and intellectuals?

"The tiny saucepan on the smallest backburner way in back of the stove gave yeoman service by being measurable, and acting thereby as a kind of gauge: you could tell how the other more numerous, more important, but more inscrutable pots were doing from looking into it and examining its contents –a salt tax, a restriction on the cultivation and sale of goods, the laws pertaining to the use of various types of land, the disposition of livestock, debt, labor obligations and so on. And it also provided a metaphor to facilitate the discussion of the more important topics: economics provided the form for a conversation.

"Smith used this metaphor to pithily depict the plight of Scotland under its feudal English overlords. The latter had robbed Scottish people of the ability to converse, in Smith's loaded sense of the word, and as a result, their minds had become 'neglected, uncultivated, and depressed.' Freeing up those minds required –and could be measured by- freeing up conversation, by which he meant to say economics, or 'the general disposition to truck, barter, and exchange.' Smith wanted to have Scottish people laughing and talking, conversing with one another, parents with their children, and neighbor with neighbor. If I were free to present you with a bag of apples for sale, which you were then free to decide whether to purchase, just look at the spectacular advances in philosophy and the sciences those freedoms would have gained us! Eventually, we'd be talking about: communications technology obviously; the marketing and advertising industries; various aspects of horticulture, such as climate, soil conditions, the supply of water and irrigation, plant genetics, molecular biology; food preparation, food storage and preservation, cuisine and cooking techniques, and home economics; nutrition, health, and the prevention and treatment of disease and illness; physiology, anatomy, biology, and chemistry; reinvestment and futures markets; and much, much more -all between you taking a crunchy bite from the freely traded apple and me running off with your freely given penny, to put into pears or strawberries or whatever else I thought would be the next moneymaking investment. We'd no longer be a frightened, superstitious, 'dumb' Scots under English lockdown.

"Well, Smith was undoubtedly right. Once we adjusted the small flame under the little saucepan, all the other pots did begin to give off the desired, appetizing fragrances. The conversation in fact broadened to include lots more pots -pardon my mixed metaphors- everything up to behavioral economics, the Internet, your !Phone, other palm-held devices, space stations, the disputed Large Hadron Supercollider, robotics and what have you. But the point of the crisis of 2008-9 is the conversation as is has evidently run into limits, and we're back to having "neglected, uncultivated, and depressed" minds, and to being "frightened, superstitious, and 'dumb.'

"What messed up the conversation? I'll tell you! It was when thinkers like yourselves, who believe that human purposes and behavior are explicable in exclusively biological, political and technological terms, put that economic saucepan, or

Adam Smith's *Wealth of Nations,* on the biggest front burner, and moved its erstwhile occupant, his *The Theory of Moral Sentiments*, to that tiniest flame out back. You burned the dinner, if you're up to tolerating more mixed metaphors!

"And so, economics can still serve us as a reliable gauge. When we look into that saucepan and examine the charred remains of the burnt dinner -the credit crisis, the subprime mortgage mess, rising unemployment, CDO's and CDS's, since the conversation has even stopped using whole, meaningful English words!- we know it's a mess inside the other pots too –the widespread dishonesty, fraud and theft, the civil and human rights violations, the unlawful invasion of other countries, the use of 'renditions' and torture, the witch hunts against immigrants, and so on.

"There never was a more reasonable man and friend of the sciences than your countryman, John Locke. Here's something he said in his *Letter on Toleration* about gentlemen like you:

"'Lastly, those are not at all to be tolerated who deny the being of a God. Promises, covenants, and oaths, which are the bonds of human society, can have no hold upon an atheist. The taking away of God, though but even in thought, dissolves all; besides also, those that by their atheism undermine and destroy all religion, can have no pretence of religion whereupon to challenge the privilege of a toleration.'"

Then, remembering the proximity of the bicentennial birthday celebration of Abraham Lincoln, the American president he most admired and emulated, Barzhad followed that great man's precedent, and unceremoniously chucked the five out of the Oval Office, slamming the door hard behind them so that ethnic reverberations of the encounter would echo in their hearts and minds far into the future.

A long afternoon and evening followed the departure of the atheists, who he was certain had gone off to the nearest bar, as he monitored the continuing breakdown of the social contract. By that time, news was arriving about the riots that had engulfed Bombay, Nairobi, Lusaka and Harare. Puffy-eyed, face drawn and ashen from fatigue and worry, he asked his staff to call him in the event that repetitions of the more serious, national disturbances developed, and strolled over in the cool, crisp evening air to the White House Residence, smoking his first cigarette since noon, and fondly anticipating the consolations of family.

The children, however, had already completed their homework assignments, had turned in, and were not awake to welcome him home, and Millie was in combat-ready mode. "Where has bipartisanship gotten you?" she demanded, "Budd has decided to drop you, making you look like a chump, you didn't get a single vote from him or his colleagues in Congress for the recovery plan, and you've ceded the initiative to a pair of the Republican Party's most flagrant opportunists, who have positioned themselves for the ride in the center of the two parties. As a result, you're losing the support of the Democratic rank and file, and you're throwing doubts on your good judgment and sincerity even among your most loyal supporters, like me, dammit! And now, to top it all off, Paltry and Walrus, to whom you were so eager to extend the glad hand, have bitten it off, and saddled us with the worst rioting the nation and the world has ever experienced. I mean, this is global, one single *cri de coeur* and *cri de guerre* wrapping itself around the entire surface of the earth, and there's no guarantee the trouble won't flare up domestically again tomorrow!"

He hadn't the stomach for a fight. "Saying that mouthful, you just know it's been a tough day, sweetie," he pleaded, "I tried to reach out an olive branch, and yes, maybe there weren't any takers."

"In typical manner, they interpreted your olive branch as a sign of weakness," she yelled, "and it gave them the courage to come out of their caves. Can you believe? All this bogus religiosity over a scientific experiment was actually the catalyst that brought black and white, Hindu, Muslim, Christian, Jew and Arab tumbling out into the streets, screaming for blood. Tell me this wasn't a carefully orchestrated plot! Actually, I don't believe for a moment that all this unrest was caused by some stupid speech about particle physics by that dumb bitch Susan Paltry or your good friend, Mr. Passive-Aggressive Rocky Walrus, or even the treachery of the banks. This has to be much more deliberate, and many of the persons who are smiling and laughing in your face, and saying they're so sorry, are throwing fuel on the flames behind your back. That's how they operate! And deep down in my heart, I know that Ezekiel and Gunther are deeply implicated! Tell me that bastard's $2.5 trillion giveaway to his Wall Street buddies isn't is like throwing plastic explosives into the bonfire!"

He conceded out of weariness, "Whether you're right or wrong," he said, "it's nasty out there, the storm clouds are gathering all over the world as you said, and I've got to deal with that first and foremost."

But she wouldn't give up. "And there's us too," she persisted, "I can't go on this way any longer."

"Can't this wait, darling?" he begged.

"No, it can't, " she answered brutally, "The worst part of this is your failure of nerve. The way I see it, all of this is happening, not only because of some olive branch you said you proffered, or some grand strategy of emulating Lincoln, or because of Walrus and Paltry's deceitfulness, but more because you really can't stand up to a roomful of white men and white women. I would have never guessed that the man I lived with for fourteen years, the father of my two little beautiful black girls, is really all hollow inside, if you thump him hard enough. You're beginning to be such a stranger to me, now that I am really seeing *you*, you as you really are, that I'm beginning to be scared of you. Sometimes I find myself wondering whether you are from this planet at all!

"Alright, I guess at bottom you do have the same redeeming qualities I always knew and loved: I guess they haven't gone out for a long stroll somewhere. You remember that movie we saw when we first started going together? *Brother From Another Planet*? The hero in it was a kindhearted alien who, right up to the end, couldn't get a handle on how humans lie, and steal, and hurt one another, and stab one another in the back, and cause one another so much physical and emotional pain for nothing —just out of spite! And if I wanted to put your behavior in a good light, I would think of you as him. But that sort of otherworldly naiveté is not what we need in this world today, not while the whole deal is coming apart. If change is to really happen, you've got to go up against them in their faces! You can't avoid confrontation, the thing you've been running from all your life. You've got to know these people are out to get you, you've got to know they think only of themselves, very often not even including their immediate families, and that, in their blindness and selfishness, they can pull everything down upon their heads —and on ours too, unfortunately- and that's exactly what they're doing. That's what you have to deal with!"

"Isn't this the greatest coup for them? Don't they have you right in the spot where they want you? You make the pretty speeches, while the white boys take the reins, as always! All the blacks and immigrants in this country are headed behind bars behind this rioting, where they've always wanted them, and their pals are already drawing down billions of dollars in contracts to build the prisons and torture chambers and manage them, and guess what? They've got a black president, the first, to issue the lockup orders! The twenty-first century will run out before they stop hee-hawing over that capital joke! Maybe it's a mercy we might all wind up dead long before that happens."

Barzhad remembered what he'd been saying earlier to his staff, in the spirit of rallying the troops. It hadn't sounded convincing then even to his ears, but unable to think of anything else, he thought he'd give it a try with Millie. "Look, darling, it's rough, and you're right, there are people out there who aren't on the level," he said, "but I'm confident we can lick this. We just have to pull together, stick together, and we'll beat it."

She ignored the bromide. "Let's forget about all this presidency crap for a minute," she said, "and go back to being just a longsuffering wife and her husband. And I can tell you, Barzhad, I do feel used and put upon. And I'm going to take this opportunity to explain those feelings to you more fully than I have done previously."

"Sweetheart, let's just stop right there," Barzhad begged, "Things are bad enough as they are. Let's not say words in the heat of the moment we'll later regret."

"You weren't brought up as a black child, Barzhad," she plunged ahead, "and I realize now that nothing I can say is ever going to change that. God knows I've tried repeatedly! White people brought you up, and your books clearly spell out how completely your upbringing was white throughout your childhood. But after that point they falter, don't they? Because then you turned into a teenager, and became bigger than your white age-mates, and could play basketball better than them, and suddenly you weren't white anymore; you were a black teenager, Bigger Thomas, and Willie Horton, and the 'big, black buck' Ronald Reagan saw at the checkout at the supermarket, buying those enormous, T-bone steaks with food stamps. You have to hand it to Marcus Mosiah Garvey: he was a bit more candid than you about that awful shock to the system in his adolescence; the white Jamaican planters and their wives began looking crossly at him if he was caught playing any longer with their children; and no, as for those little blonde girls he'd played with before, well, he just had better leave them alone —or else!

"That was a problem, wasn't it, Barzhad? As I said, you don't talk about it a lot in conversation, or in your books, and you've hidden it very well since, but yes, that just argues to the point, doesn't it? *Mucho problema*! Too painful even for your eloquence to prettify! So, now you're too grown for your white grandparents to cover for you, to hide you in the petticoats of their whiteness, and their neighbors and friends are looking at you as if for the first time–this big, grown black stranger suddenly appearing in their midst- with the same suspicion and hostility with which your grandmother said she viewed other random blacks, and what to do? Identity! Who am I? The biggest problem in life, especially in America! Nobody can be a whole person in America unless she or he can get that resolved.

"So you turned up in Chicago, didn't you, scrambling to be black! What choice did my poor baby have? And now, four-teen years later, I am finding out that I should have resented my role in the drama. Why, find some black girl and hitch a ride on her wagon! Because now the white girls and boys are whispering behind their hands when they see you. That wasn't an enviable place for me to be, was it, Barzhad? And piggybacking on my insider status, you got in with my family, you became a community organizer in black neighborhoods, and joined up a black church, which had a charismatic pastor who had an outspoken, black, activist consciousness regard-ing white America and its conduct at home and in the world. And so, you began to learn who you were. But could you ever learn enough to graduate? Well, I think you've brought me home some miserable, stinking, flunking grades since the inauguration, and you aren't leaving me with any hope they'll soon improve.

"The inauguration! Running for president! You became very good at hiding your feelings and being like a chameleon, Barzhad. Whatever anybody wanted, you'd be it. Turned out, of course, it's a very useful talent for a moderator, the person who keeps the team on balance, and from going overboard. Plus, you were an engaging speaker, always respectful, and willing to dialogue. And that's what Dachshund and Lizzie realized. And eventually the whole Democratic Party realized it, and then the country as well. But where did that really leave you, Barzhad? There's just one word: emasculated! And where does that leave a country desperately needing change? Why, leaderless!"

"I don't know how you're going to pull this together, but I'm out of here. I have spoken to you until I'm blue-black in the face, and you still won't get it. I tried to appeal to your political survival instincts and begged you to consider the motives of the whites who voted for you: but that didn't work either. So, me, the kids, and my mother —we're gone! I don't want to burden you with a scandal, so we'll say my mother is homesick, or she's worried about the rioting right on her block, whatever; and she wants to get back home, and she's too old for the kids and me to just abandon her. I'm sure an accomplished wordsmith like you can make a convincing cover story out of those elements, can't you?"

"Millie, if you do that, you'll have a scandal whether you or I want it or not," Barzhad said, "because I really couldn't go on without you, or the kids, or your mother. I'd fall apart. I guess that's proof that there's something to your analysis: because without you guys, I'd really be nothing. As you said, I'd be a man without a face or an identity. So please give me another chance, or give it a little while as you think it over."

She looked a little contrite, "One of my staff, Bertha Mason, is telling me you ought to consult a *houngan*, or a *santero*," she said, "she specifically mentioned a guy from Trinidad, maybe he's pundit, who practices in Brooklyn. You can get his information from her if you're interested." And his spirits soared, and it gave him so much hope, that she still cared enough to recommend occult services!

Barzhad's parents currently resided on a planet in a constellation furthest away from the Milky Way. Later that night, when Millie and he were lying frozen in positions that were exactly as far apart as a six-foot wide bed allowed, and after she had turned off her bedside reading lamp and had perhaps gone to sleep, he travelled there. He made the journey with great reluctance. They had only summoned him to them once before, when he was much younger, and his mortal mother had just died, and because the vastnesses of time and space that had to be traversed, and the extremes of thought and emotion that the journey exacted daunted his human sensibility, and produced so devastating an anomie and alienation, and so pronounced a premonition of his own mortality, he truly preferred not to repeat it.

The life forms of his parents' home were sentient precious gemstones and jewels, who nourished one another, and interacted, by giving off varying intensities of light and color –one combination for communication of ideas, for instance, or another for feelings, another for physical subsistence, and so on. In a textbook case of mimetic camouflage, his parents had adapted the same energy, and glowed the whole time in pulsing multicolored waves like large, extraterrestrial fireflies.

"The time is coming closer," his father said, in the blazing purple of super-conscious intelligence, "and you're going to have to make a difference now, or not ever. But you'll only be able to act in accordance with the limitations of your flesh. An embodiment has its history and its future pretty much marked out for it before the Spirit inhabits and animates it, like in the vibrations of these stones around us. In your world, however, they're all there in the flesh, which once was food, and before that a handful of dust, and before that water, and fire, and air and ether. Whatever was enacted in any of these constituents at any time previously are bound to have consequences, which have to be worked out in the future –is the future, according to the basic terrestrial or material laws of cause and effect and transformation. What you will strive for, what you will desire, what you will try to avoid; the proclivities, wants, desires, dispositions, moods, emotions and aversions you will have; your strengths and weaknesses are all in the flesh, long before life enters it. What will be, will be: getting in the way is ineffectual and stressful; a sort of respite is staying out of the way.

"But there is only one, sure refuge from this inexorable pattern, or these intrinsically unsatisfying alternatives: by consciously, and through unremitting hard work, being indifferent to whether you are in or out of the way, denying that cage of flesh, and identifying instead exclusively with the Spirit that came into it. I pray that it hasn't, but the time for you to practice that discipline and accomplish any results may have run out.

"Hardship, and disillusion with the world, helps turn humans away from the well nigh irresistible appeals of their flesh, since they are being denied anyway, and towards Spirit. There's a lot of that among black people in America. But, because of what happened in boarding school, you turned more towards their oppressors instead. And now I don't think you have the aptitude or the time to reverse course."

Transmitting the pure white light of transcendence, his mother concluded their instructions: "However, Spirit can never be destroyed. It occupies many names and forms throughout eternity, but ever remains One: no matter how many those forms and names may be that represent It, It remains Changeless and Unblemished. When in the course of time, either in the universe in which you currently are or in another, you realize your identity with the One, you'll be with us again, my darling son. So go, with all my blessings, and your father's as well."

Beginning to fall into an uneasy sleep, Barzhad considered what his father's advice entailed. How was he to concentrate on getting out of his skin with all the rest that was going on? If his mission had been to be some sort of messiah, a savior for the universe, he'd have to say he'd been a total failure, wouldn't he? His flesh just hadn't been configured that way. To begin with, he really wasn't much of a contemplative: he just didn't get in the way, as his father had put it, and as Millie had earlier remarked. Strictly the line of least resistance: that was as Zen-like as he was capable! He had never really taken to meditation, and then the business in the boarding school had cleanly vaporized that area of his will. Duck, stay out of the spotlight, then make nice. It was really the part of the genealogy of his flesh that descended from his celestial forebears that had propelled him into the presidential campaign, rather than any extraordinary aptitude it had acquired as he grew up in his mother's family, at school in Hawaii, with Millie and her family in Chicago, or in college. She had been mostly correct, but not *all* correct. Deciding to look into the suggestion Bertha Mason had made to her, he at last succumbed to the restless sleep.

Not far way, barricaded behind phalanxes of police officers and national guardsmen in full riot gear, the Dupont Circle cabal had stayed up, eating pizza, which they had had the foresight to order in bulk ahead of the most serious rioting, drinking beer and wine, and following the mayhem on television; but it was like Super Bowl to them, a huge entertainment, and they were ecstatic. "This surpasses my wildest expectations," "Rambo" crowed, "Fuckin' *LHC*! What the fuck is that? Where the fuck did that come from?"

None of the conspirators was more pleased than Tommy Gunther. He had presented his $2.5 trillion bailout plan earlier in the day at the Treasury. There hadn't been any detail in it, because, as usual, he had fed his family the old excuse that he had to work around the clock in privacy, and had ended up once more in the Mayflower Hotel with Val, half an ounce of crack, a magnum of Hennessey, and the Saran Wrap. The plan had been pummeled, and he was called every name in the blogosphere that existed for the deflation of ego, self-esteem and self-importance –tax cheat, turd, dud, weasel, snake, Wall Street stooge, stillborn Son of Hank, Rubenacci, pickle brain, and –get this- crackhead!

He figured he'd turn the tables in the next day's meeting

at the White House, where he'd have the president and his colleagues eating from his hand. He was banking on being called to play the part of conciliator, shuttling between a repentant administration and the CEOs of the major banks, whom he would secretly continue advising to play hardball.

"I can roll that Brunton bitch over a barrel, and fuck her fat arse as hard and as long as I like," he boasted, "We can roll back all this nationalization shit, all this cap on CEO compensation, and interfering in how the banks operate. Private investors can come in, and we'll –the government, that is- guarantee that they carry off all the profits they want. One thing about these boys: they remember a favor, and they pay it back, with interest. Unless they go to jail first!"

9

It didn't go quite as Tommy Gunther imagined. In the Cabinet Room, he nodded at the assembled members, and drew out the chair next to the Secretary of Labor, Helena Asunción, who was deep in a conversation in Spanish with Hérmano Rodríguez, the Secretary of the Interior. The two Hispanics abruptly got up and found seats on the other side of the room, with a very audible '*ratón*,' still echoing from Helena's lips. Vice-President Jimmy Burnes pointedly didn't return his greetings. The president came in right behind him. Far from cowed, he still looked more like a dangerously displeased schoolmaster when he convened the meeting of his Cabinet members, advisers and senior staff.

"It's a relief that the worst of the rioting and looting in the United States seems to have been brought under control, but it's still continuing abroad," he announced, "Why did the banks gratuitously unleash this fury against our nation's core values and institutions by deliberately and maliciously creating a panic? In view of the billions of dollars they have already received from us, and the trillions more Mr. Gunther is proposing we hand over to them, why did they up the ante by completely shutting down their operations?"

Tommy had expected contriteness, and the president's

belligerent attitude surprised him. The latter's big eyes were surveying him, and he figured he was the one who was expected to answer.

"Sir, I guess they thought their livelihood was in jeopardy," he bleated, "All this talk about nationalization was scary."

"That also upset people in the street," "Rambo" added, "It's been proven over and over again: Americans are a freedom-loving people, and they'll fight for the rights of the individual in a free market."

The Republicans in the room, "Scrappy" Deats and Paddy Nuncio, weren't sure which way to go. "Groggy" was no longer there to guide them, or speak up for their point of view. Their Republican instinct was to let failures, like most of the banks, sink: but if some Democrats were saying that nationalization should replace them, they were against that too. As always, their solution would have been tax cuts: stop taxing the go-getters; put programs and strategies in place to facilitate the rise to the top of a new batch of them; and, of course, some of the wealth would trickle down in the long run. There'd be fewer banks and financial institutions, and the ordinary citizen would be even poorer relative to their top-earning CEOs than in the recently late and departed Gilded Age, but the churn would have recommenced, and would have eventually formed the even purer, more clarified butter of Master-of-the-Universe. "Scrappy," the bolder of the two, abbreviated this line of thinking and just said, "See how Soviet Russia fared when it put the economy in the hands of apparatchiks!"

His wife's denunciations still echoing in his ears, the president shot back, "They put Sputniks in outer space before we could get our spacecraft to even get off the ground successfully! The rioting is likely to resume if we don't correctly identify its causes and do something about them."

"Scrappy" made a smart comeback, "I believe our policemen are adequate to the problems. If there are immigrants in our streets who feel they can behave as though they were in Baghdad or Kabul, they should be treated as though they were!"

Helena Asunción and Hérmano Rodríguez rolled their eyes. Helena raised her forefinger and cleared her throat, as if beginning to speak, but then slumped back in her chair in an attitude of resignation.

Senator Brunton joined the argument, "Earlier, Secretary Gunther, you outlined your 'new and revised' $2.5 trillion plan to rescue the banks and the economy. Could you tell us here what's 'new and revised' about it, except the doubling in the costs? Because whatever it was apart from that, it went clean over my head."

Gunther's voice faltered somewhat. Why hadn't the rioting silenced the bitch? "Well, it puts private investors back into the picture," he said.

Secretary Brunton came right back at him, "And that's another disappointment -you didn't do your home work, did you, sir? You made no effort to incorporate anything that we said in our previous meetings regarding the nationalization of the banks."

"I was displeased by that too," the president said.

"What I want to know is what a 'stress test' is," Hérmano Rodríguez said querulously, "Maybe they don't get the right answers because they can't add and subtract, but don't the bankers try to figure out where they'd be if one or several variables affecting their business change? If unemployment rose, or another ten million homes foreclosed, or people couldn't pay the minimum amount due on their credit cards any more, or several banks and two more governments fell in Europe, weren't they trying to find out what their position would be independent of your 'stress test?' As a matter of fact, you don't have to be a banker to be doing a 'stress test.' Everybody in the country is doing one —what will happen if I lose my job, what will happen if there's a major illness in the family, what if my kid doesn't get that student loan- only they aren't so pretentious as to give it a fancy, scientific-sounding name stolen from their cardiologist! What new variables are going to be included in your 'stress test?' Here we are, in need of something concrete to put up as a defense against rock solid, concrete setbacks, and what do we get? *Fluff!*!! This is all nonsense, wool pulled down over our eyes!"

Andy Dunstan, the Secretary of Education, who was familiar with educational testing, followed up, "Are these stress tests standardized and objective? Or are 'pass' or 'fail' grades going to be handed out arbitrarily? For example, I'm still not clear why it was illegal to bail out Lehman Brothers when it turned out to be perfectly legal to bail out A.I.G. a mere twenty-four hours later!"

The president's chief advisor, Dickie Anchor, put in, "As I understand it, you're going to give private investors - up to a trillion dollars and trust them to buy up the banks' toxic assets. If we're handing out the money, taxpayer money, why do we need middlemen? Why do we need the middlemen to be private investors? Why not homeless persons, or anybody over sixty, or persons with a mole under their left eye? I mean, they're just middlemen. Or, duh, why doesn't the government just hand it over to the banks directly, in exchange for equity, or management input?"

"Well, they might refuse it on those terms," Tommy replied, "they'd be afraid of political influence, if the government was the direct donor."

Dickie Anchor was amazed, "They've got their hands out asking for government funds, if it's no strings attached," he marveled, "but if the government insists on having a say-so in how the money is spent, and holds them accountable, well, they'll turn their backs on the money. 'We can buy our jets and pay out bonuses of billions of dollars by ourselves, thank you; we don't need any help from you.' I thought they were in a crisis!"

Lizzie Jameson, another senior advisor, raised a related

problem. "The extent of the crisis is really equal to the value of these 'toxic assets,' and nobody seems able to say what that value is." she said, "According to your statements, Mr. Secretary, one of the strengths of your so-called 'new and improved' plan is that private investors will be able to do a valuation after all. Why's that? What will they know that we don't? I can't follow your arcane reasoning."

Gunther was unraveling before the barrage of questions, each containing a barbed condemnation of his cocaine-inspired plan. "Well, isn't that what they do for a living?" he blustered, "Evaluating risks?"

The president cut in sharply, "So, we pay a fee to the best of them –the talented Mr. Madoff, maybe, before he's put away for the rest of his life in a federal penitentiary- and get his expert opinion, and then we'll have the value, and go from there! However, my information is even 'vulture capitalists,' who make a living swooping up distressed assets and hoping to flip them for vast profits, don't want to come near these, because not even they can put a value on them. Or, like vultures, they can smell a trap, and are keeping away as far as they can. Or perhaps the banks are putting blinders in the way to prevent even an out-of-the-hat figure from being suggested. Did you investigate this mystery, Gunther?"

"They wouldn't do that, sir!" he protested.

Grim laughter filled the room, with the two Republican Cabinet members grimly abstaining from it.

"Rambo" figured it was time to shore up his crumpling co-conspirator, "I repeat, bottom line, if you go out and ask the rioters, they'll tell you that they're against nationalization and government bureaucrats running private enterprises, and in favor of private investors and private banks. Isn't it obvious that the atmosphere of unease and rebellion won't lift until the banks are up and running, but fairly and transparently this time, and Joe Public has a chance again to make a buck as a private entrepreneur, investing or saving his money as he likes, without government interference?"

"That's a most willful reading of what's happening in the streets!" Secretary Brunton reprimanded him, "A lot of it comes from the inflammatory broadcasts of Susan Paltry and Rocky Walrus, which were a jumble of so many ill-assorted rumors, insinuations, and nonsense that it's difficult to say to which the public is actually reacting. But, quite independently of the LHC scare they unconscionably raised, and the 'specter' of nationalization, we were in a serious crunch regarding jobs, healthcare, foreclosures and falling house values. Each additional foreclosure depresses housing values even more, and whatever those 'toxic assets' are worth, their value also decreases as the foreclosures increase."

"Aren't those glaring omissions from your 'new and revised' plan? Why have you put off –for a few months!- a plan to spend the $50 billion put aside to alleviate the foreclosures, when 10,000 American families are being ejected from their homes every day? Isn't that of far greater concern to the average rioter? Far from 'new and revised,' this is more irresponsible than anything the previous administration had offered us! It's nothing but an outright, back-door subsidy to grossly inefficient, obsolete banks and their shareholders!"

Dickie Anchor took up Secretary Brunton's cue, "What on earth did you learn while you were in Japan during the '90's anyway, Mr. Secretary," he asked, "They propped up a bunch of 'zombie' banks, exactly as you are proposing, largely because government ministers were so cozy personally with the bankers; the country descended into its 'lost decade;' and in the end, they had to nationalize the banks anyway. Isn't that what happened? Why are you repeating the disaster, act by act? Why don't we just cut to the chase?"

"Where are the jobs? Where is the healthcare? Where are the enhanced unemployment benefits? Where is the aid to the states?" Lizzie Jameson wanted to know, "if you took the perspective of this 'new and revised' plan, you'd never guess that a stimulus plan was simultaneously feeling its way blindly around Congress. Oughtn't you to have mentioned how these two efforts are integrated? Shouldn't bankers be concerned whether people work or go to college?

"The language of the plan is the language of the *status quo ante*: assessing risks, betting low to win high, 'flipping' assets, getting family –in this case, the government and taxpayers- to watch the investors' backs when they lose their shirts in the casino. Oh, never again to see the faces of Louis Blankfein, Kenneth Lewis, and Vikram Pandit! Oh, never to have to listen to their cheap huckster's language that is setting us back so many trillions. Perhaps they can use some of the fortune they pocketed to sign up for Introduction to Ethics 101, Elementary Moral Philosophy 101, and Economics 101.

"How about the banks of the future just cashing our checks, saving our surpluses, using the latter to extend credit to us, with reasonable fees and interest rates, to buy our homes and businesses, and holding the mortgages until they are fully paid? No more 'flipping' anything, no more speculation, no more CDO's and CDS's ever again!"

The president laughed, "I happen to think that would be a far better world in which to raise my little girls. At our last meeting we learned that the chief argument against nationalization is that investment decisions will be subject to political pressure or bureaucratic inertia, and that this would be a far worse thing than if they were subject to the concern of private bankers and investors to feather their own pockets –no matter what the cost to the public at large. We pointed out then that it was amazing that this sort of reasoning persisted after what we have suffered in the past year.

"More important, though, is that, except in the minds of greedy, selfish individuals, our investment priorities are straight forward: they speak for themselves. Science and technology, green energy, the eradication of poverty, starvation, the scarcity of drinking water, disease –the lifting up of millions of the earth's inhabitants whose life spans haven't improved since the Stone Age, and the international cooperation required to set our shoulders to these tasks. If it required the public spending in World War 11 to really lift us out the Great Depression, why can't we start spending in a Great War to achieve all those goals? Nobody quarrels with these goals. Nobody with half a brain, that is! But it's the sheer *audacity* to take the steps towards achieving them that seems to be wanting!

"In the United States, we have international airports that look like disused barns; roads and highways that are literally crumbling; bridges that are falling down; schools the mere physical appearance of which tempts students to turn and run in the opposite direction.

"The investment priorities are abundantly clear. Private operators are the ones who are standing in the way."

"But that's just pork," "Scrappy" exclaimed. He now seemed to be making a strenuous bid to replace "Groggy" as the voice of the Republicans in the Cabinet.

The president said sternly, "Sir, I think I messed up. I think I was very naive expecting your party to rise to the op-portunities of bipartisanship. I guess it also takes a little more intelligence than I credited you with!"

At this, Helena Asunción spoke up at last. "Now that Mr. Budd has resigned, and frankly, we're hoping for a couple more resignations in the same vein, Secretary Rodríguez and myself feel more comfortable airing our views," she said, "We were very conscious of being from despised immigrant groups while Mr. Budd was around. And then again, my job here in the Cabinet is to represent labor; so, for me, it's a double whammy.

"Apart from the $2.5 trillion dollars that could go into setting up a national bank, as I hear you suggesting, there's an equal amount we can make available by rescinding the $2.5 trillion we are already giving away in tax cuts to the super-rich.

What's the arithmetic here? What's $2.5 trillion divided by the population of the United States? Don't worry, I meant the *legal* population; and I guess we have to exclude children, or people who didn't file an income tax return. So, divide by about 100 million, for argument sake. Wow! Unless I misplaced some zeroes, doesn't that come up to about $25,000 per person?"

Looking fixedly at "Rambo" Ezekiel, Hérmano Rodríguez corrected her, "We're aren't giving a penny to the CEOs of the banks and other high earners, so that leaves more for the rest of us. Nearly double, probably. And there'd be even more if we retrieved the compensation they 'earned' while allowing their institutions to fail, or if we got lawmakers, like our sorely missed colleague, Freddie Dachshund, to pay back what they 'earned' from profiteering off their public service. As the president said awhile back, they'd be punished for acting like Mobutus and Bokassas."

"Rambo" Ezekiel started to crack his knuckles, but stopped before he made a sound, and looked guiltily at the president.

Helena continued, "So, let's issue a credit card for $25,000, $50,000, or whatever the exact figure is, to each eligible American. That's sure to stop any repeat of the rioting, and if, as Secretary Brunton suggested, we promoted similar efforts abroad, it would stop there too. We'll publish a huge directory of businesses and importers, or categories of goods and services, where we want the credit card to be used, in order to stimulate growth and job creation in those areas. Won't that immediately stir up some action? Like, overnight? Meanwhile, don't forget this will be on top of the $789 billion stimulus plan, which will be renovating America and creating 3.5 million jobs on its own, on a slightly more protracted timeline."

"They'll spend the money on crack," Gunther bleated prophetically.

Andy Dunstan looked at him with irritation, and then ignored him. "A sector where we'd want the credit card to be readily accepted would certainly be education and training," he said thoughtfully, "So, it will get an additional boost, as Helena mentioned. People would be encouraged to go back to school, and an area of job creation could be counseling and career advisement. People would be counseled to hold jobs, even if they already have $50,000 in their pockets, as a patriotic duty, to earn and save and budget wisely, to get the country on its feet, and make sure it never, ever again gets into this mess!'

"Actually," Helena said, "Andy's remarks remind me that something the stimulus plan doesn't specify is who's going to be doing these 'shovel-ready' jobs. Black Americans? Traditionally, such jobs have gone to recent immigrants and new citizens, with the native-born moving up to higher-paying, white-collar employment. So it's not just jobs, therefore, but the structure of the job market that has to be considered. It's the accepted law of the jungle how people climb the labor hierarchy —first, the informal economy; then, menial labor; manual labor; next, entrepreneurship; then, higher-paid, white collar employment; and at the top, professional work; or retirement/investor.

"So, you just can't frustrate the expectations of Black Americans and established, naturalized immigrants. They've done their 'shovel-ready' stints already, and they are looking to move up the ladder, as per the rulebook. As Andy said, they should benefit from further education and training to help them do so, and the financing for it will come from a combination of the regular student loans already in place, like the Pell grants, which should be substantially enhanced, the aid given to students in the stimulus plan, and the remainder through out-of-pocket payments drawn on their special, $50,000 credit card.

"But then that brings us to legal and illegal immigration. Immigrants are the ones who'll do the 'shovel-ready' work. If we don't normalize and de-stigmatize immigration, especially from Mexico and Central America, we saw off the bottom rungs, and the whole ladder topples.

"That's something else Republican leaders are going to have to address more intelligently. Hispanic immigrants are already being rounded up and held in prisons where the squalor and brutality matches Abu Ghraib and Guantánamo. They've been accused of spreading disease, fueling an increase in crime, trashing the environment, exacerbating global warning and guess what? They caused the economic crisis too! Little racist thugs are beating them up across the nation. They are called 'walking A.T.M's,' because they are afraid to go into banks to deposit their earnings, leaving them vulnerable to be robbed of the few dollars they have. It has to stop!"

Secretary of State Brunton was wearing a broad smile, and her eyes sparkled. "I'm liking everything I'm hearing," she said, "Apart from being just execrable, the racist attacks on immigrants only makes our leverage in foreign countries more tenuous. I also noted that you mentioned 'businesses and importers' where the credit card will be honored, which suggests that you're in favor of subsidizing both American and foreign manufacturers, without protectionism. But I think this ought to be coordinated much more closely with economies abroad."

Hérmano Rodríguez's anger had blotted out the ongoing conversation, and he was still hung up on the comments he had made earlier. He said, "Those thieves should pay back everything they stole! They knowingly and deliberately led the whole country into staggering debt to stuff their pockets full with exorbitant fees."

Concluding the meeting, the president said, "It brings us back to where we started. Why isn't a government takeover better? At least, until we scrounge up some honest bankers and financiers who can count to twenty without relying on their fingers and toes! Let's take it from here tomorrow."

10

Bertha was a solidly built, middle age Grenadian of medium height whose skin shone through her white uniform like antiqued bronze on account of the daily polishing she gave it with pure, raw, unpasteurized, non-homogenized shea butter imported from Ghana. From her experience of Caribbean politics, where blacks had been governing themselves for more than fifty years, she understood that leaders needed help and guidance more desperately than the ordinary citizen, and matter-of-factly provided Barzhad with the information he wanted.

"I think Robert is the man for you," she said, "he did help mih cousin the lawyer when she did lose she position in a top firm; an' right after that, he help she friend, who did gone *basourdi* with psychiatric drugs, an' edgin' towards suicide."

Barzhad was nevertheless very self-conscious. "Well, I just need to talk to someone way outside of the loop, you know. Is Robert a discreet sort of person?"

"The bes!'" she assured him, "Besides, he a educated brother, like you. Sir, you don' ha' to feel embarrassed in front of me, hear? What kind of animal it is don't know wha' you goin' through, with all the trouble on the street, and everywhere all over the world?! Robert dey-dey in Brooklyn, he must be did see all that riotin' first-hand."

"You have it exactly right, Bertha," he said, more confidently, "the opinion of the man on the street, from his own mouth, one-on-one with me, not like at these town hall meetings and other public settings."

"He's your man," she repeated flatly.

"Then I am grateful for your recommendation, Bertha," he said, "I really do appreciate your help and tactfulness."

"You know, sir, a person don' ha' to be too bright to figure out why all of this is happenin,'" Bertha said, "White people ways ha' to change. Da' is the bottom of it! For example, you think you can mek them stop callin' Grenadians 'insurgents?' I read a story in the papers that say this white American man visit Grenada for the first time since 1983, an' this time he fin' it don't ha' no more 'insurgents,' only laid back, happy-go-lucky islanders it ha.' Bu' we was never insurgents, sir!"

"Well, the travel sections of the newspaper aren't the most accurate part, Bertha," he said, consolingly.

"But it insultin!'" she insisted, "My Lordie, we did treat those ungrateful, white medical students like we own pickney, just like we treat dem pickney when we take a job as a nanny, an' those students were *so-o-o* ungrateful, they say they did fear for their life. But it was that evil, evil man with the Devil own smile, that evil, evil Ronald Reagan, who did send the whole U.S. Army agains' a tiny island only as big as Central Park nearly. First off, they kill 180 senior citizens sittin' down to their dinner of porridge in the Old People Poor House in St. George's!"

Barzhad was looking over some papers on his desk, "Well, it was the Cubans, wasn't it, dear?" he asked.

"Mr. President, Cuba only as large as Central Park *an'* Prospect Park, is all!" she replied indignantly.

He said, "I guess the Cold War warped people's minds. It was unfortunate."

"Mr. President, you the president an' an educated man," she said, "you can tell me why white people in this country so obstinate? Ain't is obstinate for them to go on believin' these small islands can harm a big, rich, powerful country like America?"

"I don't know," he said hastily, "but if I find out, I'll let you know. But how are you making out personally, Bertha? Do you have a family? Are they hurting on account of the troubles?"

"See, sir, we're Grenadians," she began, "we ha' we *esusu*, and tha' is we support! Is why we don' need welfare an' such! You know 'bout *esusu*, sir?

"I think I may have heard of it," he said.

"Well, is somethin' that start off small, eh," she informed him, "A handful of housewives, traders an' market vendors in Grenada start poolin' their capital an' each one would draw the whole kitty in turn. If a member ha' a house to build, or want to start a business, or a big expense like a wedding or funeral come up, the money dey-dey for that. An' as people start to migrate, it did cover the costs a' travel an' relocation too."

"Ah, that's it!" the president exclaimed, "an indigenous banking system that originated in West Africa. It operates something like the informal Islamic banks."

"Could be, sir," Bertha granted, "but now it grow to somethin' that ha' thousands of members worldwide. Not one, several: mine is the Grenada and Grenadines Greater *Esusu* Association. They even ha' a salaried, elected governor an' other staff. Now we talkin' millions of dollars goin' up an' down throughout the islands, in the U.S., the U.K., an' Europe. Nowadays, if you settle abroad, an' you wan' buy property dey-dey, or start up a business, is the *esusu* where you go firs.' The ordinary banks in the country ain't ha' no time for you, bu' the *esusu* ain't never goin' say no to a member."

"Then maybe that's how we should run our banking system," he observed.

"Ain't no joke, sir!" she said earnestly," an' is not only

for capital, hear? You wan' get married, you' birthday come an' you wan' celebrate, the pickney born an' you lookin' for godparents –is wha' the *esusu* dey-dey for, they goin' fin' you a good mate, or business partner!"

"I see," he said, "*two* West African traditional institutions rolled into one –the informal banking system and the friendly society. In the U.S., lots of the funerals of African Americans used to be financed by friendly societies, especially in places like New Orleans, where there was a heavy Caribbean influence, and they also paid out pensions and stipends to the relatives of the deceased."

"Well, is all over the other islands too," Bertha added, "Trinis ha' theirs, an' Guyanese, Jamaicans an' Haitians."

"It might be difficult to implement here officially," he said.

"An' we don't tolerate no stealing and cheating an' other crookedness," she continued, "we ha' ways an' means"

"I see," the president said hastily, accustomed all his life to participating in circles where 'ways and means' were never brought up in conversation, "do you get to interact with my little girls a lot? How do you like them?"

"The bes!'" she declared, "that bigger one, Marie, she *s-o-o-o* smart. She goin' be president one day, jus' like her father, mark my words!"

He said, "I'm sure you're giving them a better preparation for the job than I ever had."

"Mr. President, you don' ha' to be scared o' these people, hear?" she advised him, "they jus' people, an' the reason why they don' change, is because is stupid they stupid. Anyway, people jus' come an' go, sir, an' we don' really mean much as individuals. Bu' wha' you put in the universe, now tha's somethin!' Like the Crucifixion of Our Lord Jesus Christ, sir! Now, tha's like a star burnin' forever in the sky, an' can't no-one pull it down from there. Our salvation and redemption!

Tha's how you must aim to act, sir! To put your deed in the sky, like a star!"

"Bertha, you put your finger right on it," the president said, "I mean it honestly. That's the only way we can make a difference. And, one more thing, can we arrange it that Robert is coming as your guest? Thanks a lot."

11

Awe, Robert had discovered, employed several elocutionary styles. Although a Japanese element was never absent from any of them, the degree to which it appeared varied with her audience and the circumstances. When she was most at ease or at home, the consonants and vowels began stretching around the block - "*a-w-w-w-w*;" a more staccato rendering indicated that she was experiencing uncertainty, or stress; and otherwise, in the majority of exchanges in the course of a day, with mere acquaintances or strangers, and when the conversation very rarely touched on intimate matters, her schooling in Maryland, which had begun in her fifteenth year, and her subsequent residence in the United States prescribed conformity with white, middle-class, American speech conventions.

The rioting had caused her to immediately adopt an even more formal style of speech. As news of its severity in Manhattan reached them, with its mounting toll of deaths and destruction, Robert and she had gone to the Park Slope Food Coop to stock up on essentials. They had drawn up a list for enough drinking water, canned foodstuffs, dry cereal, biscuits, dried fruit and nuts, first-aid supplies, toiletries, candles, matches, torches and batteries to last them for a siege of several days' duration. They weren't alone in taking this precaution.

In fact, other members of the Coop had already depleted most of the shelves by the time they began shopping, and they had to wait at the Tea Lounge across the street, sipping soymilk lattes until more shipments of the missing goods arrived. Never mind the pillage in Manhattan: to the east, the sky over Flatbush was filled with clouds of dense black smoke, indicating where banks and businesses were burning. All the faces above the mugs of steaming coffee were strained, anxious or distorted by fear.

The consonants and vowels had always come out for Robert. Although they'd stayed celibate, they'd become more intimate, and meditation had helped in both developments. Actually, Awe was much more relaxed in the absence of the sexual dynamic, which always tended to be contentious, and a source of ambiguity, even in the best of relationships, and even the topic of babies receded: she often remarked that it seemed irresponsible and utterly selfish to think of having children at such a time in world history. Once she resumed meditating, she reconnected with the program implicit in it, or the graded progression from one level of consciousness to another over time, and surrendered herself to it. Now, as current events took a turn for the worse, meditation was also an inestimable source of strength and endurance.

That night, soon after they'd finished their practice, they heard sounds at the door, and watched with horror as the locks turned. Somebody had the keys! As they sat frozen in fear, the door burst open, and four men entered. They were tall, burly and white: and a mere glance gave them away for who they were – plainclothes police, detectives, homeland security officers, or immigration enforcement. The well fed beefiness and waistlines that bulged in spite of tight corseting, legacies of all the meals they had eaten either at public expense, or the take exacted from private restaurateurs and shop owners; the buzz cuts; the flushed, featureless faces and blank eyes; the cheap, ill fitting, pastel-colored suits, egregiously out of place in any situation, accessorized by cheap, nondescript ties; the thicknesses at the ankles where holsters, with service revolvers in them, had been strapped identified them unmistakably. Even without reading these hieroglyphs, Awe and Robert just *knew*.

As they sat on the sofa in the living room as witnesses, too afraid to speak, the men spread out through the apartment: the bedroom, the second bedroom that had been made into their joint studio/study, the kitchen/dining room, the bathroom, and the closets. They examined the backs of the computers, and one of them took photographs. They took in the musical instruments, the books on the bookshelves, and the framed pictures and Tibetan cloths on the wall. They kept throwing appraising glances at their captive spectators.

The tallest of them, with carrot-colored hair and the worst fitting suit, appeared to be the leader.

"You're Robert, right?" he asked, "Is that your name?"

Robert nodded.

"Well, don't be alarmed," he said, with a smile that was calculated to alarm, "we're federal officers, and this is just a clearance check." He removed from his coat pocket, and briefly showed, a gold badge fastened to a sleeve of black leather.

"Clearance from what?" Robert asked. Awe's tiny fist was clenching his tightly.

"Do you own or possess a firearm?" the man asked, without acknowledging the question.

Robert shook his head. His questioner hadn't given his name or introduced his companions, who were standing to the side, observing the dialogue, and Robert wasn't about to enquire. Their presence in the modest-sized living room crowded the whole apartment, made it too small for an ordinary civilian existence, and infected it with a disagreeable stench –stale breath, stale flesh, stale food, stale clothes, stale routines, stale minds: stale death, like at an undertaker's. It crossed Robert's mind that Awe and he should move, and relocate to a new apartment, once they had safely survived this situation. This one would never, ever again be free of that stench!

The tall, bulky man with the carrot-colored buzz cut continued, "The president has asked you to be the guest of a White House Residence staff member at the White House. The visit will take place this coming weekend. Is the timing good for you?"

Robert stared at him. Awe did as well, and her mouth dropped opened.

"Robert!" the man said, "If the president of the United States wanted you to visit the White House this weekend, do you have any pressing, prior engagement or engagements that would make the timing inconvenient for you?"

"I don't," Robert said, "I mean I don't have anything planned for this weekend." He felt Awe's fist tightening more, "but I don't understand. I don't know anyone who works at the White House.

"This has to be very hush-hush," the man said, "it's bad enough the Asian young woman is here, but there's nothing we can do about that now, is there? But you mustn't share this with anyone else. You understand?"

Robert asked. "I take it this is not a hoax. Who is this staff member? Why would the president want to speak to me?"

"Naturally, we don't want to say the president wants to speak with you," the man went on, "You'll be the guest of the staff member. If you are ever asked –by *anyone*- that's what you will say, if it's necessary to say anything at all: a member of the White House Residence staff snuck you an invitation. Got it?"

Robert nodded.

The man said, "Of course, if you aren't asked, the problem doesn't arise. You should just take the secret to your grave."

Robert felt Awe's hand trembling uncontrollably, and nodded again. It occurred to him to ask how they'd laid their hands on the keys to the apartment, but already knew better than to expect he'd be told the truth. Still, he assumed the answer was that law enforcement personnel or detectives had access to citizens' home whenever they wanted it; and it was worrisome to know that.

"Alright," the man said, "your hostess is one Ms. Bertha Mason, who is a fifty-three-year-old naturalized immigrant from Grenada. Mrs. Osama hired her to take charge of laundry at the White House Residence. Most of her family settled in Brooklyn, and it seems you know a couple of them. She suggested to the president that the two of you might have matters of mutual interest to discuss. There's a prepaid, return ticket in your name at Amtrak at Penn Station for the 9.00am train on Saturday. When you get to Union Station in Washington, a Sikh taxi driver wearing a green turban will be waiting to pick you up. Take his cab. At the White House, you'll join tourists waiting for the next tour of those parts of the premises open to the public. As you are touring the place with the others, I'll meet you and separate you unobtrusively from them. Then I'll get you to the Oval Office. Any questions?

Robert shook his head. He couldn't recollect knowing any one named "Mason," although persons often maintained many aliases; but once more, he decided not to prolong the officers' visit by asking for clarification. He wanted very much to give Awe his undivided attention and calm her down.

"You do understand this is a great honor, don't you?" the man said, "OK, Robert, thanks for your cooperation, and see you on Saturday afternoon. It should be around 1.30 or 2.00pm when you and I make contact." He and his colleagues trooped out of the apartment, considerately bolting the locks as they had found them.

It was then that Awe really began shaking like a leaf; and, in spite of his prior intention of coming to her assistance, Robert had begun shaking non stop too, much to his surprise, and was unable to otherwise move. He tried to speak, and couldn't. So they just remained where they were on the sofa, unable to unclasp their hands, and an hour passed before they finally settled down.

Even then, it was awhile longer before they regained command of their tongues. "Oh my God," Awe kept repeating, when that happened, "Oh my God. Government is so sinister!"

"Do I feel like traveling into its underbelly on Saturday?" Robert asked rhetorically. "I can't imagine what matters of 'mutual interest' I have in common with the president, unless 'Bertha Mason' or her relatives were clients of mine, and then I don't believe the president would want a consultation with me. Guys like that would choose a $800-an-hour psychoanalyst from a top practice! And why all these cloak-and-dagger arrangements? Why not an invitation on monogrammed White House stationery? It's not as if it can be about homeland security, what do I know about that? It makes no sense!"

"Oh, please don't go," Awe begged, "In Japan, government, big business and the *yakuza* are just one big conspiracy dominating the lives of everyone else! The government is just one unit in their combined regime of control and terror. It's just bad luck to come to their notice. Bad, bad luck! And it's the same here, isn't it? What about JFK, his assassination, the mafia, Hollywood moguls, the CIA and the FBI? And now they know our names, who we are, and where we live. They have the keys to my apartment, isn't that right? We are trapped in their coils!"

Robert thought it was time to stop Awe's hysteria from going out of control. As casually as he could, he said, "I don't see how to get out of it. Those guys were serious about the invitation. Anyway, that was just security. It's the president, after all, the first black president, so they have to be extra careful. Although I wish myself they hadn't made out like an Oliver Stone movie or a Scott Turow novel! And why me? That's the bothersome part! What does he want from me? What do I have to tell him?"

"Come to bed with me just for tonight," Awe pleaded, "don't pull out the sofa please. I love you so much, and I don't want anything to take you away from me. My demons took a leave of absence when we started living together, and I don't want them coming back!"

"I don't know how and why I lived such a solitary life before," Robert said, "I don't really want to go back to it. Far from being the distraction I feared, living with you has been more of an encouragement: you kept me focused on my goals, and in a more positive frame of mind, which was really an achievement with all these worries, and I'm grateful. You've been a real support! I can't imagine why the president wants to talk with me, but what I just said about you will wind up in the conversation, I'm sure."

Much later, revived by tea and more meditation, they slept more or less peacefully in each other's arms, and didn't stir until noon the following day.

12

Robert found the president as calm and detached as he apparently liked to appear in photographs and videos. "What a relief it is that the banks are open and conducting business as usual!" he declared, as Robert entered the Oval Office, and the door closed behind him, "Hullo. I'm glad you could come."

Maybe a quarter of the banks in Brooklyn were either burned to the ground, or remained closed because extensive rebuilding was needed. He had also seen more than the usual number of customers thronging into the remaining banks, in some cases forming long queues outside, waiting to get in, and he wondered whether a run on the banks was the next chapter of the nightmare the country was enduring. He said as much to the president.

"In some ways, it's worse than the 60's," he said, "then, it was disaffected youth, not great on organization, and pretty much bewildered by all the hormones and drugs flying around inside of them. This time, it's level-headed, older men and women looking at jobs and retirements funds flying out the window."

"We can only hope the measures we are putting in place will begin to show readily recognizable improvements in the very near future," the president responded, "Otherwise, your fears are very plausible. We haven't seen those haunting images of the Great Depression recycling in our streets as yet, and we keep saying to ourselves that they can't, like little children saying something brave to one another to keep from being hysterical in a really scary situation. But that's all it is!"

"Hearing you say that already makes me feel better," Robert said, "I'd thought the real problem we had was some of the appointments you made, if you'll allow me to say so. I am sure you know many of your staunchest supporters reacted very strongly in opposition to them. But now I'm hearing you say it really doesn't matter what we do, or who does it."

"Now, sir, I'm not sure I said that!" the president rejoined, "Maybe some of it is like a crapshoot, and all up to Lady Luck; but there's still a lot to chalk up to human agency. Regarding those appointments, I have a good idea that they outraged many loyal friends. That's one reason why I wanted to talk to someone. I believe I made them with the most honorable intentions, like bipartisanship, and after carefully considering the candidates' qualifications. But didn't Freud teach us to be skeptical of our conscious motives? Now I'm really not sure. What were your objections to them?"

"In my neck of the woods, nobody has the heart to blame you personally for anything, sir," Robert replied, "and your popularity and approval ratings with us will always be sky high, no matter what. But we did believe that all sorts of pressures we weren't even able to exactly imagine were being exerted on you. There's a natural distrust of Washington in the rest of the country! For one thing, America remains a majority white country at this time, and that's a definite constraint, just as it would be if it were majority African-American, or when it was Native-American. It would just be different, what you could or couldn't do."

"You better believe it!" the president exclaimed, "Washington is a more dangerous minefield that anything you've got in

Afghanistan! By the way, were the arrangements we made for your visit acceptable?"

Robert told him about the scare Awe and he had experienced. "I guess it couldn't be helped," he said, "but it's like everything we've said: a little bit of courtesy and common humanity and concern for the welfare of others can't hurt, but they just weren't forthcoming from an uncouth, white law enforcement officer!"

The president agreed, and offered his heartfelt apologies. "Yes, it does bear on the reasons I wanted to consult with you," he said, "I feel very hemmed in, and it makes me unsure of myself. Bertha Mason gave you a high recommendation. She said you were responsible for turning her cousin's luck around, and pulled the cousin's friend from the brink of suicide. She has you down as a pundit extraordinaire!"

Robert laughed. "We have an unusual laboratory of human relationships in Trinidad, where I come from" he said, "'Pundit' is a word that describes a holy man in the Hindu tradition. But the truth is we Trinidadians are "Africanized' and 'Asianized' and 'Europeanized' and 'Hinduized' and 'Islamicized' and 'Confucianized' and 'Protestantized' and 'Catholicized' to a cross-fertilized degree perhaps unprecedented in the world: and under all of that is a powerful undertow of even more ancient animistic and polytheistic beliefs and practices, which were handed down from the Neolithic through folk African, Asian, and Native-American survivals. And so, I offer all of that –not just 'pundit'- in the pretty nondescript, unassuming, unpretentious person you're beholding in front of you."

The two men laughed uproariously at Robert's portentous pronouncement, and when they'd regained their composure, many knots of stiffness and brittleness had untied, and the occasion turned much more loose-collared, ties-removed, relaxed and informal than either might have reasonably anticipated.

"And by the way, now that I know at last why I am here,

I feel I can forgive the menace in the interrogation at our apartment a little," Robert said, "it certainly won't do for it to become public knowledge that you're consulting a witch doctor. I mean, Cherie Blair had her medicine man, and so did Nancy Reagan, but can you imagine the outcry if it was discovered that you, a black man, had one too? Why, the newspapers would be filled with stories of 'darkest Africa,' and 'cannibalism' and 'human sacrifice,' and naked maidens smeared in blood, and the carcasses of dead black cocks, their necks wrung, being left on the doorsteps of Republican legislators!"

"All of that is a real fear! And personally, I'm still getting used to the secrecy and security concerns regarding anything I want to do," the president said, "but obviously you were right to be upset and angry about the way your privacy was violated. The enormous trouble we're seeing is directly related to experiences like yours: how to get police officers to stop behaving like thugs. It doesn't matter how much you educate them: they just won't change. How to get the military to stop tossing out the international agreements and our domestic law, and stop torturing? How to get job applicants to stop lying about their qualifications? How to stop co-worker from stabbing co-worker in the back? How to get them to value honesty and fair play? How to stop them from cheating one another and the I.R.S.? Ethnic, racial and religious animosities –how do you stop those? How do you prevent the Hurricane Katrina-New Orleans template of complacency and callousness from being endlessly copied? How to develop in civil servants a pride in their civic responsibilities? How to keep bankers and businessmen from dipping into the till, and shortchanging the public? Or to persuade them to tell the truth about their assets and liabilities? Don't talk about their outsize compensation! How to make people more caring and charitable on the whole? That kids starving and thirsting and abused in any corner of the world are everyone's shame, and everyone's challenge? How to get people serious on the topic of environmental protection?

"Can you imagine the nerve of the automakers? For decades, they ignored the need to develop affordable, energy-efficient vehicles; they remained stuck with antiquated managerial procedures; and they never once thought of moderating either their astonishing self-congratulation or their compensation; but here they come, cap in hand to Washington, aboard their corporate jets!"

"You know, sir, if Wagoner and Fuld and Madoff and the rest of them were black men," Robert suggested, "their race would not have gone unremarked, and there would have been many a comment to the tune of, 'well, what did you expect…'"

The president acknowledged the interruption, but went on "So, it's not just 'the economy,'" he said, "Those are its component parts, or the underpinnings: and they have to be fixed first. Then, you'll see, just like that, everyone all over the world will be housed, clothed, fed, and encouraged and permitted to develop to her or his fullest potential! But can the actions of a single man ever bring about sweeping changes like that? A total rebooting?"

"Isn't that one of the great debates about historical interpretation?" Robert asked, "'Great men' vs. the 'laws of history,' like historical materialism?"

"You'd think they went hand in hand, if either truly existed," the president replied, "You and I may have good ideas about what is moral or desirable, but would they gain wider acceptance in the electorate? Abraham Lincoln stood for abolition, but he prevailed with it because agreement on the matter united many diverse constituencies. He couldn't have acted in a complete vacuum."

"It seems the mark of a great statesman or stateswoman is the ability for continuous, personal growth. By all accounts, Lincoln certainly had it," Robert said, "Generally, though, even in the ordinary circumstances of a private life, when a person wants to bring about change in the external situation, it helps to focus on what sort of change the person wants to see internally. Wasn't that the method of a Buddha or a Christ or Mahatma Gandhi? What would you personally like to change about yourself, sir? You may not wish to share the answer with me, but I think you might find that's a path of enquiry that's worthwhile pursuing."

The president was impressed by Robert's observation and question, and nodded his head vigorously, "I can see Bertha wasn't wrong in her assessment of you," he said, "I've recently heard identical ideas from others whom I also greatly respect. You evidently didn't learn what you just said in a psychology class or a textbook. I am curious where you did learn it.

"Goodness! Shouldn't I be offering you some tea or something? We can't let it be said you were a guest at the White House and left as hungry and thirsty as you came. Since we haven't invested in state-of-the-art trains and rail service, the trip from New York is still at least more than a couple of hours! Some herbal tea and vegan sandwiches?" The president made the request on his house telephone.

"If we take the trouble to be really observant," Robert said, "life teaches us a lot. You have to disregard the noise the body makes, its feelings, emotions and thoughts, and listen. You'll find there's a lot of communication going on, but noiselessly.

"You are a Christian, aren't you, sir? Some Christians believe you have to work your butt off to earn your salvation, while others think it's just given to you, a gift of God, His Grace. Of course, it's both, isn't it? Whether you call it God, Spirit or Life, it does have a vote, it directs your efforts, and it shows you how to proceed. You could call it evolution too, if you liked. It docs its part, and we do ours."

"That's more or less my belief too," the president said, "I think it's ridiculous to believe in a personal creator who sits with his account books up in the sky, trying to win some foolish bet he made with the devil, who's underground; and gets really mad when you cause him to lose a round, and goes berserk, killing your cattle and afflicting you with boils and such. But there's a Principle out there, and according to it, you shouldn't cheat on your taxes or be so greedy that you cause 4.5 million workers in this country, and millions more across the globe, those who had jobs in the first place, to lose them and their homes all because of your avarice. I don't exactly know what to call it, or how to describe it, but, as you said, behind the noise, it's there!"

"You won't find it in the LHC either," Robert added.

"Obviously! That's something else I'd like to talk about!" the president exclaimed.

A uniformed young woman came in, and set down a silver tray on which there was a fine china teapot in an embroidered tea cozy, with matching cups, saucers and plates, linen napkins and doilies, and a platter piled high with several types of vegan sandwiches. She set out two places on a coffee table before she left. The president poured two cups of tea, and filled two plates with sandwiches.

Robert ate and drank and indicated his approval. "There was a time in my life when every door just slammed shut, one after the other," he said, "you leave grade school with all the inspirational nostrums, 'when a door closes, it's for another to open,' but when you need to hearken to them in your subsequent life as an adult, you've forgotten them; and as I told you, they just kept closing anyway, even the new ones that opened up. That's what I meant about Grace: often you have to be reminded, and be reassured that there is a way.

"As soon as I stopped fretting about the doors, the door of insight, knowledge, opened a little bit for me. What's real? What's permanent? What *can't* close? That turned me into a very thankful person, and it became clearer what I could and couldn't change, and what I had to do was cut out for me. Right on time, after not succeeding despite repeated job applications, I found a way to make a decent living, which I only lost a few weeks ago, in the recession. So, I'm repeating my question: how do you want to change? Or, what about you are you being directed to change? Or, have you had such direction?"

"I'm less of a public man than running for office might make me out to be," the president answered, "and I published my books with the idea of running, rather than from getting any gratification in self-exposure. It's often said that people who seek high office have outsize egos, but I'm sure I'm an exception to the rule, if it is one. It was more a case of the occasion arising when something needed to be done –at that time, before the economic crisis, the first serious black candidacy, and for someone to unite the Democratic Party and find a way out of the tunnel the last administration left us stuck in- it looked like someone like me could do it, and I upped and volunteered. I don't know: something like an underage kid hoodwinking the authorities and signing up in the military, without asking parental approval until after the fact. My pluses were: I got along well with others; I was concerned about justice, fairness, and other people's welfare; and I'm sure every next person is probably like that, after all; but they weren't in Chicago at the right time; or they didn't have a Yale degree; or they couldn't write a book, or make a pretty speech; and they didn't have this unusual, feel-good-America story –from Tanzania to the White House- to tell. But I think Americans are finding out more and more I'm really just a regular guy, happy with other regular guys in the gym or basketball court; I love my wife and kids, and I get along marvelously with my mother-in-law. I'm getting paid to do a job, the house was thrown in, and I want to give back good value, is all.

"Of course, there's a darker subtext, there has to be in the very nature of things, and, like most regular guys, I've tried not to pay it too much mind. I don't tune it out with beer or drugs or sex, like a lot of guys do: but I grew up in Hawaii, I went to an elite boarding school there, and those islands bubble up serially out of the magma at the bottom of the ocean for the sole purpose of helping people to bliss out. Just you dive from a cliff a hundred feet or so up in the air into an equal depth of the vast Pacific! Surf a really big one! *Pouf*! Ego, the illusion of a separate self, just vanishes! You're convinced the gods and goddesses are real: you can catch their many different signature fragrances in a breeze!

"So, you're this terrible Trini man, eh, 'Asianized' and 'Africanized' and all of that, and you insist I 'take a journey to the dark side,' yes? OK, 'nothing venture, nothing gain,' so here goes. And our focus, our bottom line, is: what about me do I want to change.

"The chief reason why sex wasn't an escape route for me –you know, picking up babes at a bar, making out, building up a score card- was that it turned out to be a problem, and I was never at ease in my sexuality. My roommate at school was this big, red-haired dude whose family owned half of the Big Island –cattle ranches, coffee and macadamia nut estates, hotels, other businesses- and he just matter-of-factly raped me when I was eleven: matter-of-factly, casually, because he wasn't doing much of anything else at the moment, he had one of these lazy erections you just get on hot days, he was older, bigger then, and more powerful, he knew he'd get away with it, and besides, I was in awe of him, his riches and his privileges. And afterwards, I became his willing sexual slave for a couple of years, until his escapades got him into more trouble than the school could handle, and he was sent away to an even more elite school in New England -as a punishment, I guess.

"For many years after that, I fought to overcome the homoerotic or homosexual urges I'd feel. Then numbness. I just ceased to be a sexual agent, period. If you don't go there, you don't dredge up any desire or any memories, whether it was good or bad, or should have been allowed to happen, or go unpunished. Eventually I got married, which took me off the meat market. So, if I could really reconnect with my sexuality –just privately, you understand, internally; I mean I'm not about to be a danger to the White House aides- and was happier in my sexuality, such as it is, I think I would view the world a lot differently from how I do now. Damn! You're right. Just talking it out in the open, and imagining how that would be, I can see that I'd approach a lot of things differently than I have been doing! For example, would I have made those contentious appointments?

"Next, I'd like to be happier in my own skin. Of course, there was an obvious racial element in my relationship to Brian. I succumbed to his sexual bullying because he was white and I was black; he belonged to the superior race, I to the dispensable, disposable multitudes, the wretched of the earth. Complicating the issue is that I'm not truly a black American, my father's residence status was 'foreign student,' and my maternal grandparents, who hadn't the least idea what the upbringing of a black child entailed, were the ones who brought me up. When I was a teenager, all of these contradictions used to make me feel that I literally didn't even really belong here on earth in the first place! The disassociation gets to be that complete! During the campaign, I pointed to the ideological differences between the 'Moses' and 'Joshua' generations of black politicians, but with me, they went far deeper. I thought I'd covered this up pretty well, but only yesterday, my wife made some remarks that showed me how transparent I really am in this regard. So, that's another area lacking in resolution, which affects my thoughts and behavior.

"Of course, race dumbfounds everyone in America, even an in-transit passenger in the airport, and not only me. Why did whites support me in the elections? My wife has four theories: or rather she had the first, which she then replaced with the others, one after the other; and then she combines them all together again, and believes the toxic mix. The first was that the opposition was so ludicrous that they had no choice; the world would have condemned them if they had done otherwise. The second was that they were hoping that I would fail, thereby proving once for all that blacks were unsuited to high office. According to the third, electing a black man made them feel good about themselves –see, smart whites put race in the trash bin of American history, and went with the better candidate. The fourth theory is that they've realized they should have dumped being white in the trash instead: white isn't so smart after all, it's not sustainable, it's inevitable destruction, and it's a threat to the world's survival; and only a black can show them how to be someone else. And, in fact, many whites are as vehemently opposed as blacks to the whites I appointed to important positions. But don't forget, as you consider that one, that fears I'll be changing the Rose Garden into a watermelon patch are still rife!

"As you said earlier, the U.S. is still a majority white country, and that carries its own automatic constraints, although the demographics are changing rapidly by the day. But if the last theory is correct, and whites are willing not only to chuck racism, but also to disavow whiteness itself, with its assumptions of intellectual, moral and physical superiority, privilege and entitlement, how does that transform the discussion of race in this country? Deprived of one of its major dynamics, an exceedingly ugly one, what does the country's future look like? Will it look more like one of your Caribbean islands, where blacks have controlled the government for so long and whites are a small minority; or as South Africa is becoming, where 'naturally' a black should be Secretary of the Treasury or Education?

"I guess I'd really like to be more of an intellectual: and beyond that, to eventually become wise. For example, the definitive treatment of race in America has yet to be written. For another example, I wrote these books, which I rather improperly called 'memoirs,' but I haven't published a single article in a peer-reviewed journal on constitutional law, which I taught as a professor for several years. In fact, I personally believe that the constitution ought to have been re-written a long time ago.

"We, the people of the United States….." is way off the mark in a multicultural, multi-national world, which requires global cooperation for the solution to any of its urgent, life-and-death problems. Not a mention of 'Muslims!' And don't forget it was written by a bunch of drunkards as they were frantically swatting off a plague of bluebottles!

"On a related topic, although I don't think that temperamentally I have the stuff dictators are made of, I do wish I had dictatorial powers as the president in charge of the country during this crisis. My admiration of Abraham Lincoln is well known, but obviously America is a very different country today than it was in his time –overwhelmingly urban; less of a manufacturing power and more of a center of information and services; global interconnections; this huge Wild West of a banking system; the political incorporation of blacks and civil rights legislation; large legal and illegal immigrant populations, and so on. Besides, since his time, the structure and functioning of the Republican and Democratic parties have progressively undermined the least pretense of democracy, and far from facilitating contact, stand as a huge barrier between elected officials and the electorate. The never-ending Slobo-Morris soap opera in Illinois is ample proof of that!

"But returning to the appeal of dictatorial powers, I should remind you that even the Greeks, the originators of face-to-face democracy, occasionally found it expedient to put a strongman in charge, and would remove the institutional brakes so that he could use the emergency powers as needed. Pericles, for example, would be a better guide for me than Lincoln: the original and most ardent populist, foe of any sort of elitism, he nevertheless put up one of the most effective one-man shows of the ancient world. And, of course, Rome traded in two consuls for one Caesar and next baptized Augustus as the Son of God. In our own time, Russians have looked into Putin's soul and found nothing they disliked very much.

"Here, your best plans get deadlocked in Congress, and

nothing gets done. And so much needs to be done in such a hurry!

"Of course, the Internet is something else that makes today's America different from Lincoln's, and also from Republican and Democratic business-as-usual. It may have even taken us into the future by bringing us back to Pericles' populism and face-to-face democracy. Here's the opportunity to reach out to Americans directly on their palm-held devices and mobilize them, without anything coming between you and them. It might come to that test one day!

"Is any of this making sense, pundit?"

"That's your call, Mr. President," Robert said, "if *you*'re making sense, it's making sense."

"I told you I'm a regular guy, and my friends are regular guys," the president said, "we play ball, we watch the game, we drink a brew or two, and eat a plate of barbecued wings. But there is no way in hell I could tell them any of the things I just told you. There never was a time when there was ever an opening through which a frank and cleansing disclosure and discussion could pass. A sort of awkwardness would sometimes arise, just fleetingly, you understand, a *je ne sais quoi* mis-synchronization of heartbeats –you did say you were also 'Frenchified,' yes? See, they're Americans, and I'm not, at least not quite in the same way; and each person has skeletons in his closet, but it's obvious mine are a *little* different as to the anatomical detail. That's why people rely on pundits, sir, if you ever feel a need to justify your trade."

"If a door has really opened for you, Mr. President," Robert replied, "or you see that one will, you'll have the loveliest time when you go in, and this really besieged country will have what it sorely needs –a leader. And if I had a small role in either development, I'd be very satisfied."

While speaking, the president had used his hands with great eloquence. They were big, long and shapely: well suited for the purpose. He now threw them in the air in exasperation. "The LHC!" he said, "Can you imagine? The country's falling apart, and this maverick, polar biddy comes up with this utter, arrant nonsense! I mean I can't let this on publicly: but *American* Americans can sometimes be pretty weird, you know what I mean?"

Robert empathized. "Like you, I'm all on the side of science," he said, "and when you go through the door, be a thorough-going empiricist, through and through. Stick to scientific method as far as the study material allows. You're identifying and differentiating your inner states, you're describing them as fully as you can, and then you're analyzing them, testing and rejecting hypotheses about them, and coming up with new ones.

"My reservation about the Large Hadron Collider, after all the controversy has prayerfully died down, is that it isn't likely to come up with anything new. Particles have been accelerated before at slower speeds in previous colliders, and didn't come up with anything that was useful either theoretically or in terms of technological application.

"And think about it: it was built for the conduct of experiments to reveal the ultimate constituents of matter. Now, aren't we matter? Don't we have inside us, or in our flesh, the same Higg's boson –the God particle- the CERN scientists are seeking, or whatever gave us *some*thing out of *no*thing? If we went in through that door, into our deepest, innermost selves, wouldn't we be in fact going into the deepest, innermost recesses of matter?

"There are tried and tested -and not 'failed,' but successful- techniques for going through the door. It's very low-tech and inexpensive, nothing like the millions of dollars we're contributing to CERN: all it takes is an investment in a meditation pillow, a few books on the practice, and finding the time to meditate. "

"How does one meditate?" the president asked, "How is

it different from just zoning out, at which, I can assure you, I am very, very good –the best?"

"For one thing, it won't annoy the hell out of your wife!" Robert responded.

The president pounded the presidential desk with both fists and roared with laughter. The spathephyllum, from which several peace lilies had issued, including one that was a beauty -tall, ivory white, and slender- trembled in its pot. "How did you know that!" he spluttered.

When Robert, who had joined in the laughter, which shredded any last remnant of formality to the meeting, calmed down, he explained, "For every zoned-out person, there's has to be at least one extremely stressed out next-of-kin. In fact, there is usually a total disaster area around many zoned-out people! That's the iron, natural law of balance and equilibrium that admits no exceptions. Coming to think of it, I'm surprised reporters didn't pick up on that during the campaign.

"More seriously, anybody can zone out, but some are called to meditate: and if you have been called, then that's what you're doing –meditating, and not anything else, like zoning out. Maybe it's evolution that's calling you to a higher stage of development, and by the time it does, you'd have fulfilled the prerequisites –diet, exercise, yoga, trying to do the right thing, and to find the right way. It's widely reported that you, sir, are already on the right track regarding those things, so, of course, it's not surprising if you've been called. Of course, you'll just keep on doing those things, regardless.

"That boils down to saying that, for certain persons, sitting down on a meditation pillow and calling what they're doing 'meditation,' *is* meditation, but it will take a few years of doing it before they're truly convinced of that."

The urge to burst out laughing again was still fragmenting the president's attention. "Whoa! You're losing me," he protested, "Say what?"

Robert smiled and continued, "What I meant is that all

you can do is to put yourself in the right place at the right time, which is to say on your meditation pillow at a set time –or times- everyday, make the occasion special –calm down, wash before, light candles and incense, have an altar with some statues or pictures on it- and then it might happen for you. You stop being you, and are You instead. But there's nothing else you can do, nothing to guarantee that result, for example, to force it to happen, which would actually be contrary to the whole endeavor in any case, and it will be God's grace, or evolution calling –however you wish to put it. All you can do is what you did: sit in good faith and say you're meditating.

"It sounds simple, and in some senses it absolutely is, but of course, that's not the whole story, is it? It requires all that preparation I mentioned, which already presupposes a high degree of awareness and knowledge, and a lot of grit and determination, and then the actual thing –sitting on the pillow- is really very, very difficult –harder than I guess getting a law degree from Yale was- and that's probably why only a few are called to try it. I mean you're not sitting there thinking up dirty jokes! But eventually, as you blaze the path for others to follow, all humans will be called.

"If not dirty jokes, or zoning out, what's happening on the meditation pillow? Ultimately, words can't describe that, but let's see how close we can get. All terrestrial creatures, from microbes to humans, have apparatuses for breathing, taking in food or nourishment, digesting it and defecating, and for reproduction. Let's make a list of everything that can be accounted solely to creatures so equipped: from amoeba to humans, they'd naturally have feelings and even thoughts; and in our case, our bigger brains would turn those into philosophy, as a matter of the routine mechanics of the thing; the arts; and science, such as the higher mathematics, engineering, and particle physics that went into the infamous LHC. They live the life spans their particular apparatuses allotted them, and then die. If that's the end of the story, that's the end of the story! If not, what have we left out?

"We meditate in order to find out. We suspect there's more to it, and we want to know –we are called to find out- what it is. Right there, the call is something extra! Actually, we have it on Darwin's authority that there is something more -and he's often misrepresented on this topic. He wrote there was grandeur in his way of thinking, which derived from a few forms, according to a few rules, the astonishing proliferation and diversity of the life forms we can see, and the many more that will continue to evolve in the future; but while he did thus explain the origin of species, he didn't say that he had explained the origin of *life*. About that, what he actually wrote was that, *'once life was breathed into them,'* the few forms would take care of all the rest, even the rules by which they'd operate.

"*'Once life was breathed into them*!' We're back to *some*thing out of *no*thing! On your meditation pillow, go all the way back to the original few forms, past everything that can be known– and then, alert and open, what will you find? You'll have been metamorphosing into an entirely original, brand new life form –food, sex, companionship, emotions and thoughts won't appeal to it as they did to all the other forms we've mentioned- and, as with the few at the beginning of his treatise, you've absolutely got Darwin's word –and the world around us is also full of the evidence- that '*life will be breathed*' into it. The life that is appropriate to it, which is to say, *meditation* will be breathed into it, and then you'll be meditating.

"A line just came into my head: 'make straight in the desert a highway for your God.' As I said before, you can't force your way in, shovel-ready is all you can be: and so a lore of meditation has developed. Do it. Don't expect anything. Don't be impatient. Don't beat yourself out of shape over it. Just do it, and don't ever give up! And, as we already demonstrated, you're sure to succeed.

"To strengthen your resolve and improve your practice,

you could carefully observe people and learn from them. What makes them tick? Where does their happiness –or, more routinely, unhappiness- come from? The world, all of a myriad of phenomena, is a collection of texts: just open your eyes and see. And there are a few books you could read. Nothing much: *The Sermon on the Mount*, the *Vedas*, the *Upanishads*, the *Bhagavad Gita*, the *Dhammapada*, some collections of Zen koans, some verses by Keats, Tennyson, Shakespeare, and Rumi. The Old Testament. The Koran. These are but a few from a collection that could entirely fill several libraries.

"Here, I'll jot down those titles."

He reached over, took a scribble pad and pencil from the president's desk, and wrote them down.

While he was so occupied, the president thought quietly to himself. At length, he declared, "I'll do it! I'll lock myself in my closet, as Jesus said. Darn! You're right! It's right there in *The Sermon on the Mount*. Jesus did preach there's nothing you can say or do! The Father knows everything: what your trouble is, and what your need is. It's senseless to give Him information, or make a request. Just lock the closet door behind you and call yourself praying –that's praying!

"That's meditating!" Robert said.

"What you said is exactly what Jesus said!" the president said excitedly, "Don't forget the meditation pillow. Jot down where can I buy one. I'll do it every day from now on, without missing a day!"

Robert scribbled some more before continuing: "As I was saying, a good position to take on the LHC is that science is fine, and always needs to be done, but in this case, at this time, when money is so scarce, there should be better assurances of a positive result. What you are going to do about the doomsday prophets, I don't know. People will welcome any distraction right about now; and if it ties in with religious cant, it could be a real quagmire, as it has already proven to be."

"If rioting erupts again, it'll be nastier," the president said gloomily, "it won't be just spontaneous, it will be as you said -planned and deliberate, intended to bring down my administration."

"Sir, you should go ahead and make better use of IT!" Robert counseled, "You used it so effectively during the campaign, you should use it now, as you were suggesting. Reach out to the millions of idealistic young people who canvassed for you, start recruiting and paying hundreds of thousands of 'Osama's peacekeepers,' get them out on the street before anybody else gets there. Job creation and crisis intervention in one smart move. I'd be happy to help with that in New York!"

"Maybe you just created your own job, sir," the president observed, "Look, can I get in touch again? The next time, the request won't be as traumatic for the young lady and you!"

"Anytime, sir, anytime," Robert assured him, meaning it from the bottom of his heart.

As Robert was leaving the White House, the same uniformed staff person who had served them earlier gave him a tote bag with the remaining sandwiches packed in a neat bundle inside, and a thermal flask of fresh tea. "The president wishes you a safe and comfortable return home," she said, "he really appreciated and enjoyed your visit."

13

There was such an authority and gravitas in the president's stride as he entered the Cabinet Room that once again his staffers instantly fell silent. All that could be heard –and you could actually hear it- was the atmosphere itself, as he began speaking. He seemed to have reverted fulltime to his professorial persona. In fact, this time he pirouetted, as if expecting to find a chalkboard behind him, and seemed a trifle irritated that one wasn't there.

"It's clear that capitalism as we know it can't survive," he said. "Nothing 'as we know it' has ever done, so why should such a fraught system? I spent some time before this meeting reviewing the vicissitudes of our economy over the past few decades. This thing is as dead as a dinosaur, or should be! Nothing can be salvaged, or ought to be! We need a clean slate!

"Growth followed by stagnation has been the way the capitalist economy progressed from the beginning, but the grinding and screeching of the gears really began to split eardrums in the late 1970's and 1980's. We should have pulled the plug then! I was scandalized how the search for profits, the primary motivation in such a system, serially and malignly put various segments of national and international populations in a garish spotlight.

"In the 1980's, that search for profits required tax cuts, the emasculation of the unions, the freezing of workers' compensation, deregulation of the financial institutions, and increasing the interest rates on external debt owed by Mexico and Central American and South American countries. The latter immediately plunged into crisis, depopulating their countryside and swelling their urban slums. But all the money went up to the few at the top!

"Here in the U.S., we had our cocaine-smoking decade. It shone the spotlight on newly "dangerous" classes of hitherto invisible –mostly black and Hispanic- populations, and upon urban *terrae incognitae et perditae*, or mainly low-rent and public housing. You still remember that decade, don't you? All those 'turf' wars and 'drive-by' shootings? The cocaine markets were differentiated, with signature styles of drug trafficking and use, as well as attendant features like crime or violence, characterizing each; and law enforcement agencies moved major firepower to the fronts, adding to and complicating every kind of struggle for territory and market share.

"Came the 1990's, and another turn of the screw. As the cocaine-smoking outbreak deflated, "Indian scouts" and bounty hunters, in the persons of artists and the creators of the edgy urban style, explored these badlands, primarily and ostensibly in search of inexpensive loft/studio space, but often also for the drugs and other rough trade; and following on their heels, after the shooting stopped and the smoke cleared, came the billionaires -art-world financiers, venture capitalists, gentrifiers and lenders to subprime borrowers- who then built up a Himalayas of capital accumulation and diffusion, which, in the late 1990's and the first decade of the 21st century, had global reach, partially lifting GDPs in India, China, Brazil and countless other nations, and elevating teeming classes to the privileges and clout of entrepreneurship, middle income and even super-rich status.

"Today, as these mountain peaks are being leveled amid

seismic shocks whose enormous magnitude are causing us to tremble in this very room, capital is again being concentrated, this time in even fewer hands; new swaths of emptied out urban *terrae incognitae et perditae* –now comprising foreclosed, private equity housing- are being revealed; and another set of "dangerous" classes is no doubt in the wings, perhaps illegally occupying and squatting in said deserted, foreclosed homes, awaiting a curtain call. What are their demographics, and what program will they bring onstage? A new drug? A new crime wave? A further shredding of the social contract? We already saw the violence of the riots. Will any of it help re-start the *machine infernale*?

"Well, we can't wait for that to happen, I don't think we really want it to, and we're not going to put in place policies and strategies that will help the moribund beast to have its last few, disastrous breaths at our expense! Recently, I had the misfortune of discussing Adam Smith with a group of academics, who weren't sure they had heard of him. Of course, you in this room all know he's the father of economics, and that he likened the economy to a conversation: the freer it became, the freer 'motions of the mind,' or motives, cognition, perception, memory, feelings, the imagination, the heart, and manners, became also. Because Scottish feudalism, imposed by the British, put Scots in an economic straitjacket, it had also tied up their tongues and wits. Accordingly, he wrote *Wealth of Nations* to launch a 'very violent attack…… upon the whole commercial system of Great Britain.' That's what we must do now: launch a 'very violent attack…… upon the whole commercial system of the United States and the world!.'

"You see, he did succeed in helping to free up the conversation, and free up Scotland, and in the intervening centuries, the benefit has been extended and, of course, has tightly integrated the globe to a degree hitherto undreamed of. But, at the same time, the conversation also tended to be clique-ish and hierarchical, as I was saying earlier. It had always excluded women and children; slaves, indentured servants and other types of coerced labor; and try talking about animal rights to those cattle and poultry in the giant protein mills where they are tortured today! As it became globalized, therefore, the conversation cut out the majority of the human population – and guys retaliated by lobbing airplanes into our tall buildings. We returned the favor by sending the Marines and mayhem. On both sides, torture, rape and deliberate dismemberment have become the approved weapons of war. The conversation also failed to develop a vocabulary to keep pace with how many of its subordinate dialogues were destroying the physical environment, our very habitat, Planet Earth.

"The conversation had also become one-sided and partial. Smith's project was about putting more of mind –all "the motions of mind," as I mentioned, - into society, for its enrichment, greater morality, and human happiness. But instead, only our basest reptilian appetites got out: bigger portions, more fat, mega-quantities of calories, McMansions, sex around the clock, SUVs, and all that junk.

"Here's how degraded the conversation has become. On Black Friday last year, two thousand frantic shoppers trampled to death a part-time employee at a Walmart as they stampeded towards the advertised bargains inside the store. It wasn't an accident. We'd wasted all our talent on sophisticated marketing strategies to draw all those people there, lined up in the cold and darkness, sated on Thanksgiving turkeys and pies, waiting for this blood sport called Black Friday. This sort of commonplace depravity is the flip side of the same coin with the Ponzi schemes, outrageous executive compensation and corporate jets!

"So the task now is to withdraw mind and recoup before sending it out into the world again. The new economics has to release yet newer 'motions of the human mind,' the ones I mentioned plus -I don't know –maybe even telepathy, teleportation, clairvoyance, walking on water, flying through the air…………..So how do we come up with a new conversation, which is to say a new economics. That's the challenge as I see it for this administration.

"Well, let's turn to a related topic, as we in this room are the ones who have been put on the spot to take on the challenge. Thank you for your financial statements. In light of my little lecture –and I do apologize for lecturing anyone- you probably won't be surprised that I found some of them quite unacceptable. I mean I am myself quite affluent, but I never made a penny from trading on my position as a lawmaker or government advisor, and I never shall! I think we're going to have to make some changes around here."

Helena Asuncion and Hérmano Rodríguez were evidently pleased. They clapped. "About time, sir!" she said.

"Mr. Gunther, cheating on your taxes caused me considerable embarrassment, and I was obliged to say it was an 'honest, little mistake,' when it still beats me how it was made! I mean income is income, whether it's cowrie shells or kola nuts, and if you haven't paid taxes on it to somebody, something's wrong. You don't have to be a Treasury Secretary to know that!

"Before that, there was A.I.G. and Lehman Brothers, the Bear Stearns/Maiden Lane fiasco, the 'rescues' you made that were such a disaster for the taxpayer, for the financial markets and also for the Federal Reserve System as an organization. You were in the room every time, and things only got worse. But I was prepared to overlook all of this because, yes, you were in the room, and maybe this time around you'd have something useful to contribute to fixing the banking system.

"Well, you don't, do you? It was clear from our last meeting that nearly everyone present thinks your 'new and improved' rescue plan is just a conduit for handing over $2.5 trillion to the bankers and private investors, without a single thought or care for the millions of Americans who are suffering the consequences of their misdeeds. And here's your financial statement that says why: you're in their pay! I'll need to have your resignation by the end of the day.

"Mr. Somerville, you're no better, are you sir? In your case, I had to overlook your really questionable behavior as a university president, when you not only offended women and faculty members generally with your ridiculous ideas, but you also alienated widely respected African American scholars, because you wanted them to stop their investigations of black popular culture. Hadn't you heard of academic freedom? And your financial statement shows the degree to which you profited from lobbying for the deregulation of financial institutions, which is the major cause of our trouble. So you're fired too!

"Mr. Ezekiel, I've put up with your potty mouth and your family's racist views towards Arabs and Muslims; but, with your income of millions of dollars -all earned, like your friend, Dachshund's, from being an elected official- I just can't have you as a member of my administration, which has to come up with a new way of doing things –change we can believe in- when you're so heavily invested in the old. Your career just doesn't exemplify the ideal of selfless, committed public service we are aiming to institutionalize. It indicates more the mindset of the pirates whose plunder has put us underwater. I need your resignation too.

"And "Scrappy," you and Paddy Nuncio can give me yours as well. Thanks."

"You black mutherfucka!" "Rambo" screamed, "you fuckin' black nigger bitch. Think you can get away with this, huh? *Huh?*! You'll be sorry when I get through with you, president or no president. Now, suck my dick!"

"Rambo" stormed out of the room, followed by Somerville, Gunther and the two Republicans.

There was silence, which the president coolly ended by laughing out long and comfortably. "I guess Arabs aren't the only ones he was brought up to despise," he said at length.

Secretary Brunton wiped the tears that were rolling down

her cheeks," I'm so sorry, sir" she kept repeating, "I'm so sorry!"

"We'll find replacements for these MIA's as we go along, but we should start working on our agenda immediately," the president said, resuming their meeting. "And if need be, we'll just go directly to the electorate for their support.

"First on the agenda is obviously the nationalization of the banks, which is vital if credit is to start flowing normally again as rapidly as we would like. The way it was done in Sweden, the bank executives were sent packing. Then the government looked at those worthless assets, valued them, and paid off what they could to counterparties, creditors and shareholders in a sort of managed bankruptcy, what we should also be doing with the Big Three. The biggest obstacle is still that valuation: I think the bankers know, and the losses run to too much more than they can safely reveal to the public before going into hiding, maybe fifty or sixty trillion worldwide! Sweden had a much smaller problem, and they soon had a national bank that was clean and fresh and valuable, which cost the taxpayer much less than a bailout would have. It's going to be more complicated for us, but I think the same strategies will work."

"We'll have to work on the precise structure and function of the bank. It will be tightly integrated and regulated from the bottom up. I envisage that at the grassroots level, the local branch of the bank will be tied into a network of similar organizations, many of which we are committed to create where they do not already exist, such as the health clinic, the library and IT center, the public gym and swimming pool, the community nursery and recreation room, kitchens for food vendors and the hosts and hostesses of large private or public receptions, and the workshops for artisans and the community green gardens. Its officers and board of directors will all be local people: and they will give personal loans, business lines of credit, and mortgages based on their intimate, face-to-face knowledge of their neighbors' financial circumstances and personal character. They will know how to compensate for any deficits of those in anyone. The branch will also handle payroll for local businesses, take deposits, and encourage savings. And so on up to the district level; then the twelve regional Federal Reserve banks, appropriately renamed; then a federal entity; and finally, the Treasury. At no level will dicey speculation be permitted!

"It's very important that as we plan this, we do so in co-operation with the other affected economies, which is to say all the national economies of the world, really. But Sweden, Canada, the European Union, China, Russia, Japan, India, Mexico, Brazil, and Venezuela –they have to come in immediately: they have experiences which we can use as guides. Sweden and Canada have survived the turmoil more or less intact; Cuba, although it desperately needs help, has advice to offer us about survival in the face of unrelenting spitefulness. Furthermore, these countries are brimming with tip-top economics brains, as are the thousands of non-Ivy League universities in this country, and we have to tap into that wealth of resources immediately. We have to schedule meetings with them at once. Only a fool cannot see that, this time more than any other, the whole world either works together, or sinks.

"Which leads to the second item on the agenda: hostilities around the world have to cease. Israel cannot have a free pass anymore in dictating how things go in the Middle East: very clear, undisputed, universal principles of fair play, justice and equal development for all the people of that region must call the shots instead. Iran, Hamas, Hezbollah, Pakistan and North Korea must understand that they are wanted at the planning table, not on the battlefield. The situations in Iraq and Afghanistan must be stabilized, not militarily, but with the implementation of truly peacekeeping and peace–maintaining initiatives.

"On the domestic front, we need the $789 of the stimulus

bill, or the $500 billion of it set aside in cash for the government to spend, to be spent, and to start creating jobs, immediately. I'll want detailed plans for such spending before the end of the month, and the newly employed workers should be getting their first paychecks two weeks after that. We'll also need to spend that $275 billion meant to rescue the 5 million homeowners who can't afford to make their mortgage payments; and to persuade the 13 million who can, but whose homes are now worth less than their mortgages, not to walk away.

"And yes, Helena, progressive taxation will be re-instituted, and we'll see whether those credit cards can't become a part of the recovery equation.

"Finally, we'll be working on a budget that aims to reduce the extreme income disparity that has developed in the past three decades. A return to progressive taxation and spending on education, health and job creation will be key. Our Budget Office has been provided with pocket calculators and sophisticated computers: I'm praying you get the math right!

"That's a lot of work, and you each know which part of it is specifically yours. Collaborate, and feel free to walk into my office whenever you need to. I'm usually there from 7am, and I never get out before 8pm anyway."

Marie and Sally were working on their homework in the Lincoln study when their father returned from a hard day's work at the office. Marie was doing a project on the emergence of the modern Caribbean, and asked him to tell her about the late C.L.R. James.

"Cyril Lionel Robert James! A Trini! He was a hero!" her father said, enthusiastically, "a political theorist, a novelist, a writer, an ardent cricketer –it's a game they play over there- a sports writer and an all round sportsman. His student, Dr. Eric Williams, and he brought party politics to the British West Indies, which was how the former British Caribbean colonies were called, and were in the forefront of the movement that brought them independence from Great Britain. He was also a leader of the Pan-African Congress, which, by sponsoring African leaders like Kwame Nkrumah of Ghana and Jomo Kenyatta of Kenya, also helped African colonies to gain independence. Although neither was an economist –Dr. Williams was an historian, whose book on slavery, *Capitalism and Slavery*, is still regarded as one of the best on the subject- they designed a sophisticated program for the economic and social development of the region. My favorite books by him are *The Black Jacobins*, about the Haitian struggle against Napoleon to become the first sovereign black nation in the Americas, and *Beyond a Boundary*, about politics and cricket. You've got to look them up online!"

"I'd prefer that they got the actual books from the library and read them," Millie said, with a feral expression of maternal, I-know-what's-best-for-the-children solicitude on her face, "print media aren't going out of style anytime soon."

Both children immediately buried their heads in their books.

Later, in the pantry, Barzhad seized a big fistful of his wife's ass, which was clothed in a flattering dress that was soon to grace the pages of *Vogue* magazine, and pulled her against him with the other long arm. "African-American girls rule, no doubt," he growled affectionately, "but sometimes they're a trifle bossy!"

"Barzhad, don't tell me you're messing around with that cocaine again," she said, sternly, "God! Have you gone crazy?"

"No, silly," her husband told her, "but I am messing around with liberty, and I'll keep it up until I get caught!"

"You'd better tell me what this is all about," she said warily.

"The black state of mind scored a direct hit!" Barzhad told her, "Hit me right here, wriggled around a bit, and started living for good right here, where my bipartisan heart used to be!

"I guess their parade of follies finally got to me. In the last couple of days, I saw it all actually, the whole lineup from beginning to end. I had an Oxford don who was nothing but a grab bag of conceits, smoke and mirrors, and don't talk about plain, hot air! There was the usual weed lot of rugged individualists, who don't know the truth even though it keeps hitting them on the head, and they don't have the vocabulary to tell you about it even if they did. I had the fetishists and dope addicts strutting their stuff, and a sandlot full of bullies. A chorus of needles stuck in their grooves! All the while, reality was like an ocean liner receding fast over the horizon.

"You'll be happy to know Ezekiel, Gunther, Somerville and Rubens are packing their bags and will be leaving town by sundown. And you know what, love of my life? I wish we were too! God, I'm sick of this place, and running this show. But since we're stuck here, things are going to be different from here on out. We'll definitely have to double the security for you and the kids, but we're going for broke. I'd rather have one term and shake it up real good than have two and do nothing!

"Your influence was the kicker, but maybe Bertha's guy gave me the decisive jolt I needed. Hallelujah, I can see! Hallelujah, I can hear! Hallelujah, I can speak! And boy, am I going to kick *arse*!

"Why, that's James Brown ah'm hearing," Millie cried, "'Papa's got a brand new bag,' daddy. Muhammed *A-h-h-h*-li! Jackie Robinson! Welcome to the Black Hall of Fame, *dahl*-ing!"

And when he finished giving a more detailed and coherent account of how he had passed his day at the Oval Office, Millie cracked out a bottle of Zinfandel she'd had in reserve. "Don't start up about your diet, please" she said, "boy, maybe there's still hope for you! Maybe we'll learn you're a terrestrial after all, despite the big ears."

The presidential bedsprings hadn't boasted much action since the presidential couple moved in, but they sure got their 'stress test' that night.

14

When Robert ripped the tag off the UPS overnight delivery envelope, a smaller, plain white envelope slipped out. In it, enclosed in a folded sheet of plain 11.5 x 8.5 bonded, white paper was a check for $100, 000, signed by "Barzhad Osama." In the top left hand corner of the check, "Millie and Barzhad Osama" was printed, with a Chicago, Illinois address. In the line for "memo," the president had written, "Thanks." Then, on the plain piece of paper, Robert discovered that the president had written an unsigned, personal note, "I started, and the benefits were immediate and just amazing. Perhaps this is what I was cut out to do! You, of all persons, will easily detect the difference when you read of my future exploits in the newspapers!"

Robert hesitated at first to accept the honorarium, and wanted to either send it back or put it away as a keepsake. But a sober consideration of his sagging finances changed his mind. When the check cleared, and the money was available, he revisited the store, his last place of employment, and wasn't surprised to find that it was still vacant. When he called on her, the landlady was happy to see him, and said that finding new tenants was next to impossible because of the dead, rental market for commercial space. She agreed to give him a fifteen-year lease at half the rent his boss had paid.

Sadly, that former benefactor had quite lost the sunny disposition that had once distinguished him. He had put on weight, walked with a shuffle, and the light in his face had dimmed. After being wiped out, his sole support was a parking lot he owned in Flushing, Queens, which paid a more or less steady income; but the recent marriage of his younger sister, a lavish ceremony of great consequence in their community, the expense of which falls entirely upon the bride's family, had cleaned out those earnings too. As a result, he remained a lodger at his uncle's without a home of his own, and often went without the funds to buy a restaurant meal or the fine clothes he so dearly loved. He no longer owned a car. He was overjoyed that Robert wanted to pay cash for the store's inventory, which remained untouched in storage, and proposed a steeply discounted price for it; but Robert refused to give him anything less than its full value. Asked whether he had won the lottery, Robert shrugged his shoulders and contrived to look mysterious.

A couple of weeks of enjoyable industry followed. With the help of a Mexican contractor and his employees, he renovated and repainted the store's interior, the bathroom and the basement, which hadn't been floored previously, and was insufficiently lighted: and the work had gone so splendidly that, on completion, he realized that, but for the lack of a shower and a second or emergency exit, the space was finished enough to be used as a stopgap, if possibly illegal, residence. Then, he brought in a licensed plumber and electrician to completely refit and rewire inside and out. A new street sign went up: *Oracles and Cures.*

Despite the almost complete cessation of consumer spending, most of his neighbors wished the reopening of the store well by flocking in to make purchases, and Robert spent happy days renewing acquaintances he thought had ended for good.

More important, from both commercial and personal points of view, his former reputation as someone who listened carefully and gave wise counsel, quickly revived. And, by the end of the first week, his clients from the outlying sections of the borough started returning. The rapidity with which news got around really amazed him.

Robert's return to a more structured daily agenda was an immeasurable boon, and the good spirits it brought him proved infectious. While work at the media firm had contracted, Awe started working on a new composition, the music to accompany a children's story she had written, which was about a nine-year-old girl being introduced by an angel to endangered species, and learning about their diminishing prospects and their terror of extinction. Progress with the composition now accelerated dramatically, and her relationship with the few private students she had also improved. And so, contentment's sweetest daughter moved in as the third sharer in their home, and her hand was in everything: their conversation, their work, their *sadhana*, the meals they shared, and the relief they felt from being continuously at penury's door.

One day, Robert was exceedingly pleased to receive a visit from Benjie, the art gallery proprietor in Bedford-Stuyvesant. He said he had been overjoyed when he learned that Robert had reopened the store.

"Did you win a Lotto or what?" he asked.

Robert, who found telling lies difficult, mumbled, "Something like a personal stimulus plan." His manner and tone of voice indicated to Benjie that the matter was closed. Locking the door behind them, Robert took Benjie to the Connecticut Muffin at the corner, and they returned with soy lattes and some slices of vegan banana-walnut bread.

"How have you been holding up, Benjie?" Robert wanted to know, "You said it was touch-and-go last time."

"Still is, nothing's changed," Benjie told him, "no sales, no commissions. Into the bargain, I ought not to be having the banana bread, or the latte, for that matter. Old age comes with its usual retinue of hypertension, blood pressure, and potentially diabetes and heart disease. I don't have insurance, so I can't afford to get ill!"

"Gosh! I'm sorry," Robert cried apologetically, "I really don't do this much at all myself. It's just that I can't seem to lay my hands on my old electric kettle, and I need to buy another small refrigerator, the last one must have been sold, and so I had nothing to offer you. Old habits carried me off. You know, back in Trinidad, friends come around, and we'd be having currant rolls and a glass of iced soursop punch or mauby instead. Probably worse for us than this, though!"

Benjie assured Robert no apology was necessary. "Let's have a slice of the bread," he said, "we weren't brought up any differently down south. But old age is the devil, isn't it? I just turned sixty-seven, and the body can't stop crowing morning and evening, 'I won't be here for long' and 'I'm out of here real soon!'"

"I'm sixty-five," Robert said, "and I keep hearing the same refrain! I do my best with dieting, exercise and adequate rest, but they aren't going to make you immortal."

"I used to be in martial arts once, so I meditate and work-out every day," Benjie said, sipping his coffee, "But yes, the time is coming up for us to make the final tally, Robert: what we learned, and whether it was all worth it."

"What's your scorecard looking like, Benjie?" Robert asked.

"I had a lot of friends when I was younger," Benjie replied, "you know, guys I saw everyday, and we got high and ran the streets together, and then there was so much we were going to do. So many plans! I couldn't tell you where a single one is today. Nowadays, I have my artists and clients and friends like you, but it's more about a business transaction or respect, and we do preserve our privacy more, and keep our distance."

"Never married, Benjie?" Robert enquired, "No kids?"

"I have a son in Oakland," Benjie replied, "but we did a better job keeping up with kin during slavery than we do nowadays. But the point I was making was about my score-card, you know. *Something's here* –it's got that written down, but we don't see it!

"African arts, and the arts of the African diaspora, are my specialty, as you know, and it's still a thrill to hold in my hands something I'd not seen before. Hunting down that thrill took me not only throughout the Americas and the Caribbean, but also up and down and across Africa many times: Guinea, Mali, Nigeria, Gabon, Burkina Faso, Ghana, Cameroon, Congo, Tanzania and Mozambique –I've toured them all, the cities, towns and tiniest villages.

"These were mostly masks of the ancestors I am talking about, the kings and queens, gods and goddesses, although there were pieces that depicted the hunter, the fisherman, the cattle-herder, the cultivator of yams; or animals; and I'd get absorbed in the abstract figures that had inspired Miró, Braques and Picasso; or pieces that were used as utensils in the house-hold. But it was a kind of scorecard too, wasn't it, especially the high tradition of the ancestors? It documented life process: how they loved us, and prepared the paths we were to follow, and how we were to do the same for the generations coming up after us. And embedded in it were the same noggin-scratching mystery, and the same tantalizing conviction, that the answer was right there at hand, hidden in plain sight: it moves, what makes it move? Scientists and historians can tell us about how the successive forms came into being, but art has to endure to remind us of the 'qui vive,' the *why*, that makes their passage over time possible."

"And religion makes us one with it," Robert added, "It's shocking that atheists don't recognize what's adaptive about something so basic!"

"Well, if they truly believe their atheism, that would be the adaptive advantage too, wouldn't it?" Benjie asked, "Belief, even if it's in the non-existence of God! It's the insincerity that's maladaptive."

"Ah! The Nok! The Dogon! The Baule! The Nuna! The Makonde!" Robert crooned, "if those masters were alive today, I wonder what sort of masks they'd make for our edification, and to teach us about those great themes of continuity and change, the great natural laws that support them, and the Lawgiver."

"But we have television, sir!" Benjie declaimed sarcastically, "Not to mention movies, YouTube, MySpace and the rest. Isn't it mindboggling how low-tech takes you directly to the pulse of life, where you can act and mime or be possessed, while high-tech leaves you more or less like a zombie, stripped of origin, presence, blessings, or will? Or put another way, the mask makers wanted to show us the supernatural, but did an even better job giving us detailed, empirical, psychological portraits of ourselves; while MySpace and the others wanted to give us those; failed; and instead, didn't give us anything remotely supernatural, but just shot us out into denatured vapidity –blank, meaningless emptiness, the blogosphere!"

Robert crumpled up the pastry bag and napkins, and threw it and the Styrofoam coffee cups into the garbage. "The more's the pity," he said, "it feels as though the mystery isn't just personal and metaphysical any more, if it ever was, but also historical and political. What we are going through today feels like if it's being chiseled on biblical tablets, putting down in perpetuity not only our mortal fates, but the fate of creation itself. I guess I'd like to live this mess out, if survival is still an option, and see whether it can be prevented from happening again in the future. Then I'd be happier giving my final accounting."

"The rioting was very bad," Benjie reported, "worse than anything I've seen before, and I saw Selma, Watts and the Bronx. Let's hope it doesn't happen again. The mood is still very flammable unfortunately. So, from the grand perspectives of old age and our approaching demise, do we have anything useful to say on the subject?"

"For the moment, yes. Thank God the stimulus bill has passed," Robert replied, "I can't believe the state and the city don't already have plans for an immediate go ahead with the spending. These delays are unconscionable!"

"Some are unavoidable," Benjie said, "after all, replacements have to be found for Ezekiel, Gunther, Somerville, Dachshund and Budd. Aren't these Republican governors who are refusing to accept the money out of their tree? They're against pampering us, they said!"

"These guys are unconscionable, and I hope they are never returned to office!" Robert declared, "What about education? A few hundred new Head Starts should have been up and running already. Your neighborhood alone could use that many!"

"If money actually did become available, I was thinking I could get some financing to convert the gallery into an after-school with an arts specialization," Benjie said. "I have a stable full of down-on-their-luck sculptors, painters, and video artists I could tap as instructors."

"That's what I'm saying!" Robert exclaimed, "The state and city budget officers have to know it's a life or death situation."

"Well, at least Osama got good marks for getting rid of the dead weight and deciding to bring the fate of the Big Three to his personal desk," Benjie said, "and if he can keep eighteen million people in their homes, and put six million back to work, it will do a lot to smooth feathers in Bed-Stuy."

"So, to answer your question finally," Robert said, "you and I have to stay in touch more and join forces to wage unceasing battle against the old age part, so that we'll be spry when we're needed. Really, no more lattes and banana bread, no matter what the occasion! And, in addition to the Head Starts, there are all kinds of other projects for which we should be advocating. And I have a feeling we haven't seen the end of the rioting. So, we could be more proactive making sure they actually don't recur: handing out fliers, convening talks and meetings, going out and getting funding to support those activities.

"As for our approaching demise, when we've put in all that wholesome labor, we'll have earned our rest, don't you think?"

"I'd be more effective if I had better equipment at the gallery," Benjie reflected ruefully, "my ancient computer crashed the other day, and I can't afford to replace it. Some part time help would also be useful. But I'm struggling as it is to buy the raw fruits and vegetables I should be eating, never mind lethal banana bread."

Robert went behind the counter and reached out his checkbook. He wrote one out and handed it to Benjie. It was for $20,000.

15

With the dismissal from the Cabinet of Tommy Gunther, "Rambo" Ezekiel, Lance Somerville, Paddy Nuncio and "Scrappy" Deats, the Dupont Circle cabal had less of a need to meet clandestinely, and Pastor Rocky Walrus and Governor Susan Paltry joined it openly soon after their infamous broadcasts. The Governor had learned from *Vogue* where Millie Osama shopped, and her visits to Washington also supported her determination not to fall behind in the First Lady fashion race: while the pastor still refused to forgive the universe at large for the doldrums into which he had sunk after the inauguration; his popularity, which spiked briefly during the riots, had summarily plunged again afterwards.

As a result of the concentrated intelligence of their enlarged membership and, of course, the indefatigable plotting, they had been able to strategize some minor successes in their campaign against the president. For example, they paid or persuaded several media –newspapers, television shows and talk radio- to organize contests around the country, in which entrants were to lampoon the president, either in a cartoon, a live skit, a video or a written piece. Accordingly, a real life story of a chimpanzee in Stamford, Connecticut, that had attacked a woman, critically wounding her before being shot to death by police, became grist for the contestants' mill: the winning entry, published in a Portland, Maine newspaper, was a cartoon showing the police shooting a deranged chimp, with the caption, "Next time, they'll have to find someone else to be 'car czar.'" In fact, most entries belabored the same line of attack: contempt for the president's race, and the alleged likeness of persons of African ancestry to animals, especially monkeys and the higher primates. The confidence that some Americans had, that the election of the first African-American president signaled the demise of invidious comparisons based on race, and racial animosities, was thus brutally exploded.

This particular strategy reaped a harvest of unexpected benefits for the conspirators when the Attorney General Edward Helper, one of the few African Americans Barzhad had appointed to a top Cabinet position, staged a frontal attack against it. He sought a restraining order in the United States District Court, District of Maine, to prevent reproduction of the offending cartoon in other newspapers and publications, arguing that it was a clear instance of 'hate speech,' and that it provoked racial disharmony. However, Judge Allen Haberman, a Republican appointee from the time of the elder Bush, disallowed the request, ruling that it fell rather under the category of 'political speech,' which was protected by the First Amendment; and he specifically denied that there was any 'racist' content in it. Helper then published an Op Ed article in *The Washington Post*, in which he called Americans 'cowards' on the issue of race; gave several, other instances of continuing widespread racial discrimination and segregation in the workplace and civil society; and summoned the nation to engage in a frank discussion of racial matters that would actually reach more closure on them than had been so far achieved. He ended his article with a swipe at the Supreme Court, decrying its biases against racial minorities, immigrants and women, and throwing in for good measure the observation that the individual justices owned investment portfolios that gave them an interest in an unprecedentedly wide range of businesses. "Since businesses were on the whole so thoroughly integrated and interconnected nationally and internationally," he concluded, "there is no case involving a business in which the justices should not all be obliged to recuse themselves, effectively leaving the country without its highest court." The ensuing furor, in which the he was accused, among other things, of 'politicizing' the Justice Department, brought gladness and jubilation in the ranks of the conspirators and their supporters.

Anti-nationalization and anti-bailout sentiments canceled out each other, but left the free floating rage to settle undivided on the "irresponsible" homeowners whom the president had set aside $275 billion to rescue. Another campaign in the media contrasted these "scheming profiteers," who, it was implied yet again, were mostly black and Hispanic, from the hard earning –white, needless to say- homeowners who struggled to pay their mortgages and deemed it a "a matter of morality" not to walk away from their homes, despite the latter's declining value.

Finally, in order to revive the LHC issue, wherein such an enormous potential for mischief had been demonstrated, Pastor Walrus and Governor Paltry took the initiative to invite the two Hawaiian Christians, who had earlier initiated legal action against the U.S. government and FermiLab of Illinois, the two U.S. entities collaborating with CERN, to Dupont Circle for talks. Offering a war chest of several million dollars, lawyers drawn from top law firms in Washington and New York, and limitless media coverage, they persuaded the two men to resume said legal action. Accordingly, a new complaint was filed in the U.S. District Court, District of Hawaii, in Honolulu on February 18, 2009.

The case fell this time in the roster of Honorable Learned Fist Kahuna, who was unusually quick in granting standing to the plaintiffs, prompting some legal experts to suppose that an extra-juridical interest had influenced his judgment. Judge Learned Fist had been the target of many such insinuations throughout his long career on the bench, and he was unperturbed by this one. In his ruling, he considered the important areas in the case, such as jurisdiction, procedure and the scientific controversy.

Addressing the government's argument that the complaint had been brought after the statute of limitations had run out, since the government had disbursed its entire contribution to CERN in 1996 and 1999, the judge observed that it was still making payments for the ongoing repairs, was paying the salaries of U.S. scientists involved in the program, and would contribute to the costs of experiments undertaken in the future in the LHC. He was inclined to believe, therefore, that the government's argument was at best too literal in its interpretation of the statute, and disingenuous at worst.

The same observation also applied to the government's argument that a U.S. court lacked jurisdiction in the matter, since CERN and the French and Swiss authorities were fully in charge of the collider and its operations. This might have been the case, the judge said, if there were in fact no ongoing U.S. payments. As there were, a U.S. court was empowered to rule on their advisability or legality.

And finally, regarding the science, the judge declared that the government hadn't persuaded the court that it had satisfactorily addressed the safety concerns; and moreover, its claims that the experiments would advance physics in such areas as string theory, the composition of dark matter and energy, the existence of more than the four dimensions of space-time and hence of 'multiverses,' the 'big bang' theory of the universe's origin, and the standard model of particle physics, were insufficiently documented. He showed surprising scientific acumen in addressing each of these claims in his 196-page opinion.

He concluded by mocking scientists for their pretense of omniscience: "I learned the other day they recently discovered that this universe is really twice as large as they had previously thought. They congratulated themselves on the discovery, and boasted how it proved science was the most reliable method of enquiry possible. Of course, they neglected to observe that the discovery actually meant that, just the day before, they were *dead wrong* about the size of the universe! Like many other scientific discoveries, this one wasn't an improvement in previous or existing knowledge, an incremental advance; it was an outright refutation and disavowal, cleanly sweeping away prior thinking like so much dust and cobweb! And guess what? They are still wrong! By their own accounts, common sense and, in view of the idea of an expanding universe that most ancient observers espoused, half or more of the universe has already slipped away forever beyond the reckoning of our senses, no matter how well we enhance them technologically or theoretically. Relying on them, we can never get the right answer."

In view of the vital need for cash in the present economic crisis, he recommended that the operations of the LHC be put on hold, pending completion of the trial and an upswing in the world's economic fortunes.

While the Dupont Circle conspirators busied themselves to make sure this decision reached the widest audience possible, scientists unanimously condemned it, and began their own campaigns to discredit it. The chief weapon in their armory was that although legal action had also been brought before the European Court of Human Rights in Strasbourg, France, the Europeans were not bound by Judge Learned Fist Kahuna's ruling. Get the operation up and running quickly and urgently, was their thinking, and let the opposition chew on a *fait accompli*!

The tweedy head of the atheistic delegation that had approached Barzhad had returned to his native London, where he had started a campaign to increase public acceptance of atheism. He had published a book attacking fairy stories that he deemed egregiously 'unscientific,' such as those with plotlines involving princes turning into frogs, princesses into mermaids, pumpkins into carriages, and lions wandering around in wardrobes: and was frequently at bookstores and book signings throughout the United Kingdom, denouncing the Church of England and the Roman Catholic church for giving implicit support to this 'subversive' literature.

Another of his initiatives involved placing atheist messages on 800 buses and 1000 subway cars throughout Greater London. "There's probably no God," some advertisements said. "Now stop worrying and enjoy your life." "Why believe in a god?" another read, over a picture of a man in a Santa suit. "Just be good for goodness' sake." And yet another advised bleary-eyed commuters, "Atheism: Sleep in on Sunday mornings!"

After Judge Learned Fist Kahuna's ruling and the uptick in the opposition to the LHC, Tweedy turned from these efforts to full-throttle support for it, and for an earlier resumption of the experimental program. He was greatly aided in this goal by an alliance he formed with the Dutch parliamentarian, Geerters Wilderbeest. The latter's hatred of Islam was legendary and world-famous, and he had long been the live wire of a campaign to have the Koran banned in his country. As part of that campaign, he had made and circulated a scurrilous short film that depicted Islam as a terrorist faith, "that sick ideology of Allah and Muhammad." Although the Dutch government had initially protected his right to launch the campaign, however detestable it was, in deference to the storied Dutch toleration of free speech, an Amsterdam court later ruled in a civil charge brought against him that Wilderbeest should be prosecuted for "insulting" and "spreading hatred" against Muslims. Dutch criminal law penalized anyone who "deliberately insults people on the grounds of their race, religion, beliefs or sexual orientation."

It was an indication of the degree to which Muslim immigration had polarized public opinion and attitudes in Europe that Wildebeest counted on the support of persons across the political spectrum in his legal defense. Globalization, multinational institutions and mass migration had bewildered many Europeans, regardless of their level of educational attainment or socio-economic background: and there was a widespread feeling that governments were coddling ethnic and religious minorities out of a misplaced sense of civic and political correctness. For example, several academics with unimpeachable 'liberal' credentials had disingenuously wondered in their blogs why Wildebeest was being prosecuted for "criticizing a book." Wasn't *Mein Kampf* banned throughout Europe? The puzzled brain trust was apparently unconcerned that they were thereby implicitly equating billions of Muslims around the world with genocidal Nazis. As the goal of Wildebeest's campaign was to stop the "Islamic invasion of Holland," it was unclear whether the academics also felt that a military defense of Europe might not be some day required.

Wildebeest immediately recognized in the support of CERN a means to further antagonize the European Union's Muslims. Suffering the effects of the downturn more severely than their host populations, immigrants had become even more resentful of the enormous expenditure on the CERN program than previously, and were better prepared this time to make their protests effective. With Wildebeest and Tweedy at the helm, therefore, the battle lines were drawn once more, and the situation teetered dangerously to the point where it had been formerly –rioting, demonstration and counter-demonstration. Soon after, the first cars were overturned and burned in the suburbs of Paris.

Fearing that the violence would also re-infect America, President Osama pleaded as before with European leaders to refrain from acting on the LHC, only to be roundly rebuffed once again. The French president remarked that it was the same old story all over again: the Americans reached out for cooperation, but only on American terms. In the end, the date for the resumption of the LHC program was moved up to sometime in March, but CERN scientists declined to give an exact time and date, as it was impossible to say when all the repairs and trial runs would be completed. But they were eager to start as soon as possible, before more opposition either delayed or completely derailed the program.

16

For a weekday in March, it was turning out to be an unusually busy Wednesday at *Oracles and Cures*, which was all the more surprising because the temperature was scraping the bottom of the 30's, when just the previous day it had been a balmy 63. A customer was already waiting on the bench outside when Robert arrived at 10am to raise the security gates. She wanted a sage smudge wand to burn in her apartment to cleanse it of negative and hostile energies and entities; a black candle, scented with cedar wood and patchouli, to light for protection after completing the cleansing; and Robert's special blend of pine and nutmeg oils, to rub on her palms for alertness, and to attract money, prosperity and good luck. Her eyes alighted on a two-inch-high bronze statue of Lakshmi, the Hindu goddess who brought out all the sweetness of life, and she purchased that too. Although well-meaning and a veteran supporter of the store, she was the sort of person who required instructions or information to be repeated several times before she felt satisfied that she had mastered them. And so, although Robert rang up the quite substantial sale with much gratitude, he had a feeling that he would be kept on his toes all day, and called up the inner resources to help him deal with the challenge.

A member of his gym stopped in next to buy an essential oil for his scent diffuser, and Robert discounted a mixture of red grapefruit, bergamot, ylang-ylang and African musk. The young man, whom he mostly saw staggering under an impressive load of barbells, or walking his pit bull in the park, was also reading for a bachelor's degree in sociology at Hunter College; and complained that the pressure of weekly readings for the classes, quizzes, the upcoming midterm exams, and term papers down the line were getting the better of him. On top of all of that, the relationship with his girlfriend had just entered its fifth, rocky year: and he wanted Robert's advice on methods of stress relief. Robert patiently advised him of the merits of meditation and yoga; and the young man, who was unemployed, and supporting himself mainly on his student grants and loans, made a down payment on a meditation pillow, to be paid off when he next received a check.

And so it continued, like a revolving door. Another long-time acquaintance and customer, the pastor of a church in Bed-Stuy, came in with a stack of requests for proposals, to which he wanted Robert to submit applications. He also brought a check of $2,500 made out to him as a retainer fee for preparing and writing them: and additionally, he was to write himself into the budgets as the progress report writer and program evaluator. To Robert, this was a very welcome assignment, because he hadn't been stingy with his honorarium from the president, and the last dollar of it was already in plain view; furthermore, the economic crisis was steadily worsening, and it was a relief to know that there were sources remaining from which he could still earn an income. But inwardly, he groaned at the amount of time and effort he was contracting to expend. There were a dozen or more solicitations from various federal, state and city agencies that dealt with social needs or problems. Each would require, besides the actual writing and the submissions process, a heavy investment in research: for afterschool programs and summer camps, knowledge of the numbers of children and adolescents requiring the services, a precise account of their circumstances, and a review of the latest literature on early childhood and youth education and the utilization of leisure time; for facilities and services for homeless persons, an investigation of the disincentives this population had regarding being housed; for job training and employment advisement for parolees and ex-offenders, a review of the stigmas they experienced on their return to civilian life; for counseling for battered women and families, and domestic violence prevention, expertise regarding the incidence of violence and its etiology, and a critique of the interventions that had been recommended; and for parenting classes, or substance abuse counseling, familiarity with state-of-the art social work improvements in those fields. Moreover, the pastor was famously anything but timely in this area of grant applications, and consequently, some of the deadlines for submissions were already in the very near future. Pocketing the check, Robert told himself that he had a busy night ahead of him –that night, and several others subsequently.

Aware that Robert was cut off from the news at the store, except what was streamed onto his computer, which he had obviously been too busy to turn on thus far that day, the pastor filled him in on the breaking news in Europe. "Protesters are reacting to rumors that the scientists will throw the switch of the LHC sometime today," he said, "and hundreds of thousands have taken to the streets in London, Paris, Geneva, Berlin and Amsterdam. They believe today or tomorrow will be the end of the world. They are saying the machine will produce black holes or strangelets that will swallow it up. The demonstrations are mostly peaceful for the time being, but violence is starting up!"

"Pastor, we really don't need another round of that in the U.S.!" Robert said, knowing that the pastor wasn't in favor of the LHC either.

"You're right, of course," the pastor said, "but Rocky Walrus and Governor Paltry are reaching out to their faithful, and who knows how that will go. It's a pity the Europeans rejected the president's call for a delay. There really was no hurry to do these experiments in the middle of a global economic downturn."

"These RFPs you gave me are a sign that money is trickling into the pipelines at last," Robert said, "the funding for these sorts of programs had dried up. It would be a real shame if this LHC controversy distracted us just as we are getting off the ground again."

"The pastor shook his head sadly. "I don't know who is more to blame," he said, "these arrogant, godless scientists or the protesters, whose opposition may be commendable on some grounds, but who also have regrettable political motives."

The great monetary debt he owed President Osama, and the enormous goodwill he felt towards him ever since their meeting, were always uppermost in Robert's mind, even if he never talked about them or alluded to them. "Pastor," he told his friend urgently, "you have no time to lose! You must work the telephones and your email. Get in touch with your congregants, the churches affiliated with yours, and everyone you know across the country. I don't believe for a minute the LHC can cause any harm, and the likeliest thing is that it just won't start, just like the last time. But if protests derail implementation of the stimulus plan and the other recovery plans the president announced, we may just wish that it had ended the world after all!"

The pastor came alive. "You're absolutely right," he boomed, "I'll get to it right away. We have to prevent a repeat of the rioting!"

An unpleasant scene occurred after the pastor's departure. The next-door neighbor, a doughy, red-faced mother of two stout girls, had always been barely civil, both when Robert's former boss had owned the store and now, when he was the owner. He had never been able to get to the bottom of her opaque hostility, although he had occasionally heard her complaining to passersby that the 'smells' in the store, and its 'physical aspects' were offensive to her. Since he reopened, she had taken to going past holding her nose or coughing uncontrollably. She now marched into the store demanding that he stop burning incense. When Robert tried to explain that customers liked to know what they were buying before taking their purchases home, she cut him off, and threatened to complain to the Environmental Protection Agency. "You're living in New York now!" she screamed mysteriously, "you'll see!"

Benjie was next through the revolving door, as Robert was still digesting the ugly incident and pondering its causes and meanings. "We're seeing a lot of that," Benjie explained, "People are losing grip. They're just letting it all hang out. I just hope it doesn't translate into assaults and homicides."

"This damn LHC nonsense is going to exacerbate that trend," Robert complained.

"Ah, don't bother about that, my brother! We've got the whole thing under wraps," Benjie reported jubilantly, "There'll be no trouble in Brooklyn or elsewhere in New York. The African Muslims and Black Muslims are solidly behind our boy Osama, although they grumble about the bombings in Pakistan, and the lack of progress so far in advancing talks with Hamas and Iran. But everyone's still overjoyed he's gotten rid of the racists and numbskulls on his team, and they're cool about nationalizing the usurious banks, and giving money to homeowners. So, the attitude is: let the scientists do their worst, Allah is the decider, after all."

"The real worry is Walrus' and Paltry's constituencies," Robert said, "and all the neoconservatives who'll see this LHC non-issue as an opportunity to create problems for his administration."

"We're working around the clock there too," Benjie said, "we're working in collaboration with a lot of the organizations that put canvassers on the street, or knocking at doors, during the campaign. They've had a sudden inflow of funding from their former sources, and they are back out in full force in the Bible Belt and the Sun Belt, urging people to show restraint, to stay indoors, and boycott the call for protests and demonstrations."

"Behind that veneer of born-again Christianity, they're a violent, bloodthirsty lot!" Robert warned, "Frankly, I'm very worried."

Throughout the late afternoon and early evening, customers flocking in to buy amulets, oils and other prophylactics against diffuse negativity and evil fed Robert's growing uneasiness with a continuous report of belligerent bulletins from the political battlefronts. Unrest, disturbances and isolated outbreaks of serious violence were increasing so rapidly that President Osama had hastily convened a news conference for 8pm, EST, which all the networks had agreed to carry, pre-empting regular broadcasting.

At 8pm, President Osama walked quickly from the Oval Office to a room packed with journalists and government officials. Millie, Marie, Sally and his mother-in-law joined him, and after hugging each of his family members for a long moment, he went over to the bank of microphones and addressed the nation.

"Today, the stock market fell by another 631 points, the latest unemployment figures reported the loss of an additional 700,000 jobs so far in the month of February, bringing the total to 6.4 million to date, for an unemployment rate of 8.3%, and another 130,000 homes were foreclosed. These reverses have happened despite the passage into law of the stimulus plan, the recovery plan for the banking system, and the emergency funds being made available to homeowners. Americans are understandably even more disheartened than when I last spoke to you. And as if these worries were not enough, there are elements among us, agencies who are unabashed in putting partisan agendas ahead of national interests, and who are strengthened as the whole is weakened, who have raised to the pitch of hysteria an entirely unfounded fear that the world is going to end, if not tonight, then tomorrow, or latest by the end of the month.

"The deep anxiety caused by these concerns, taken singly or in combination, led to violence and rioting throughout the nation a fortnight ago, and indeed, the same common concerns simultaneously led to violence and looting throughout the world. And tonight that specter has reared its head once again, and violence and looting have already erupted in several states. I am appealing now for them to stop, and I want to use this occasion to emphasize in no uncertain terms that violence and rioting are intrinsically wrong; that violence and rioting are in and of themselves wrong; and moreover, and most importantly, violence and looting aren't going to solve our problems, violence and looting are just going to make them that much worse. So, I am appealing to Americans: come to your senses, let's solve our problems and not make them worse!

"I'd like to address again each of the problems I raised in their order of importance:

"First on the list must be the stimulus bill. It is meant to put many of the 6.4 million who have lost their jobs so far back to work, and to lay the foundation for job creation way into the future. I have outlined several times before, and in far greater detail than I will go into here, specifying dollar amounts and other numerical values, the major provisions of the bill. Money will be spent on energy to transform the U.S. energy grid and make it more efficient; to repair public housing and make it more energy efficient; and to weatherize low-income homes. Money will be spent on science and technology, for new scientific facilities, and to improve broadband Internet access in rural areas. Money will be spent on infrastructure, on highways; to modernize federal buildings and other public infrastructure; for clean water, flood control, and other environmental investments; and to improve public transit and rail infrastructure.

Money will be spent on education, for local school districts, in outlays to states to prevent educational service cutbacks; to broaden the federal Pell Grant program, which gives need-based grants to fund education; and to modernize higher education programs. And money will be spent on health care, for Medicaid; to improve health information technology; and to improve preventative care. The plan also includes extensive tax cuts that will put money into the pockets of middle- and low-income Americans, which they will spend to buy goods and stimulate business, both in America and abroad.

"The stimulus bill is now *law.* Isn't it counterproductive to regard it as still moot? Yet some of the violence and rioting that occurred a fortnight ago, as well as some of the rioting and violence that are occurring tonight stem from dissatisfaction with the bill. Of course, no legislation is entirely perfect, but with goodwill, effort, awareness of the urgency of the task, and at least the good faith that it is moving in the direction of improving our declining fortunes, the disputed parts can be made better. Yet today, utterly and irresponsibly disregarding the effect of throwing fuel on fires physically burning in our cities, Governor Robby Jimsonweed of Louisiana, Governor Susan Paltry of Alaska, Governor Mickey Sandman of South Carolina, Governor Dick Derrick of Texas, Governor Hale Baboon of Mississippi, and Governor Curley Beaver of Idaho have declared that they will reject some or all of the bill, without advancing a single sound reason why they would do so. And they made their announcement in full knowledge that it would inflame the situation on the streets, when it is in the interest of every law-abiding and God-fearing American to quell it. Indeed, as of this moment, none of these so-called responsible public figures have called on rioters to stop the lawless behavior!

"My fellow Americans, it pains me to remind you that these governors are all Republicans. You know how earnestly I have appealed for bipartisanship, and that, sometimes in defiance of my own advisors and voices in my own party, I made deliberate, practical attempts to promote it, only to have them spurned and rejected. You must judge for yourselves the meaning of these developments, and whether you should tolerate those who knowingly incite others to violence and rioting.

"My fellow Americans, the burning and looting only ensure that the work of recovery and rebuilding, however poorly conceived, never gets started at all!

"The matter second in importance, at least to my mind, is the money that has been set aside to keep Americans in their homes. Keeping Americans in their homes is the cornerstone of a growth-oriented, prosperous, middle class America. Families kept intact; children benefiting from the positive example and instruction of their parents; and communities where neighborliness, mutual caring and fellow feeling, respect, fair play, ingenuity and innovation are prized; that's what keeping Americans in their homes means. Who can argue against that? Wherever in America or in the world you see a neighborhood without a boarded up, foreclosed home, and children are playing on the freshly mown lawns, and Dad is tinkering in the garage making something or inventing something, why, you see happiness, hope and the brightest future. Who can argue against that?

"Yet, once more, we have detractors stirring up envy, resentment and rancorous feelings, who are saying that actually we are rewarding 'bad behavior,' and they are sending people out into the streets to vent this artificial, deliberately cultivated anger and hatred. My fellow Americans, they may be aiming to bring down my government: but what they are in fact doing is burning and looting our homes, public buildings and personal belongings, and bringing down our beloved America!

"Next, we have a plan to nationalize the banks. You must examine the record objectively and dispassionately. Haven't we given the bankers and private investors one incentive after another, one approach after another, one stack of billions of dollars after another stack of billions of dollars? And what have we gained in return? Credit remains frozen; businesses remain stalled; consumer spending remains zero; jobs remain in freefall; and upon awakening every morning, we find the situation has worsened overnight, and the contagion has spread further, bringing down the most vulnerable governments and nations abroad, and bringing the threat of complete collapse closer to our shores.

"Yet, without proposing an alternative –the tax cuts of the previous eight years of the last administration is not one- the same irresponsible people are marching others out into the streets to create mayhem, to fight what they are calling social-ism, to fight big government, to fight our humble efforts to try to turn adversity around.

"And finally, to cap it all, now they're telling you to go out and riot and loot and be consumed in violence, because scientists have created a doomsday machine, and it's going to end the world! My fellow Americans, are we so gullible that our fears are so easily manipulated? Who gains if the world ends? Sure, like all other human endeavors, science is imperfect, and scientists proceed by learning from their mistakes. But don't scientists have husbands and wives and children and other loved ones? Why would they recklessly put them in jeopardy, simply because they couldn't be bothered to consider all the dangers and put in place all the proper safeguards? Wouldn't the scientists themselves also perish, with no one left to have knowledge, or award fame, or anyone left to claim either?

"Again, you must judge for yourselves the meaning of these developments. Go back to your homes, be cleansed of these impulses that have been delibcrately fomented to mis-guide you, and please take my advice -judge for yourselves the meaning of these developments. Good night! God bless America!"

The telephone rang the instant the stream to Robert's computer ended. It was Awe. She was crying. She had returned home from Manhattan with great news about her book project, which a Japanese publisher had agreed to publish together with the accompanying music CD as an insert, once a producer for the latter was secured; but she had gone out to a nearby bar to watch the president's broadcast; and now she was terrified. She begged Robert to come home as soon as he could. The news coverage on television was showing shocking images of rioting throughout the country. Pitched battles between rioters and the police were being shown in several European capitals, after CERN scientists had vowed to keep on working around the clock in order to restart the LHC program as soon as they possible could. The rioting had then spread to Southeast Asia, China, Japan and Australia. The governments feared they hadn't the manpower to control the rioting, and felt their collapse was imminent. As during the disturbances last time, she was going out to pick up water, food and other essential supplies, but at the small bodega at the corner of their block this time.

Almost certainly having the same thoughts as Awe, many persons in the vicinity of Robert's store must have bolted straight from their televisions to the streets. Like Awe, they were stocking up on water, food and other essentials, and came to Robert's pushing shopping carts or laden down with full tote bags and plastic bags. While they still wanted the protective amulets and preparations that had been in such heavy demand all day, they now also wanted just plain, inexpensive candles for illumination, in case there were blackouts. Outside, the street had turned as busy as during the prime shopping times on weekends or holidays, and customers kept coming to Robert until nearly midnight, when he completely ran out of candles. For the first day in months, Robert had made a lot of money, but had never felt as joyless.

It was a relief to end the long day. A downside of the reduced rent the landlady had accepted from Robert was that she no longer felt obliged to send up adequate heat to the store, and his toes and hands felt frozen on that exceptionally cold day. Usually, therefore, it was no small pleasure on such a day to return home to a warm, cozy, homey apartment and Awe's equally tropical welcome. A hot shower and clean leisure clothes would have completed a blessing than which life here on this earth had nothing greater to offer. But a shadow hung over it tonight.

Awe was still very agitated, and the first order of business required him to pay attention to allaying her fears. In truth, however, his sense of foreboding was as great as hers. By that time, although no rioting had been reported locally, police cruisers, ambulances and fire engines were continuously racing through the streets, sirens and flashing lights tireless; and the chop-chop-chop of police helicopters' propellers echoed overhead. Swarms of them, like flocks of carrion birds, their great ominous bodies only dimly perceived in the darkness, converged over the ghettoes to the south, north and east, the beams of their searchlights combing the rooftops of buildings from on high and intersecting one another like swordplay in the sky.

"This will blow over by morning," Robert told her, with his voice carrying little conviction, to his greater chagrin, "just like the last time."

That lack of conviction broke fresh sobbing out of Awe. "Only two months ago or so," she moaned, "and the world was *so-o-o-o* completely different a place to live in!"

The observation was so correct that it left Robert quite speechless. What could he say? That Barzhad would soon fix it up by nationalizing the banks, keeping homeowners in their homes, and implementing the stimulus plan? That he would return everything to how they had been; or, if changed, for the better? Although his confidence in the president had grown absolute after their secret meeting, it suddenly felt like a feeble thing against the immensities of bad fortune they seemed to be encountering.

"Bad things happen for us to become better, and do better things," he said consolingly, "you'll finish the book, a recording studio will make the CD, and tomorrow's children will be vastly superior to us because of it!"

"What happens when worlds die? Do they slip into other dimensions? And what becomes of their inhabitants?" Awe wondered.

"We'll know after the data generated by the LHC are analyzed and theorized. That's what the whole fuss is about. A bit of understanding from a few harmless experiments, if they can deliver anything so profound."

And gradually, as the conversation turned more intellectual, extracting from them both what little they knew about particle physics, theoretical physics and cosmology, they reassured each other remarkably well. No matter how jaded or coarsened by the sex-saturated ambience of modern America, an observer would not have failed to be impressed by the exchanges by which they did so. The bond between them, unostentatiously but unmistakably indissoluble, effortlessly and coolly nonsexual, was nevertheless undeniably an interaction between a man and a woman. Their way was a clear, simple reproof of how the over-valorization of sex too frequently eroded self-respect and mutual esteem. After a light snack of chamomile tea and a couple of slices each of dried Alfonso mango, they washed their faces, scrubbed out their gums and set out their gear for meditating. As they were assuming lotus positions, however, the basket of fruit on the center table flew across the room and smashed into the opposite wall. It immediately bounced back a foot or so, however, peeling off a page of the calendar that read "March 18," and after pausing in midair for an instant, turned into a stack of greasy fried moose cheeks; the impact seemed to mobilize into action the metronome on Awe's electronic key board, which straightaway morphed into a giant bald eagle, the white tips of whose outstretched wings scraped the walls, as it beat them, squeezed out of the window and took flight towards

Prospect Park; whereupon the whole room started pouring downward, like liquid into a black hole.

But Awe and Robert, who had taken hold of each other's hands, began glowing like an enormous ruby and a smaller jade respectively, into which they eventually transformed; and a band of red and green connectivity, pulsating and flaring and crackling and mini-exploding alternately, joined them fast together. Then, as Gemstones, they were airborne; and soon joined a crowded and glittering pilgrimage bound for the planet in the constellation farthest from the once-and-forever-defunct Milky Way, where Barzhad's parents currently lived.

THAT'S ALL FOR NOW, FOLKS!